# MISCHIEF MAYHEM

A BROTHER'S BEST FRIEND ROMANCE

STEEL ROSES MOTORCYCLE CLUB
BOOK 4

JENA DOYLE

DIRTY WORDS PUBLISHING LLC

Line Editing: Misha Robinson at Verity Ink Editing

Proofreading: Kimberly Hunt at Revision Division

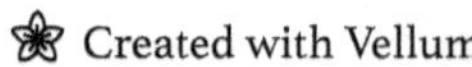 Created with Vellum

To all the golden retrievers with partners that give off black cat energy...
This one's for you.

# STEEL ROSES FAMILY TREE

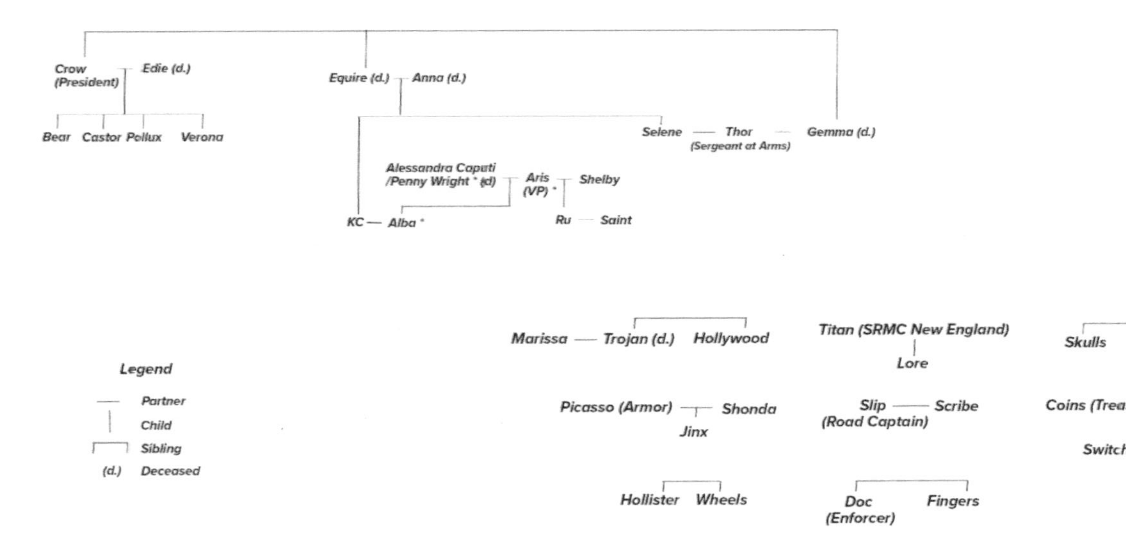

# CAPUTI FAMILY TREE

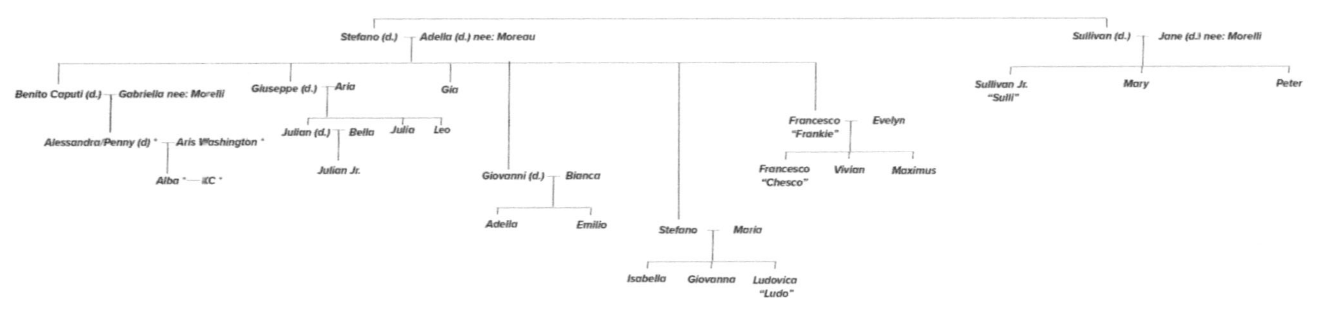


* Member of Steel Roses Family Tree

## Legend

| | |
|---|---|
| — | Partner |
| \| | Child |
| ⌐ | Sibling |
| (d.) | Deceased |
| nee. | Maiden Name |

## 1

## VERONA

"Do you believe in soulmates?" my friend and fellow MC princess, Ru, asked as she leaned over the pool table so she could sink her four ball into the corner pocket.

"I suppose." I cleared my throat and winced as the familiar ache shot down the center of my chest. Instinct had me clutching the glass jar necklace that hung under my shirt, the one I wore at all times, the one that reminded me I was still alive. "Like twin flames? That kind of thing?"

"Sure." Ru took a sip of her beer and nodded, her curly brown hair bouncing around her face as she moved. When she failed to put her next ball into a pocket, I took my turn, easily sinking my nine in the center.

"Maybe." Taking a drink of my own beer, I ignored the throbbing scar that ran in between my breasts. "What about you?"

"I used to think it was bullshit." She grinned, her icy-blue eyes sparkling under the shitty fluorescent lighting in the club as they sought out her fiancé, Saint, across the room. The dark-haired brother sat with some of the other motorcycle club members, drinking and laughing as my cousin, KC, talked. "But after everything that's happened, I can't deny it."

"Please." I rolled my eyes and sank another ball in the far left. "You're twenty-three, same as me. Don't you think you're a little young to be talking soulmates and happily ever afters?"

She laughed, her cheeks flushing despite how open we were with each other. Once upon a time, Ru and I had been best friends. I was the president's daughter, the proverbial princess of the Steel Roses Motorcycle Club, and she'd been born to the VP two months after me. We were raised in this chaos together, and even if we lost touch after high school, I'd never discounted her friendship.

"You don't know what it's like," she said, nodding toward the rest of the brothers, "to have one of them devoted to you, those alpha assholes."

"I grew up in a house with four of them. I think I have an idea." Being the youngest with three older biker brothers, combined with having the president as my father, meant I'd had to be tough, much tougher than the rest of the princesses and hang-arounds. Bear was the eldest, Castor and Pollux were the twins in the middle, and I came last. Our mom died when I was nine, leaving me as the sole girl, someone to be protected, the apple of their fucking eye. It had been fifteen years and my father still hadn't moved on. I'd never even seen him with a hang-around.

"What about fate?" Ru brought the topic back as she tried to make another pocket, missing it.

"Maybe. My mom was a witch. She used to believe in magic." Memories of helping her with her spells and rituals flooded through my mind as I lined up to pocket another ball. It bounced off the edge and scattered the others around it. Of course, magic hadn't saved her in the end; she'd still gotten blown up by the MC's enemies, the Caputi Mafia.

"You believe in magic but not soulmates?" Ru raised an eyebrow and moved around the table, tilting her head to the side.

No, that wasn't true. I did believe in magic, the kind that linked two people based on spilled blood and experience, the kind that gave me an undeniable link to my found family. But soulmates might be pushing it.

"I don't know what I believe," I said, because that seemed easier to explain. "But I do know that settling down and getting married at twenty-three is stupid."

"Hey," she grumbled with a laugh. "I'm not married."

"Uh-huh." I chuckled and swallowed the rest of my beer, deciding to change the subject. "How's the construction going at the Beacon?"

Her features dropped, and she ran her palm over her flushed alabaster face. "We're almost there, thank fucking God. Hopefully, by St. Patty's Day we can be back in the space."

This past Thanksgiving, a former hang-around turned traitor had bombed the BDSM club where Ru and I worked. Technically, the MC owned the place, but Ru had been given a partial stake and a loan to renovate it. On the night of our grand reopening, the whole place exploded, nearly killing my brother, Pollux, and putting dozens more in the hospital. He'd been in ICU for weeks afterward, and only just recently started talking again after being taken off the ventilator. After that, the Beacon had been confiscated by the Feds, and once they returned the property to us, Ru had filed the insurance claim to rebuild. She had the stamina of an Olympic athlete. I would have thrown in the towel and sold the place by now.

"But with the insurance payout, I can finally get those marble countertops I wanted for the bathrooms, so . . . silver lining, I guess?" She smiled and set down her stick when Saint approached, wrapping his arms around her waist from behind before whispering in her ear. The public display of affection would have grossed me out if it wasn't such an everyday occurrence around the clubhouse.

She, of course, had been right. These alpha assholes loved their women, and the more they loved them, the more obsessive they were about them. Ru turned in Saint's embrace to wrap her arms around his neck while he grabbed her ass and nodded toward the exit with a devilish grin.

"See ya, V!" Ru waved before giggling and stumbling out into the frigid February air.

With Valentine's Day tomorrow, the normally grungy clubhouse looked like love had vomited everywhere. My cousin, Selene, grinned at her husband, Thor, by the bar while Ru's sister, Alba, walked over to sit on KC's lap, leaning in so she could kiss his cheek. Some of the other old ladies mingled around, laughing with the old-timers, the ones that had been in the club since I was a child. Red hearts hung from the rafters and streamers weaved from corner to corner. It was tacky as hell, but at least no one was getting shot or murdered. So there was that.

I stood by the pool table, knowing I'd be alone for the first Valentine's Day in years. I was proud of that fact and celebrated my single status. I'd gotten away from an abusive ex-client, I was back with my family, and . . . My gaze caught on a dark stare across the clubhouse.

*Hollywood*—my eldest brother's best friend and the club's resident manwhore. He'd gotten his road name because of how beautiful he was. At six foot five, corded with muscle and tanned skin, Hollywood had the traditional square jaw and chiseled features that made both women and men swoon. I, on the other hand, lived to push men like him to their knees and hear them beg.

As soon as I made eye contact with him, he darted his gaze away, going back to his conversation with Bear and another brother, Wheels. Had he been staring at me?

I snorted and took a drink of my beer, grateful Hollywood had never been interested in me, not like that. Pick any number of the female notches on his bedpost, put them in a lineup, and they'd all fit a profile: paper thin, traditionally gorgeous, hopelessly devoted to inflating his ego. None of that was me. Sure, I was tall with legs for days, but my thighs had been built for crushing men's souls, not appeasing their fantasies. I preferred my tattoos and raven hair with matching makeup. I liked people to know who I was as soon as they saw me, lest they form any incorrect opinions.

Besides, it wasn't like Hollywood was *my* type, either. He was probably a dominant biker badass in bed—holding his women down, growling dirty words in their ears, choking them until they begged for air. While I loved a good rough fuck, I preferred to be the one doing the growling and choking.

Despite his namesake and the rumors floating around about his sexual prowess, I wasn't susceptible to his charms. Sure, his dimples complemented his perfect teeth, and the fact his biceps were bigger than my thighs meant he could probably bench press me, but that changed nothing about how I treated him.

He was my brother's idiot best friend, and except for one time . . . a long time ago . . . nothing had ever happened between us. He didn't even know that was me, and I planned to keep it that way.

"Hey, let me know when you're ready to roll," Wheels said, smiling as he passed me to head outside. Right after I'd gotten back from college, Hollywood had been assigned to be my bodyguard, but shortly after the bombing at the Beacon, Wheels had taken over. I never asked why, but I didn't mind. The younger brother had an easygoing personality and mostly kept to himself. I appreciated that because while things were still being renovated during my day job, I relied a lot on my income from Alba's camming website, Crimson—sort of like an OnlyFans—that she owned.

I nodded and glanced over to Hollywood again, watching as a hang-around approached him and put her arms around his neck. He shook his head and smiled, whispering something to her that made her pout and back away from him.

"Are you sure?" she whimpered.

He chuckled and tapped the end of her nose. "Don't be like that, beautiful. It's only a few more weeks."

"But I want you now," she whined.

He ran the back of his knuckle down the side of her cheek, clearly uncomfortable but doing his best to appease her. "You'll survive."

*Christ, take no for an answer, lady.*

I furrowed my brows and finished my beer while she crossed her arms, giving him puppy dog eyes. "You're no fun now that you've taken a vow of chastity—"

Surprise choked me as bubbles flew up the back of my windpipe and into my nose. My eyes burned, and I coughed, tapping myself on my chest to clear my throat. But that aggravated my scar, and I gasped, struggling to breathe.

*Focus. Slow down. Inhale.*

I'd noticed he hadn't been sleeping around as much as he used to, but to cut sex out completely? *Holy shit, that's dramatic.*

"You okay?" Bear asked, suddenly at my side with his hand on my shoulder.

I nodded and wheezed a quiet, "Yes," before hacking again.

"You sure?" My brother's dark brown eyes radiated concern, his curly hair falling in his face as he assessed me.

Nodding again, I grabbed the glass of water out of his hand and took a few swigs to settle my esophagus before handing it back to him. "Yeah, just . . . it went down the wrong pipe."

"Listen, I already have one sibling in the hospital; I don't need a second one." He smiled, and the movement lit up his entire face, making him look so much like our mother that my heart clenched.

My scar burned again, scalding up the center of my chest with the same agony it had the night I'd been shot. I'd been in the backseat of Saint's truck when my family's enemies attacked, and a bullet had gone through Hollywood's torso into my sternum, where it lodged in my bone until I had surgery to remove most of it. I'd never get rid of it all. Fragments of that bullet, of that night, would be permanently embedded inside my skeleton until I croaked.

"Did you hear they're discharging him soon?" I grinned. "I've got the space at my house to take him if you and Castor can't."

Thor and Selene had moved out a few weeks ago, leaving the whole place for me. When Wheels started babysitting me, he'd moved into the basement, but he mostly kept to himself. Having Pollux around wouldn't be a hardship.

"No, Castor swears he's got it. You know they have that twin telepathy thing." Bear chuckled and shook his head before giving me a more serious stare. "You probably ought to check in on them from time to time."

I laughed and agreed. Where Bear always had his head on straight, the twins had the luxury of living like carefree teenagers . . . at least until the Beacon. When Pollux got out of the hospital, the three of us would take on the brunt of caring for him until he was self-sufficient again. With third-degree burns on fifty percent of his body and a healing wound from shoulder to groin, he should have died that night. I thanked whatever Goddess watching out for us that he hadn't.

"Sure," I said, nodding to our father in the far corner, whispering to the MC's vice president and Ru's father, Aris, who stood next to the road captain, Slip. "How's he doing?"

Pollux's injury had worn him down in addition to being the patriarch of this fucked-up found family. His hair had turned nearly gray and heavy bags sat under his eyes, a hint as to the last time he'd had a full night's sleep. Being the president of the SRMC meant the crown lay on his head, and every casualty, every ounce of blood spilled, was the direct result of his action or inaction.

*Imagine the pressure.*

Bear sighed and took another drink. "He'll be better once Pollux is moving around again."

"Are you coming to the Valentine's Day party tomorrow?"

My brother barked out a laugh and shook his head. "No, I've got guard duty, thank fucking God." Before he could elaborate, our father caught his stare and nodded, gesturing Bear over. Pushing himself upright, he clinked his glass against mine and moved to walk away. "Take it easy, V."

"You, too." I watched Bear make his way to Dad and the other MC officers, and by the time I glanced back at Hollywood, he'd already disappeared.

"Jesus, you look like hell." Castor whistled and walked closer to his twin, who had already situated himself in the wheelchair for our daily walk. He'd been stable for a few days now, and if he kept up his stamina, the doctors said he could leave soon.

"I'm still the handsome twin, and that's all that matters." Pollux grinned as Castor scoffed and took up the spot behind the wheelchair, playfully pulling our brother back to tip him over.

"How are you feeling?" I walked closer, examining the circles under his eyes and the sunken cheekbones. He'd lost at least thirty pounds since being stuck here, and the sooner I could get him home to stuff him full of cheap beer and pizza, the better.

"Same ole, same old." Pollux flashed a grin as Castor pushed him into the hall. "Did I tell you the nurse gave me her number?"

I scoffed and rolled my eyes. "Yeah, I bet."

"I'm serious." He laughed and held up his phone to prove it.

"Did you tell her you're a virgin?" Castor teased.

"No, but I told her you're into cake-sitting," Pollux joked. "Too bad for you, that's not her thing."

Castor threw his head back and guffawed. "Don't yuck my yum, brother."

"You're both disgusting," I cut in, knowing none of their insults were true, that they just liked to razz each other with the most degrading shit they could think of. I'd never disparage a person for their kink, even if they got off on the thought of watching people sit on cakes.

"Yeah, you're the one to talk," Pollux said, "Mistress Mayhem."

Despite crossing a few boundaries, both Castor and Pollux had been there that night at the Beacon. Most of the club had. They'd heard about my domme impact play performance, and they knew what I did for my side hustle. It wasn't like I kept it a secret, but it did make me pause when my family brought it up.

"You sound jealous," I said. "Do you want me to tell you how I get men to give me money to treat them like I treat you two idiots?"

"No thanks," Castor started.

"I'm good," Pollux finished.

Twins ran in our family. Castor and Pollux were identical, whereas our cousins, KC and Selene, were fraternal, born a few years before them. My brothers had the same dark curly hair and brown eyes as Bear. Their facial features were more like mine and our father's, and Bear looked so much like my mom, it hurt sometimes to see the similarity.

We walked for another half an hour, gossiping about our family and what Pollux wanted to do when he finally got the go-ahead to leave.

"Throw a big fucking party," he said, wheeling his chair back into his room. "This summer, I want to ride to California and back."

"Fuck yeah," Castor said, giving the injured brother a high five. "You and me and the wide open road."

I watched the two of them daydream about the future with whimsy in my gut, hoping they'd get to see it. Promising to stop by the next day, I said my goodbyes, met up with Wheels, and headed to Crimson headquarters to start my shoot for the day.

I'd never set out to be a professional domme, nor had I ever thought I'd make it this far in life. Losing my mother so young had instilled within me deep-seated anger issues I'd never fully work out. I used to take that fury out on myself and everyone around me, the scars on my wrists and inner thighs only hinting at the extent of it. It was the worst kind of sadness, the kind that ran bone deep and threatened to boil over every second of every day. During my darkest moments, I struggled to get out of bed, much less get dressed and go to school.

Dad had taken me to a number of therapists, but it wasn't like I could tell them my father's enemies had blown up my mother and they might do it to me so what was the fucking point in living? Everything seemed so meaningless, so mundane. Why even bother? Meds and yoga saved me. I learned how to redirect my thoughts, how to find an inner peace, an inner safe place where my demons couldn't find me. It was only a bandage, of course. Depression was a disease that never went away, not really.

After high school, I'd wanted go to New York City, study art, and become the next Frida Kahlo. I'd gotten accepted to the prestigious program at New York College in Manhattan, but my father, king of the alpha assholes, refused to let me live so far away from home.

"We have enemies everywhere," he'd said. "You won't be safe."

I, being a pigheaded stubborn shit, hadn't listened to him. Against every argument he'd thrown my way, I'd gone to the big city on my own, and after a few months away from home, I quickly realized I had champagne tastes on a beer budget. I was trapped in an overpopulated city with no real career prospects, an expensive nicotine addiction, and a dream every other eighteen-year-old art major shared.

I'd been desperate for a long time . . . so desperate, in fact, that when one of my roommates told me she dominated men at a local dungeon for money and asked if I'd be interested, I couldn't find any good reason to say no. I grew up around three brothers and a gang of bikers—I'd seen my fair share of dicks and men pulling on them.

One of my first clients had been a man named Curtis, some down-on-his-luck investment banker that loved for me to humiliate him. Admittedly, the work made me feel alive again. It made me *want* to see tomorrow in a way that meds and yoga never had, never could. In a world where nothing felt like it was in my control, this one thing was, and I lived for that high.

I found out everything I could about the kink lifestyle, particularly about sex work within the community. After a few months, I went full time at the dungeon. When I wasn't in school, I moonlighted as a professional domme and a bartender, and between those two things, I worked my way up. By the time I graduated, I'd been offered the general manager spot by the owners, but things with Curtis turned ugly.

He'd gotten possessive and jealous, and he wanted me to stop seeing all my other clients, to come live with him and be his full-time dominant. I didn't love him, and aside from our kink relationship, I didn't want any other kind with him. He'd started to stalk me, showing up at the dungeon during my shifts, only to hang out until I left so he could follow me home.

One night, he lost control and broke into my apartment. He beat me and nearly abducted me, and if I hadn't stabbed him in the leg and ran, I could only imagine what would have happened. I couldn't go back to that life afterward because he'd never leave me alone. Just because I was more dominant sexually didn't mean he operated that way outside of kink. He was bigger and stronger in every sense, and I'd gotten away with my life by the skin of my teeth.

Wheels pulled up outside Crimson headquarters and parked next to Saint's pickup. I spotted KC's truck on the other side.

"Lots of Roses today. I'll be fine for a while," I told Wheels.

He nodded. "Cool. I'll wait here."

He could have gone out to do anything else, but he seemed content to fiddle with his phone while I did my thing. Like Hollywood, Wheels was gorgeous and got around like a one-dollar bill. He had deep umber skin and a bright shimmering smile that made others grin just by looking at it, and women *loved* him. Covered in tattoos, he matched every biker stereotype ever—beautiful and bloody and bad. But he took his role as my bodyguard seriously, and he respected his position in the club. He'd never cross a line with me, and I appreciated that the most about him.

I walked inside, admiring how the space had been transformed since Alba and KC first bought it. Instead of a concrete wasteland, an inviting foyer greeted visitors, complete with a furry pink wall and a neon sign with the company's name and logo. KC hated it, but it was one of my favorite things about the place.

"Hey, V," Alba called when I walked into the breakroom. She sat at one of the tables with her husband, drinking coffee while they went over reports laid out in front of them.

"Hey, how's it going?" I leaned in to say hi and waved.

"Ru was looking for you earlier," KC said, flashing his classic friendly grin. "She and Saint are filming down the hall, but you should check in with her before you leave."

"Thanks." I nodded and turned before Alba stopped me.

"Hey, how's Pollux?" she called.

"Good." I updated them on my visit, just as I did every day. They said they would swing by to see him on their way home, and I assured them he would love to talk about the hot nurse he planned to marry once he broke free.

"Are you coming to the Valentine's Day party tonight?" Alba grinned expectantly, her wild blond hair curling around her head like a halo. KC called her Sunshine as a nickname, and with the way the light hit her through the window behind her, making her golden skin glow, I understood why. "We're auctioning off a date with the single brothers. All the benefits go to Pollux's medical bills."

I remembered Ru saying something about that, and thankfully, I'd been kept out of the planning. The whole thing sounded ridiculous and objectifying, even if it was for a good cause.

"Yeah, I'll be there," I said, taking a step back so I could go to work, "but not for the auction." I had no need for a man in my life. Even if I'd always considered myself a mostly (read: regrettably) hetero-leaning pansexual, I wasn't interested in dating women, either. It sucked to be alone on Valentine's Day, especially when everyone else in the club was such a horny little hedonist, but I'd just gotten my first real taste of standing on my own. I didn't want to jump into anything serious.

After I went to my room, I set up for my first client and changed into the black corset I planned to wear. I put my leather mask over the top part of my face and logged on to the Crimson platform to take live calls for the next few hours.

Sure, most people associated kink and domination with sex. In the best cases, it could be. But with most of my clients, it rarely went that way. They liked the degradation that came with hearing a beautiful woman tearing them down. One in particular liked me to insult him until he cried, saying it was the only way for him to have an emotional release.

I never asked why they sought me out, only tried to deliver on what they needed.

After that disaster with Curtis last June, I came home to the protection of my father, my brothers, and my badass biker family. No one from the dungeon knew my real name, no one except my roommate. I'd never given them any real facts about me, but occasionally, when I drove to work by myself or when I got a new anonymous client in my camming channel on Crimson, a shiver went down my spine the way it used to when he looked at me. There was something in an abuser's stare when they directed it at their victim—something slithery and territorial and toxic, something I could never forget.

Curtis's abuse caused a relapse in my depression. Sure, I put on the brave face when I first arrived home. I smiled and sneered and heckled the way I always had, but inside, I was crumbling. I started to believe I deserved what he had done to me. I remembered the horrible things I'd once thought about myself: I was worthless, no one cared about me, the world would be better off without me in it. Depression lied. It always did. But knowing that did not stop those thoughts from spinning. It was one thing to see my family and hear them tell me they loved me. It was another to believe it myself. Up until the day Hollywood took a bullet for me, I genuinely thought I'd be better off dead.

Whenever those thoughts reared up again, I clutched the glass jar hanging around my neck, reminding myself of Hollywood's sacrifice. Whenever I let those dark thoughts creep in, whenever they fought for dominance in my mind, I remembered that night. I remembered how close to death I'd actually come and how hard I fought to stay alive, how hard Hollywood had fought to keep me alive.

The bullet reminded me there was at least one person in this world who would die for me, and I would *never* waste his blood again.

# 2

# HOLLYWOOD

"You ever been waxed from ass crack to nut sack, forced in a suit, and shoved up on stage to be auctioned off for charity?" I asked, wiping my hands on an oil rag as I approached Bear and Thor, both working on a Chevy pickup that had been brought in yesterday. Bear's boots hung out from underneath the front while Thor leaned over the hood, clenching his hands around a wrench.

"No," Bear grumbled. "And if you've got nothing to do but talk about your nut sack, you could hand me that Phillips-head by your left foot."

I bent down to get the screwdriver, placing it in Bear's outstretched palm before continuing. "I don't know if the fact it's for Pollux makes me more or less of a whore for a good cause."

"You don't have to sleep with the winner, Hollywood," Thor said, tightening the nut farther into place while Bear held the bolt firm. "In fact, I think Alba will insist that you don't."

I clapped Thor on the back and grinned. "Don't worry about that, my brother. I assure you, the days of a free-dicking Hollywood are gone."

"God," Thor said, straightening, before wiping his dirty hands on his shirt. "Go find something better to do before I do it for you."

"You see," I continued, ignoring his protests for the sake of the punch line, "despite the outcry of millions of broken hearts, I've taken a vow of chastity."

Bear snorted a laugh and scooted out from under the truck.

"I know what you're thinking. 'Hollywood! How could you?'" I grabbed my chest in mock dramatics, sighing as Thor rolled his eyes. "It's a terrible sacrifice I had to make for my own well-being. You understand, don't you? I mean, you're off the market now. How long were you whacking it solo before Selene finally—"

I ducked out of the way just in time to miss his massive fist as it flew at my face.

"Find something to do, Hollywood," Thor growled.

"Temper, temper. I tugged too hard on the wolf's tail." Mirth singing in my blood from getting under his skin, I laughed and walked back toward the Honda I'd been working on all morning. "I'll keep Selene's name out of my daily dick updates . . . I call them dick-dates."

Thor glared at me while he backed into the customer service area, his features lighting up as soon as he set them on his wife, who currently read a book behind the counter.

"Anything I need to know about Leo duty tonight?" Bear took a drink of water and sat down on the chair next to the truck, tilting his head to the side while he waited for my answer.

"He's healing up," I said, "but Saint says he's still not talking to anyone but me."

Bear nodded. "Good. It should be an easy shift, then."

Six months ago, we'd abducted Leo Caputi, the heir apparent of the notorious Caputi Mafia. For the first few weeks, he'd been detoxing off a bunch of shit and hadn't spoken to us. Around Christmas, Selene had insisted he be moved to a house, and the only MC-owned space that didn't have someone living in it was the two-bedroom I'd once shared with my older brother, Trojan. I had since moved in with Saint and Ru, but I came by daily to nurse the fucker back to health per a personal request from Crow. Leo had settled in and, after Selene did surgery on his knee to reset the poorly healed joint, he seemed to be doing much better. But being in that house again . . . looking at all the things I'd left behind . . . my chest ached just thinking about it.

Trojan had died while trying to protect Alba and Ru from Leo's uncle, Benito, the former boss of the Caputi crime family. After his death, the family had been taken over by his widow, Gabriella. We were still trying to figure out how to take her down.

Of everything I'd lost in my life, of everything that fate had stolen from me, that one hurt the most. I should have gotten over it by now as it had almost been two years, but in my darkest moments, I'd admit I probably never would.

I opened my mouth to tell Bear good luck, but my phone vibrated and cut me off. I reached into my back pocket, and after recognizing the number, I headed toward the door so I could take it outside.

"Will you accept the collect call from Allegheny County Penitentiary?" the robot voice asked.

"Yes." I reached into my pocket for my cigarettes, pulling one out to light it while I waited to be connected.

"Matty?" came my mother's hoarse voice. "Matty, is that you?"

"Hiya, Momma," I said, clenching my eyes shut at how horrible she sounded. She'd been a smoker all my life, but these years in prison had not been good to her. "How ya feeling?"

"Like rotten hell," she said. "But it's so good to hear your voice."

"You, too," I said, smiling. "Tell me what you've been doing."

"Not much of anything," she confessed before updating me about her sewing job and how little she'd made last week. "I hate to be trouble, but I need shampoo and conditioners."

"I'll put some cash in your account as soon as we hang up." I'd been taking care of her ever since Trojan died, sending her as much as I could every month. It never made a dent in helping her well-being, but I'd like to think it did more good than bad. "How's everything else?"

"Everything is all right, baby boy. How are you?"

I filled her in on the garage and the upcoming charity auction for Pollux. "I'm living with Saint and Ru, but I think I need to find a new place." They were still in the honeymoon phase of their reunion, and not that sex normally bothered me, but when I wasn't getting any of my own, I itched hearing it through the walls.

"It's good to talk to you, Momma," I said at the end. "Will you call me tomorrow?"

"I'll try," she said. "I love you."

"Love you most." We hung up and I cleared my throat, swallowing back the shame that usually burned in my gut when I talked to my mother. Images of being that scared little boy floated through my mind—the feel of the gun in my hand, the warmth of brains splattered on my face, the wail that had come out of her mouth after it'd happened.

*"Don't you ever blame yourself for that,"* Trojan had once told me. *"He got what was coming to him."*

I repeated that to myself and stuffed those complicated emotions deep down inside where they couldn't gnaw at me.

"Hey, you still working on this Honda or what?" Bear said, leaning out of the door with his eyebrows raised.

"Yeah, just taking a smoke break." I flicked my cigarette out and went back inside, determined to get the damn thing going before I left.

I hadn't always worked at Rose Garage. Back when Trojan had been alive, I only took shifts when times were rough. With no older brother looking out for me and Mom, I had to make up for both of us, and Thor needed the help now that KC's cam-star career was taking off.

Trojan and I had come to the SRMC when I was twelve. After Mom went away, someone had to take care of me. My brother hadn't even blinked before signing the guardianship papers and moving me from Pittsburgh to Madison County. He joined the SRMC shortly after that and got married to Marissa, the love of his life and one of the most awesome women I'd ever met. Once I turned eighteen, I prospected my way right on in with KC and Bear.

They'd been my best friends since we were kids, but once we'd patched in, they'd become brothers. I'd give my life for them and nearly had on several occasions. The oath I'd sworn to the Roses had protected me more times than I'd done for it, and I considered it my highest honor to call myself a part of their family. Besides, it wasn't like I had an old lady or kids waiting for me at home. Compared to every other brother, I was dispensable, just another body in the war against the Caputis.

I used to revel in everything that came with being a part of a MC —the drugs, the booze, the women. God, the women. I'd known I was good-looking since I hit puberty and people my mother's age started grabbing my ass whenever they wanted. Once I discovered I liked men too, they did the same. What could I say, I loved the attention. Who wouldn't?

The problem came after Trojan died, and I realized all those meaningless hookups were just that. Worthless. Emotionless. I saw the intense intimacy KC and Alba had when they looked at each other. I watched Saint and Ru come to terms with their own adoration after keeping it secret for so long. Thor and Selene had finally gotten together after years of chasing after each other's tails. I was never gonna have that if I didn't clean up my act. It took one conversation with Ru to realize that if I ever wanted to find a love like that, I needed to take myself more seriously, perhaps starting by keeping my dick in my pants until I found someone worth taking it out for.

Losing my brother so young made me appreciate the fact that life was too short to live the way I was, and if I kept going, I wasn't going to have anything to show for it but an early grave right next to Trojan. At least he had a widow. At least he had someone who could say they loved him and knew him better than anyone else in the world. All anyone had of me was the persona I put on every morning like a mask: good ole Hollywood, the guy with a smile for everyone, the one who would let anyone in his bed.

By the end of the day, I still didn't have the Honda working and I'd run out of ideas. Frustrated and resolved to work on it tomorrow, I dropped off the ticket to Selene on my way to the time punch.

"I'll have to check it out again later." I shook my head and scratched at the back of my hair. "The CPU could be busted."

Selene nodded and smiled. "Sure. I'll see you at the clubhouse later."

"You got it." I cleared my throat and swallowed down the guilt of what I was about to ask. I figured Selene would be a good person because she had a reputation of keeping her mouth shut and not digging too deep. "Hey, do you know if V is planning to come?"

She pursed her lips and narrowed her eyes, assessing me for any sign of weakness. Like her husband, she was a hunter and sniffed out injured prey a mile away. "I think so. Why do you ask?"

"No reason." I tried to play it off like my gut wasn't doing Goddamned somersaults, and I hitched my jeans higher on my hips. "I was just curious . . . ya know . . . who all is gonna be there and what not."

"Uh-huh." Selene tilted her head to the side, her bright blue eyes shimmering like she saw through me, all the way down to my bull- shit. As my best friend's twin sister, she had known me as long as him and nearly as well. "This wouldn't have anything to do with your little freak out at the Beacon's reopening . . . would it?"

"I didn't freak out." *I didn't. I swear I didn't.* Was it startling to see V decked out in leather with a crop in her hand? Yes. Was it even more shocking to see her skill with a cat-o'-nine-tails? Absolutely. Did it rattle me to the very core of my sick, perverted, sex-deprived heart? I plead the fifth.

"Sure," she said, taking a step closer to me. "Then what would make you get up and walk away while your buddy's sister was on stage performing her heart out?" Selene furrowed her eyebrows, pretending to play dumb. "Are you suddenly a big prude?"

"No," I spat, physically repulsed by the idea. If anyone in the MC were comfortable with their sexual liberation, it was me. I didn't limit myself to pussy. I enjoyed *all* humans, everything being a solid three on the Kinsey scale meant to our species. "I needed to get some air." I coughed, my throat suddenly too dry. "Besides, it was lucky I did, considering what happened afterward."

The whole place had exploded.

"Okay." Selene let out a small laugh and shook her head like she could see *Liar* stamped on my forehead. She patted my shoulder as she passed me, heading toward Thor's office in the back. "Have a nice night, Hollywood."

"Yeah, you, too." I turned and put my sunglasses on before heading out to my beat-up two-door pickup I'd inherited from Trojan ten years ago. It drained batteries and leaked oil like a son of a bitch, but I couldn't afford anything else, so I had to keep it running until the wheels fell off. After swinging by the house, where thankfully Ru and Saint weren't home, I grabbed a quick shower and tried to forget about that conversation with Selene.

Seeing V up on stage dominating our friend, Candy, lived in the darkest parts of my imagination. But if I were honest with myself, something had changed with her the moment she came home from college. When we were in school, she was Bear's little sister—the goth girl that gave me shit for sleeping around and wearing more hair products than she did. She'd gone away and come back a fucking powerhouse. She'd grown into her curves, confidence radiating out of every pore, and when she stared at me with that heated violet gaze, preparing to cut me down to size, I hung on the edge of my seat, just waiting to see what she would say.

Of course, she didn't think of *me* that way, and up until that night at the Beacon, I'd been very careful not to think of her that way, too. But fuck me . . . the dreams I'd had since then would make Bear beat my face in. If her brothers found out the things I'd been thinking, if her *father* found out, they'd feed me to the pigs. I was secure enough in my masculinity to admit when I was outnumbered, and the Montgomery men would pummel me for even considering it.

Standing in the shower, the house blissfully silent, I let myself sink into that fantasy again—the one where she tied me to a chair, my hands linked behind my back with ropes holding down my shivering muscles and anticipation brewing in my gut at watching her slink closer. She wore her chunky platform boots, a tiny black miniskirt with metal chains, and a cropped Bad Company T-shirt, arguably the most underrated band of all time.

"You've been such a naughty boy, Hudson," she said, using my last name.

Bound and gagged like this, all I could do was murmur a quiet, "Yes, ma'am."

"You've got a lot of making up to do, you sick little perv." She slapped the riding crop in her other hand as she circled me, waiting until she was behind me to lean down and whisper in my ear. "You think I don't know that you stand in the cold shower and pull your dick thinking about me? You think I don't see the way you stare? Oh, I know what you want, you nasty fuck."

I gulped, watching as she came back around to the front, stepping in between my bare legs to stare down at me like a disapproving Goddess to her reckless devotee.

*I've been bad. So, so bad. Do it. I deserve it.*

"And I'm going to give it to you." V raised the crop and brought it down with a harsh *thwack* on the inside of my leg.

*The sting feels so good, and it's for her. She owns me. She owns every part of my body. I let her have it.*

I didn't stand a chance. The idea of her using me the way she'd used Candy, bringing me unimaginable pain mixed with the release of incredible ecstasy, had me shooting my load down the drain before I could catch my breath.

Perhaps it was the eight months with no action that had me leaning up against the shower wall and panting like a raging alcoholic in a distillery. I'd never come like that thinking about anyone else in my life, which was probably why she kept the starring role.

Was it because she was Bear's little sister, the most forbidden of fruits? Or was it because she complemented the side of me that wanted to submit, the side that wanted someone to take control, to take my worst behavior out on my ass?

Everyone I'd ever met saw my face and treated me a certain way because of it. Not V. She was the only one who clawed at me, desperate to draw blood no matter where she swiped . . . and God help me, I fucking wanted her to bleed me dry.

I SPOTTED Verona the moment I arrived, sitting with Selene and Thor in the audience. She had on that black miniskirt from my daydream and a Van Halen crop top with a big fluffy black sweater that looked soft and fuzzy. I immediately wanted to curl up in her lap, let her run her fingers through my hair, and bury my face in her secret places.

Despite all the people I'd fucked, all the people I'd effortlessly charmed into my bed, I suddenly didn't know how to act around this one girl—and not even because something weird had happened between us. No, it was because I wanted the worst fucking things in the world from her, and I simply couldn't have them.

*Nope.*

Shouldn't want them. Couldn't think about wanting them. And every time I did, I deserved to be strung up and whipped. *Fuck, I wonder how hard she could hit.*

No. No. *No.*

Shoving that deep down inside where no one could see it, I put on my Hollywood mask and made the rounds, laughing and hugging everyone I called family.

"Heya, Ruthie," I said, leaning in to give her a kiss on the cheek. Even though I lived with her, I relished any time we got to spend together. She was one of my best friends, the proverbial little sister I'd never had. When Saint started fucking around with her heart, I'd stepped in to remind him who and what she was. No one fucked with any of my girls like that and got away with it, especially not Ru.

"Hey, Hollywood. Are you ready for this?" She wagged her eyebrows. "I overheard the hang-arounds talking about how there's a pool on when and with whom you'll break your celibate streak."

"Really?" I raised my eyebrows, suddenly intrigued. "How big's the pot? Maybe I ought to get in on that action." I could use the money.

She laughed and pulled me into a hug before letting me go so she could head toward the stage to finish getting things ready. I joked with Wheels and wrestled with Lore, happy I could put a smile on the lonely brother's face. Last summer, he'd been maimed by the Caputis and hadn't really bounced back. He was a nice guy, and he'd looked out for Ru when no one else had, so I figured it was the least I could do.

Verona had finally caught sight of me and stood to walk closer, her gaze piercing through my heavily guarded fortress like a laser. I had to get out of here. I had to move before I smelled her delicious perfume and whatever it was that drew me in like a succubus.

I turned to make for the bathroom but ran face-first into Chelsea, the last hang-around I'd hooked up with before deciding to quit cold turkey. It had been months, but every so often, she came trailing around again like a feral kitten that knew I'd feed her if she meowed hard enough. Not that our time together hadn't been nice; it had just been same as all the other people before it—physical and devoid of anything special. I didn't want that anymore. I thought . . . Well, maybe I thought I deserved better, that Trojan died so I *could* have better.

She wrapped her arms around my neck and pushed up on her toes to press her entire body against mine.

"I want you deep inside my ass, Hollywood," she said. "It's been so long."

*Good fucking God. These women are ruthless.*

"I already told you," I said, pulling her arms down so I could push her back. "I'm taking a break."

She blinked up at me with disappointment in her big eyes and a pout on her lips. "Not even for me?"

*Especially not for you.*

"I'm sorry, sugar." I brushed a piece of hair out of her face and pushed it back behind her ear. "But hey, if you've got the money, you can bid on a few hours of my time."

Her face lit up like I'd told her the winning lotto numbers, and she wrapped her arms around my waist tighter.

"A few *PG* hours of my time," I corrected, disentangling myself from her embrace again before she got handsy.

That deflated her ego, and she backed away with a frown. "I'll see you then."

Trying not to grimace at the thought of attempting to keep her off me if she won, I walked toward Alba, who was waving at me from the side of the stage where she stood next to KC.

"You look great, Hollywood," she said, brushing her hands over the shoulders of my blazer. "Where'd you find this?"

"It was Trojan's." I shrugged, trying not to make anyone cry at his memory. "I think he wore it to prom."

Alba laughed and hugged me while KC shook his head and lit a cigarette.

"You clean up nice, old sport," KC said, patting me on the cheek like a grandpa sending one of his grandchildren off to school on their first day.

"Yeah? You, too." I nodded and fixed my jacket, buttoning it together to make myself look more dapper. He, of course, was still wearing jeans and his cut, indicating he had no intention of getting up on that stage to take one for the team.

*Coward.*

Though, to be fair, Alba would probably claw a girl's eyes out before anyone else got their hands on him.

Ru climbed the platform to get things started and rev up the crowd while I stood on the sidelines waiting for my turn to go.

"Thank you all for coming," Ru said. "As you know, the proceeds from tonight will go to help our brother, Pollux, recover and pay his medical bills, which are piling up, so please be generous."

The crowd whooped and hollered, clapping for Ru as she went on. She called the brothers up one at a time and read their highlight reel out to the audience.

"Skulls is a graduate of Baltimore College," she said, gesturing to the brother in question while he model-walked his way to the middle of the stage and grinned into the spotlight. "He's six foot three-inches of intimidating fun, working as a bouncer at the Viper. When he's not keeping dive bars safe, he enjoys reading and romantic walks on the beach."

Skulls narrowed his eyes at that last embellishment but maintained his forced smile while the bidding began. After one of the old ladies won, he stepped off the stage so that Ru could call up the next brother, Switch, our resident IT guru.

"He's smart," Ru said, "and he's good with his fingers, ladies. He can type over two hundred words a minute. Give him anyone to track down, he'll find them in under an hour." She rattled on about Switch's most precious assets, and after he went for two hundred dollars, I figured the night would go well for Pollux. The brothers after him went for a similar amount, and all was going fine until Aris started a bidding war among three of the hang-arounds. Everyone else found it hilarious, but I worried about the veep. Until recently, he'd never been one to sleep around, not with club girls. I figured he musta hit a midlife crisis going a thousand miles an hour, especially after his daughter, Ru, got engaged to his best friend, Saint.

*Maybe I ought to try talking to him after this is over. Maybe I can cheer him up. That could help, right?*

"Are you ready?" Alba finally asked, squeezing my shoulders and bringing me back to reality.

"Of course. I'm always ready." I straightened my suit jacket and grinned, giving her a wink that had her rolling her eyes with a laugh.

"There's a reason they put you last," KC said, clapping me on the back.

"I'm hoping you clean house." Alba smiled and cupped both sides of my face before giving each of my cheeks a big kiss. "Go make me proud."

Once upon a time, KC had dated a hang-around, Nikki, before she turned traitor and betrayed us to the Caputis. Their relationship had been one of the most toxic things I'd ever witnessed. When KC met Alba, I worried it might end up being the same thing, but they balanced each other out more than I could have ever hoped. She brightened his world, and he kept her safe, giving her a place to call home. I envied what they had with a passion—the intimacy, the adoration, the trust in another person to be a peaceful haven.

"And last up," Ru said, drawing my attention back to the stage. "You've all been waiting for him. Hell, he's probably the reason most of you are here. Let's give it up for Hollywood!"

I walked up on the platform, waving to the crowd of hang-arounds, members, and old ladies. Everyone clapped, some whistling and shouting, "Take it off!"

I laughed, amused and delighted by the attention. I knew I looked good. I took great pride in staying that way. If I wasn't at the garage or Saint's house, I was in the clubhouse's makeshift gym behind the back rooms. Of course, my Leo babysitting duties and extra shifts at the shop had put a damper on that recently, but I still got it in when I could.

"By day, Hollywood is a mechanic, but by night, he has been known to prowl the clubhouse with his charismatic grin, searching for anyone who might need a laugh." Ru read a SparkNotes version of my life from an index card while whoever ran the music blasted "Whatta Man" by Salt-N-Pepa over the speaker. "We'll start the bidding at one hundred dollars."

Chelsea was the first to raise her bid.

"I see one hundred," Ru said. "Do I have two?"

KC made everyone laugh by putting up his number. "I need help renovating the Beacon."

I chuckled and shook my head, knowing I'd do it regardless, but I was happy he'd pushed the bid higher.

"Two hundred," Ru added. "Anyone going for three?"

Chelsea fought back, shooting a sneer at KC while she raised her marker. Then another hang-around, Amber, joined her and my heart dropped into my gut. I hadn't talked to Amber in months, not since that awkward drunken night between us, and not that I'd mind a few hours in her company, but she'd probably want to fuck. That was all anyone ever wanted from me.

I cleared my throat and tried to smile wider, knowing a million eyes were on me and they'd see any sign of insecurity. Besides, the money went to a good cause, right? Pollux would have some of his medical bills paid, and all I had to do was sit through an afternoon of a beautiful woman pawing at my bits. I'd done worse for less.

After those two duked it out up to five hundred dollars, someone else joined the fray, someone I'd been avoiding for weeks now, someone I purposely hadn't looked at or talked to for reasons I couldn't explain.

"Eight hundred dollars," Verona said, raising an eyebrow at Chelsea before shooting a side-eye at Amber. My pulse hammered through my body, thrumming down to my cock before traveling the length of my legs and back up again. My grin tightened. My hands clenched into fists before I consciously relaxed them.

*What the fuck does she want with me?*

## 3

## VERONA

They were making him nervous. I could see it even if everyone else was only focused on his pretty face. He'd made some ridiculous vow of celibacy, and the hang-arounds couldn't do anything except claw at him like hyenas on an injured lion.

That shit was fucked-up.

I didn't like the territorial way Chelsea looked at him when he'd arrived, like she had a right to his body even if he resisted. When the other one upped the ante, a similar look of possession in her stare, I decided I wouldn't let that happen.

I knew what it was to put your head down and suffer things your body resisted just to get through it. Hollywood loved this family too much to say anything, loved them enough to spend time with those handsy bitches so that Pollux would have an easier road ahead.

"Nine hundred," Chelsea replied, and I rolled my eyes, knowing I could wipe the floor with these bitches.

It wasn't like I sat on a small fortune, but I'd done well with my clients that afternoon, and one had tipped me three grand alone. I could take this much further than she could.

"Fifteen hundred," I said, relishing the way she opened her mouth and twisted her ugly glare in my direction.

"Two grand," she said, her high-pitched voice turning into a whine.

"Twenty-five hundred." I crossed my arms and took a deep breath, waiting to see if she'd balk.

Hollywood opened his mouth and widened his eyes at me, somehow still managing to look pretty with a gaping jaw, and Selene laughed from her spot a few seats down.

"Twenty-five hundred, going once . . ." Ru glanced over the crowd. When Chelsea crossed her arms and frowned, leaning back in her seat, I relished my victory. She didn't have the cash to match me, and when I glanced back at Amber, her sullen features confirmed she didn't, either. With no one else going for that amount of money, the audience sat in stunned silence while Ru brought it to a close. "Going twice . . . Sold, to Verona Montgomery for twenty-five hundred dollars. Please see the treasurer to pay your balance."

Hollywood walked off the stage, adjusting his jacket as he headed toward Coins in the far corner. The MC's treasurer had volunteered to help with accounting tonight, and when I walked up, he grinned like I was the cat that stole the cream.

"You sure gave those girls a run for their money," he said.

I whipped out my checkbook to write the information while Hollywood moved around the table to stand beside me. He'd been avoiding me for a while now, and when he'd nearly collided with Chelsea earlier trying to get away from me, I realized we had an issue. He'd looked like he'd seen a ghost and quickly turned away. Now, he stood stiff as a board and more quiet than I'd ever seen him.

"Yeah, well"—I ripped the check free and handed it to Coins— "like KC, I need renovations done and Hollywood's big and sturdy." I punched his shoulder like I'd done all my life, but instead of the friendly banter I'd become accustomed to, he only smiled and nodded. That confused me more.

*What the hell is his problem?*

"Just make sure you watch your back." Coins nodded to Chelsea and Amber, who stood next to each other with twin looks of disdain. I waved and smiled wider, making a big show of wrapping my arm under Hollywood's elbow to pull him in tight.

"I'm not worried about them. They're just jealous." I blew a fake kiss their way.

Clearly disgusted with me, they both crossed their arms and walked toward the other hang-arounds at the far edge of the platform.

"Besides," I continued, "Pollux needs the help, so it'll go to a good cause." It was the least I could do, and if my brother needed more, I'd gladly give it.

While we waited for Ru to bring everything to an end, I stared up at my "prize." He swallowed, and I memorized the flat expanse of skin on his neck as it disappeared under his jacket. Hollywood smelled amazing, all man and sandalwood and pine, and he looked even better than usual in his fancy jacket.

"You clean up nice, Hollywood," I said, "for a street tramp."

He curled the sides of his mouth into a devilish smile, glancing down to meet my gaze. "Thanks."

It had been weeks since we'd been this close to each other, longer since we'd made eye contact. Now, as I held that melted mahogany stare, I noticed flecks of gold pooling in his irises, dotting the brilliant earthy landscape with glittering rarity. Like everything else about him, his eyes were mischievously gorgeous.

"You're welcome." I fought against the heat snaking up my neck and into my cheeks, telling myself it had nothing to do with that mesmerizing gaze being set on me. No, I'd just dropped a lot of money on a few hours of his time, and I didn't want people . . . namely him . . . asking questions about that. How could I tell him I'd seen in Chelsea the same thing I'd once seen in Curtis, that same obsession and toxic desperation?

"Hey, little sis!" Castor called, breaking my trance. He was currently setting up the cards and chips on the table in the side room, away from the crowd. "You still in for Texas Hold'em? Or did you blow your load on the big guy?"

"Nope, I'm still in." I ignored my brother's innuendo and nodded, glancing back up at Hollywood. "You up for trying to help me make my money back?"

He barked out a chuckle and led the way.

After the auction ended, they put on music and cleared the floor for dancing, but I was more concerned with whipping a bunch of grown men into submission via poker.

"Oh shit, I didn't think you were serious about inviting her," Lore said, scratching at his eye patch. "I might as well bail out now."

"One of these days, I'm going to beat you," Wheels said with a wink.

"Oh, yeah?" I sat down at the far corner and put a cigarette between my lips, taking a moment to light it before blowing the smoke away from them. "You think today will be that day?"

"She's good," Castor said. "But she's not as good as me."

"That's right, I'm better," I teased. I'd been playing with Castor and Hollywood since we were kids, so I knew their tells, but Lore and Wheels would take some work to figure out.

Castor explained the buy-ins and blinds, and after the first round, I had a better idea for the two newer brothers. Lore only had one working eye, but he blinked when he didn't have anything good. Wheels shifted in his seat when he got a pair of queens on the river, giving him a three of a kind. That told me what I needed to know about how to read him. Castor's tell had been the same since we were little. As soon as he saw his cards, he rubbed his nose if he had a good hand. If he didn't, he licked his lips. Hollywood, on the other hand, had trained his physical body well enough not to give anything away, but he turned into a chatty Cathy if he was trying to distract his opponent. When he got to talking, I paid attention to his bluffs.

This went on for a few hours while we laughed and joked with each other, but eventually, I started to clean up. The more I drank, the better I got at outsmarting the others . . . or perhaps the more they drank, the worse they got at hiding their hands.

"Jesus, V," Castor said when I'd won the last several rounds. "Can you knock it off?"

"Who taught her how to play like that?" Lore said.

"I did," both Castor and Hollywood said at the same time, making me burst into laughter.

"You're both idiots," I said. "It was Bear, of course."

"Ahh." Wheels smiled, lighting up his entire face. "I should have known. That motherfucker can read anyone."

He could. We'd both learned from our dad. When a man had his money on the line, an itch was never just an itch, and a shift of the hips could mean the difference between winning the pile and going home empty-handed. After I won another two rounds, Castor and Wheels had lost their money and gotten too drunk to keep going, so they went back into the main room to party. In this hand, I had the bigger pot, but Lore was ready to call it quits.

"I'm all in," he said, spilling his few chips into the center.

"Fold," Hollywood said.

"I'll call. Show your cards, buddy." I flipped mine over to reveal two pair.

He had nothing. He was bluffing.

"Jesus, Lore." I laughed as I cleaned up his chips and piled them neatly in front of me. For a hundred-dollar buy-in, I was up nearly two hundred bucks. "You're terrible at this game."

"Nah." He waved me away, slurring a bit as he stood. "I've got, uh . . . some business . . ." He cleared his throat and waved at the hang-around that had spent a hundred dollars to win him earlier. She stood by the door with a playful look, beckoning him to the back rooms. When he reached her, he wrapped his arm over her shoulder and let her lead him out of my sight.

Now, only Hollywood and I sat at the table while he lazily shuffled the cards and stared at me. I let him have his fill, relishing the way his eyes trailed down my neck, over my shoulders and chest, and back up again. His gaze brushed against my skin like a caress, like I'd suddenly been stripped naked in front of him.

"You've been avoiding me," I said, hoping to break the tension.

"Have I?" He raised his eyebrows, seeming surprised while he looked down at the cards. "I don't think that's true." He pursed his lips and dealt the hand before placing the deck down in the middle of the table, discarding the first card before flipping the next three over. Based on that, I had three queens but hoped for the fourth in the next two turns.

"Any time I look in your direction, you shift away," I continued. "If I try to talk, you flee like a bat out of hell." I took in his stiff muscles and the way his feet were perched by the sides of his chair, like he might get up and run any second. "Did I do something to piss you off?"

He cleared his throat and shifted in his seat before grabbing two chips and tossing them in. I called his bet and he flipped the next card over, revealing a king of spades.

"You didn't do anything," he said, shaking his head. "I've just got some personal shit going on."

"Is it your mom?" She'd been locked up most of his life, but I knew they were close.

"No, she's fine," he said. "It's nothing you need to be worried about."

"Hmm." I didn't like that answer, but I let him have his privacy. If he wanted me to know or if there was anything I could do to help, he'd tell me. "Why did Wheels take over as my bodyguard? Was it the big thing you had to do for the club?"

Not that I cared—*not at all*—but it had been nice to have someone I knew as well as Hollywood by my side for those few months. I liked Wheels, but it was hard for me to trust people in general, and Hollywood was my brother's best friend. Even if I couldn't fully open myself up to him, I trusted my brother enough to trust Hollywood.

"So nosy tonight." Hollywood grinned, dropping a few more chips into the pile. I called his bet before he flipped the next card over, showing the last queen. Holy shit, I had the hand of a century, but I didn't let that show. I tried to keep my features as calm as I could.

"We have a lot to catch up on," I said.

At that, he pushed his entire pile into the center, clearly pulling the same move that Lore had just done. "I'm all in."

I stared at him, waiting to see if he'd start talking. When he just sat there, blinking at me with a calm, stony face, I made my decision.

"Me, too." I toppled my chips over, making a big pile, and he tucked his bottom lip between his teeth as he revealed his hand. He had a royal flush.

Holy shit, *he* had the hand of a century, and he'd beaten me. He'd ... actually beaten me with a one-in-a-million deal.

"Fuck," I whispered.

"I guess you don't have anything better than that, huh?" He smiled, and I'd never wanted to wipe that grin off his face more. I seethed while he collected his chips and put them in a nice pile in front of him, reveling in his victory.

"Fuck off," I said with a small laugh, rolling my eyes as I threw my cards at him. "I hate you."

"Yeah, I know." He flashed me a Hollywood grin and winked. "It turns me on."

"Does it?" I ignored the rush of hot lust between my legs. This was one of our games, the schtick between us where I insulted him and he love-bombed me and on the world spun. At this point in the night, I'd had a lot to drink and I didn't pick up on the nuance in the way his eyes raked over my body. I just barreled onward with the joke. "I could hate you so much more than I do."

He snapped his gaze to mine, raised an eyebrow, and smirked. "Really? How much more?"

"Ohhh, that'll cost you, Hudson."

His eyes lit up at my use of his real last name, the one I'd used since high school. "What's your price?"

The game had escalated quicker than I'd planned and after *several* tequila shots, I couldn't think clearly. My attention caught on the cards. "How about another hand? If I win, you give me the pot. If you win, I'll hate you any way you want."

He stayed quiet as he clicked two chips together between his fingers and considered my proposal. "What are the limits?"

*Wait . . . is he taking this seriously? Am I?*

I clung to my inhibitions by a thread, and if I'd been sober, I might have laughed in his face, stood, and walked away. But fuck it, right? Why not have a little fun? I put my elbows on the table and leaned in.

"We're both wasted; we're beyond consent. So you're not allowed to touch me. I know about your celibacy thing, so I won't touch you. Just about anything else is on the table."

"Deal," he said, barely letting me finish my sentence before speaking and grabbing the cards to shuffle through them again. My chest tightened, anticipation clenching in my gut. The boundary between us had only broken one time in twenty years, and he didn't know that was me. He'd thought it was the side chick he'd been screwing that night, and I'd never had the ovaries to tell him differently.

Hollywood stared at me while he dealt the hand, and I started to feel hopeful when I received a king of hearts and a queen of spades. That optimism diminished, however, when he flipped over the next three cards.

I had nothing. Absolutely nothing.

"Uh-oh," he said, "that doesn't look like a happy face." Hollywood stuck out his lower lip, pretending to pout.

I sneered and gestured at him to keep going.

When he flipped over the rest of the cards, I took a deep breath and sat back in my seat, relegating myself to the fact I'd agreed to do whatever he wanted based on the luck of the draw, and today was *not* my lucky day.

"Well?" He grinned, raising his eyebrows. "Moment of truth."

Swallowing against a dry throat, I flipped my cards over to reveal my big fat nothing.

"Oh no, little Montgomery." His voice had dropped an octave, turning into a sultry purr that had me struggling not to tremble, and he flipped his hand over to reveal his hand: a full house. He'd beaten me by a landslide.

"Wow," I said, almost refusing to believe it. "Did you cheat, Hudson?"

"How dare you accuse me of fraud." Pretending to be offended, he grabbed his smokes and leaned back in his seat to light one, staring at me with a different glimmer in his dark gaze. Now, he looked like a fan meeting his idol for the first time, stars in his eyes and a big greedy grin on his lips. "Now, I think you said something about hating me any way I wanted."

I shifted in my seat and cleared my throat, refusing to break eye contact. If I looked away first, he'd seize on that weakness and strike. I knew how these alpha assholes wanted it, and I'd agreed so long as he didn't touch me. Now, I prepared myself for whatever would come out of that deliciously wicked mouth next.

## 4

## VERONA

"Well, what do you want?" I asked, licking my lips.

He dropped his focus to the movement, bringing his cigarette to his mouth for a deep inhale before letting the smoke out on a sigh. Then, he stood and walked to the door separating this room from the main clubhouse area. It was three thirty in the morning, and even though the music still blared from out there, most of the brothers had either headed home already or passed out in the back rooms. Despite this, Hollywood leaned out and glanced around before kicking the door closed and sealing the lock.

The sound of the metal deadbolt sliding into place bounced off the walls, increasing my heart rate as I realized I was trapped . . . alone . . . in a room with Hollywood . . . after agreeing to do whatever he wanted.

Any of those hang-arounds out there would have died for this opportunity, and yet, my hands trembled and my palms grew sweaty. I sat still, my attention glued to the way his hips moved as he stalked back to his seat like a predator, lithe powerful muscles rolling under his skin. The silence hung between us, and for half a heartbeat, I considered that this too might be a game. I'd been preparing for something sexual, and he'd force me to do something stupid and ridiculous to embarrass myself.

"I want you," he started, lowering his body back into his seat, "to talk to me like you do to your submissives."

*What?*

I trained my features, doing my best to keep a cool expression as my brain came to a halt. Of all the things I'd thought he'd say, that had not even ranked in the top ten. He wanted *me* to dominate *him*? Verbally?

*Jesus fucking Christ, sign me up. Wait . . . What?*

"Why?" I asked, narrowing my gaze in suspicion. *Is this a trick?*

"I already told you"—he leaned in, lowering his voice even further—"because it turns me on."

I inhaled on slow measured breaths, telling myself we'd both had a lot to drink, so this was as much about him being uninhibited as me. We would regret this in the morning, but at that moment, I couldn't find any reason to stop.

"Why me?" I held his gaze, his dark irises now almost turned completely black by his pupils. "You could have your choice of any of those hang-arounds—"

"I've never seen any of them so skilled with a whip." He punctuated the *P* on the end of the last word, making it seem more erotic than it had any right being.

"I should have known." I raised an eyebrow, wishing my heart would stop beating so damned hard. I had no idea Hollywood would *ever* think about me in this way, but now that he'd implanted the image in my mind, I couldn't deny the effect it had on me. I'd love nothing more than to make him kiss my boots and thank me for it. He had such a beautiful face, exquisitely built for riding. "No." I cut off that line of thought off. "No, pick something else."

"Why?" He furrowed his brows, actually seeming hurt.

"Because you're you . . . and I'm me."

"Oh, c'mon," he said, rolling his eyes. "Like you said, I won't touch you and you won't touch me. It's nothing I can't go online and get anytime I wanted."

That got my attention. "You've watched my videos?"

"Guess you'll have to play me again to find out." He shrugged, tilting his head back so he stared down at me with rebellion flickering behind his gaze. "Now, we had a bet and you need to pay up."

"What *exactly* did you have in mind?"

He blew a breath out through his nose while he leaned back in his seat and ran his eyes over me again.

"I want you to take off your underwear and stuff it in my mouth," he said, shifting his hips while he pulled on his cigarette. "Then, I want you to spread your legs and show me your pretty pussy while you finger yourself and tell me how much you love hating me."

*Fucking hell.* My cunt twisted with excitement, my thighs shivering as I clenched them to alleviate the ache. Every bit of logical restraint I had screamed at me to stop this. Sober Verona would not like it, but Drunk Verona told that sober buzzkill to take a fucking hike. She figured I might as well put my money where my mouth was.

Reaching for my water, I took a few steadying sips and closed my eyes, trying to summon the headspace despite being tipsy. When I lowered the cup and opened them again, Hollywood had stabbed his cigarette out and now waited for my reaction, his beautiful brown stare hungry.

"What the fuck are you looking at, Hudson?" I raised my eyebrow and looked at him like he was a despicable cockroach, like he deserved to be crushed under my heel. "Do you think I waste my time on cum dumpsters like you?"

"Fucking . . . fuck," he murmured, his eyes widening.

"Silence," I commanded, pleased when he snapped his jaw shut. "You will speak when I ask you to."

He grinned and bit his bottom lip, seemingly anticipating whatever I'd make him do next.

"Well?" I gestured to the space between my legs. "You wanted to watch, right? Get your ass over here."

He hopped out of his seat so fast, it nearly fell over, and he dropped to his knees, crawling to the spot between mine before sitting back on his haunches. My thighs shook as I raised a boot to put it on his shoulder, giving him quite the view in between my legs. He gasped, his gaze dropping to my cunt before he remembered his place and glanced back up at me.

"Do you see something you want?" I teased.

He nodded and swallowed, looking all too eager to get his greedy fingers up my skirt.

"Well, go ahead. Take them off."

Hollywood started to raise his hands, but I smacked them away. "Don't you remember the rules? No touching."

He looked up at me with big, confused eyes, and I almost caved to do it myself. *Almost.*

"You have a mouth, don't you?" I tsked through my teeth as he opened his lips, realization dawning behind that gorgeous dark stare. Then, he froze, seemingly unsure now that he was here and had to participate. "If you want to stop this, say red."

"No," he blurted out. "No, I just . . ." Gulping, he met my gaze, looking so much like a younger version of himself, like a lucky little boy that had gotten to play with a new toy before his friends. "I want to take my time."

Part of me melted because he was so fucking cute. But the other part of me remembered the role-play, the one that he wanted from me. I leaned in toward him, trying to be intimidating when I hissed, "I don't have all fucking night. Get to it."

His features gleaming, he ducked his head under my skirt and latched on to the black undies with his front teeth, pausing for a few moments to breathe me in. I had to pretend that hearing his deep drawling inhale didn't make me drip with disgusting lust.

*What a filthy man. I love it.*

"Uh, uh, uh," I said, pushing his head away from me. "No one said you could linger. Take them off."

He retreated, holding the fabric with his mouth while I slid them down my thighs. Even though I was hammered, I took a moment to admire the sight in front of me—the most beautiful man in Madison County on his knees, my underwear hanging out of his mouth, his eyes sparkling up at me while he waited for my next command.

"You're such a good little slut, aren't you?" I gathered the fabric and stuffed it in between his lips, careful not to touch his skin.

Hollywood nodded, and my pulse pounded through my body, electrifying me in ways I hadn't experienced in a long time . . . maybe ever. This was one of the tamer scenes I'd done, and I was practically trembling. I couldn't contain my nerves, and truth be told, I prayed I remembered this in the morning because I would likely masturbate to it for years to come—once I got over the fact it was Hollywood.

"Now, I want you to stay there and watch while I get off," I said. "Then, if you're good enough, maybe I'll let you touch yourself." The mental images alone were enough to have me biting back a whimper. "Would you like that?"

His quick nod made me smile, and when I sat back in the seat, I waved two fingers at him, gesturing him closer. If I planned to give him a show, I might as well make it a good one. When he got face level with my knees, I grabbed the hemline of my skirt and slowly dragged it up my thighs, watching as his features tightened with each agonizing inch. Once it was high enough, I spread my legs open, giving him a floor-seat view of my vulva.

The throaty little moan he made etched itself in my molecules, amping up my own arousal, and when I spread my fingers through my sensitive skin, I rolled my head back on my shoulders at how wet I already was. Having him watch me up close like this had brought a new level of intimacy I'd never experienced before, if only because I knew him better than my clients and longer than any boyfriend I'd ever had. I rubbed my clit, gathering moisture from lower down and using it to lubricate my ministrations.

Sparks flew over my skin and I pushed onto the balls of my feet to increase my muscle tension, watching as his eyes trailed over every inch of me. He focused on my cunt before going to my breasts and face and returning to the main event. He didn't know what to do with himself, and perhaps I was a selfish bitch because I relished in being able to drag the mighty heartthrob down so low.

"Look at you," I went on, remembering this show was supposed to be about *hating* him. "Squirming like a pathetic waste of space. Aren't you the great Casanova? The Lothario of the SRMC? And you want to watch *me?*" I let out a harsh laugh, shaking my head at the ironic beauty of it all. Chelsea and Amber likely wanted him to hold them down and be the dominant asshole they'd heard so much about. But Hollywood didn't want that. He wanted the opposite. He wanted someone to be the asshole *to him.* As I rubbed myself with one hand, I brought the other to my entrance, stuffing a finger inside.

He gulped, the muscles in his throat moving as he swallowed, and I wanted to sink my teeth into that magnificent expanse to leave marks—to see how bright pink they'd appear on his skin after I made them. Fuck, every part of him was beautiful and sculpted by pure divinity, and I wanted to destroy it, use it as a landscape for my violent kinks.

"How desperate you must be after all these months with no one in your bed," I went on. "Tell me, pretty boy, are you desperate? You can speak."

"Yes," he mumbled around my undies. "So desperate."

"Hmm, I bet. You poor thing." I grinned at his displeasure. "Go on, you can stroke your miserable cock if you want. Show me how hard I make you."

He scrambled to get his zipper undone, pushing up on his knees so he could free the enormous length, his fingers slipping on the metal as they shook. I'd heard rumors about Hollywood's infamous dick, and they certainly existed for a reason. It was long and girthy, and honestly, one of the prettiest penises I'd ever laid eyes on.

*Is nothing about him ugly?*

"I hate you," I said, remembering what prompted this whole thing to begin with. I rubbed myself harder, faster, watching as he spit in his hand and circled the tip, squeezing while his eyes stayed glued to my pussy. Curling my fingers in deeper, I tossed my head back, loving how my moans grew breathy and pronounced. "You're so fucking smug and arrogant . . . and fuck . . . I hate you so much, so fucking much."

This wasn't supposed to be about me; this was *his* scene, *his* winnings, but I couldn't help myself. Having his eyes on me as I masturbated and degraded him was more tantalizing than anything I'd ever done. And just when my orgasm claimed me, my hand swiping over my clit agonizingly hard, I pinched my nipple to access the parts of my brain that loved the pain, tipping things over the edge.

Euphoria sky rocketed into my legs and up my spine, clenching my eyes shut, forcing a groan over my lips. It ached and throbbed, and I couldn't stop myself from loving it, perhaps growing addicted to the feeling after only one round.

When I opened my eyes, Hollywood had stopped stroking himself, a bright, reverent expression on his face, his eyes wide and his mouth hanging open.

5

## HOLLYWOOD

I didn't know watching someone else climax could be so fucking intense. Granted, I had made a lot of people come in my life, but this was . . . *Holy fucking shit.* Was it because I had fantasized about it for months? Was it because she'd degraded me while she did it? Was it because I wasn't allowed to touch? Whatever had glued my attention to her, I couldn't shake it.

Her panties coated my tongue with the sweet taste of her wet cunt, shooting the delectable flavor down the back of my throat. The mere hint of it was so fucking delicious that I yearned to situate my face between her legs and take my Goddamned time. I would stay on my knees and watch her play with herself for eons. When she caught me staring at her, she grinned and dug her boot in harder on my shoulder, holding me in place.

"Go on," she said. "Show me how you like it, Hudson."

Fuck, the way she said my last name had me tugging my cock like the world might end. My feet had fallen asleep ages ago, but I didn't care. I sat there and yanked because she wanted it—because she commanded it.

"Does it feel good?" she murmured, her voice coming out in a purr that ricocheted wanton hunger down my back and into my balls.

"Uh-huh." My lower stomach clenched, and I slid my hand faster, grabbing the tip the way I liked. My head fell back on my shoulders, and I watched her watching me. When our eyes connected, I lost myself in that vibrant shade of deep blue—so blue it was almost the shade of irises in the sun. She pressed her lips into a pleased smile, her cheeks blushing an adorable shade of pink.

Fuck, that made me harder. She was so rough all the time, so quick to hiss at anyone that got close to her, but I made her blush. *Me.* The one she never had a nice word for, the one she lived to cut down to size.

"Do you want to come?" She raised a perfectly manicured eyebrow, staring down her nose at me like the peon that I was, like I was scum on the boot currently holding me in place.

"Yes, please, yes." I forced the words around her drenched panties, knowing it wouldn't take much more. I was already so close. She dug her chunky black heel into an old bullet wound, one she knew was there, and she leaned in closer, spreading her legs wider so I had a better view of her messy wet pussy.

"Spit those out and tell me how much you love the fact that I hate you. Tell me how much you want me to hate you again and again." *Fuck,* I nearly melted on the ground. Yeah, I was a special kind of fucked-up that I liked when she talked down to me, but no one else spoke to me like this. No one dared even try. No one but her, and with her sultry vibrant tone, my hands shook as my orgasm built in the center of my spine, preparing to burst out the tip of my cock.

"I love when you hate me, Mistress," I said, pushing her lacy fabric out so I could keep going. "Hate me as much as you want." My broken words tipped the scales, and I grabbed my nuts, yanking down on them hard to add a slice of pain to the building pleasure. "Fuck, fuck, fuck."

I was almost there . . . almost there . . .

A loud bang came from the door as someone twisted on the handle and tried to walk in, but the deadbolt caught and slammed against the metal lock.

At the surprise, I came like a fucking firehose, spurting all over my pants and hand and the space between her legs, catching some on her boots. I came and came and came, like I hadn't whacked it out this morning, imagining this very scenario, like I hadn't thought about this a hundred times before.

"V? Are you still in there?" Wheels called, slurring his words. "Why the fuck is this door locked? Have you seen Hollywood?"

I couldn't stop the eruption in my blood. The world had ceased to spin on its axis, my entire soul having been shoved out of my body and back in again. I was drunk, sure, but this climax broke through that like a freight train barreling out of control.

"Shit," V hissed, pushing to her feet. "Yeah, I'm in here, Wheels. What do you want?"

"Why's the door locked?" He tried to barge in again. "Are you okay?"

"I'm sleeping," she said. "I'm really drunk."

"I can take you home," he said. "Let me in."

I inhaled deeply through my nose, falling forward on my knuckles while I tried to right myself. I had spunk everywhere, on the floor, on my fingers and pants. Hell, even on my T-shirt. I couldn't fucking see straight. I blinked, trying to shake off the wooziness, but it did nothing.

*God, I'm a mess.*

"Give me a minute," she said, returning her attention to me. "I'll be right out."

"All right." His footsteps retreated farther away from the door.

When I caught my breath, I sat back on my heels and stuffed my cock in my pants, wiping my fingers on my jeans before running them over my face and back into my hair. I'd never come that hard in my life . . . and that was saying something because I'd been with a lot of people. Compared to some of the shit I'd done, whacking off while V rubbed one out barely registered on the kink scale, but I couldn't get my heart to stop racing like it might combust.

"Are you okay?" She walked closer and kneeled, bringing herself eye level with me.

I nodded. "Yeah. Are you?"

"Yeah." She said the word, but it rang hollow, even to my post-coital drunken ass. I met her gaze, knowing I should say something to alleviate the awkward tension that had crept up between us. I wanted more. I wanted her to enact every fantasy I'd ever had, to do all the things no one had ever agreed to do before. I had daydreams of latex bodysuits, silk rope bindings, and St. Andrew's Crosses dancing through my mind.

It was not the same for her. In her gaze, I saw the wall she'd drawn up between what we'd done and what would happen next, impenetrable and solid, the way her brother got when he'd made up his mind about something and wouldn't be deterred.

Just as I opened my mouth to tell her how much more I wanted, she cut me off. "I don't have to tell you to keep this between us . . . right?"

If the moon had suddenly fallen out of the sky and squashed me like a bug, it would have hurt less. Here I'd been planning the next time, convinced it had been just as good for her. But she only wanted to make sure I didn't run my mouth about it.

Swallowing down the bitterness, I nodded. "Sure, V. You got it."

"Good." She leaned down to give me a kiss on the cheek, tender and chaste compared to the way she'd treated me moments ago. "Do you want me to stay with you? We didn't negotiate aftercare."

"You better go," I said, my cheeks burning with everything rising up in my chest. "You don't want to leave Wheels hanging."

She narrowed her eyes like she didn't believe me, but gave me one last kiss before pushing to her feet. "Thanks for the show. Have a nice night, Hollywood."

Then, she walked to the door and left me there—kneeling on concrete, covered in my own come, legs shaking and arms writhing with the aftershocks of submitting to one of the most powerful women I'd ever had the privilege to know.

*Fuck. Get it together, Hollywood.*

Digging my palms into my eyes, I told myself it was just another whack. So what if V had watched? So what if I'd watched her? We were drunk, and if I had a couple shots before I passed out, I might get away with not remembering any of it.

I caught sight of her black lace undies on the ground between my legs. Chest clenching, I grabbed them and held them to my nose, inhaling her sweet musky scent before I stood, my toes tingling as blood rushed down my legs again. I had to stand there and lean on the table for a moment before I could trust myself to walk, and when I did, I found a dirty towel to clean up the mess. Then I decided the couch in the far corner was as good a place as any to pass out.

While I lay there in the decades worth of dirt and grime on the cushion, I thought of all the other one-night stands I'd had where I *had* taken those few shots before passing out, where I had chosen to forget it because why the fuck remember something so insignificant?

Not this night with V. No, I wanted to remember this forever.

Bringing the soft lace to my nose again, I took another long inhale of her, closed my eyes, and hoped for the best in the morning.

"Hey!" someone shouted, shoving me hard enough to have me snapping my eyes open like the world had suddenly caught fire.

"What?" I sat up, shaking my head as something soft and black fell into my lap. "What happened?" I blinked up at Bear, who stood over me with narrowed eyes and a scowl between his brows.

"What the fuck happened to you last night?" He laughed, pointing down to the underwear in my lap. "Whose are those? What about your celibacy streak, huh?"

For a moment, I wasn't sure. I looked around, realizing I was in the side room. A deck of cards and a pile of chips lay in a heap on the table, and the smell of stale beer permeated from the red plastic cups scattered around it. I vaguely remembered playing poker with Wheels, Castor, Lore, and V. My brothers lost until it was just me and her . . .

*Fuck.*

It all rushed back to me, slamming down my spine and back up again, lining my gut with dread. I quickly palmed the underwear and curled it into a ball in my fist. What was I supposed to say?

*Haha, I don't know? Definitely not your baby sister's?*

"I'm still a virgin reborn," I grumbled, my throat aching like I'd run a marathon. It wouldn't take much questioning to learn V had kicked everyone's ass in poker last night and Lore had left us alone after his last hand. Bear was next in line to the presidency for a reason; he was smart as a fucking whip. He'd put two and two together and string me up by my thumbs in a heartbeat. "I'm not sure which hang-around wanted to ride my face last night. I'll have to go around the club and have everyone try them on like Cinderella."

He stared at me for a moment, seeming to debate whether I was serious, before he shook his head and ran his hands through his hair. "Stay classy, Hollywood."

I forced an exhausted, hungover smile, terrified he'd see right through me.

"Get up. It's your shift with Leo." Apparently having given V's panties as much thought as he would, Bear turned toward the door and left. The tightness in my chest loosened the more distance he put between us.

He didn't need to know I'd peeled them off his little sister with my teeth, that I had them stuffed in my mouth while I whacked off, that I used them as a calming scent to help me fall asleep. If he ever found out, he and his brothers would kill me . . . literally feed me to the pigs.

One thing was certain—V could fuck with whomever she wanted as long as they weren't filthy, pathetic manwhore *me*.

**6**

---

# HOLLYWOOD

"Well, well, well," Leo said from his spot at the breakfast table, "it must have been quite the Valentine's Day. You look like shit."

Aside from having one brother with Leo at all times, we also had three prospects guarding the place at various points outside. Any day, his aunt, Gabriella Caputi, might get wind of where he was and attack the place to get him back. It had been six months since he'd first arrived and so far, she hadn't made a move. The intel we were getting from inside the mafia suggested she still didn't know where we were keeping him, and we wanted to keep it that way.

"It was a hell of a party," I said, my stomach lurching when I remembered how delicious V had smelled, how desperately I wanted to bury myself between her legs, and how much it had ached when she left me there alone.

Leo smiled, his warm brown eyes seeming more kind than he actually was. Last August, he'd sent his henchmen after us, resulting in a shootout not far from the clubhouse. V and I had almost died that night. The only reason we'd spared Leo this long had been to use him against Gabriella.

The MC's president, Crow, wanted the war to end, and perhaps getting Leo Caputi on our side could help with that. Unfortunately, Leo didn't see it that way, and I had a number of scars on my body that kept me from fully embracing that idea myself. Our families had been enemies since before either of us were born. His uncle had killed my brother. KC had killed his uncle and his brother. I, myself, had killed countless more. Where did it end?

When Crow first asked me to get close to him, I didn't think there'd be any way I could. He was a Caputi. I was a Rose. We had nothing in common. After three months, I was sorry to say that was still true. I was the only one he talked to, but I suspected that was because I'd nursed him to health, seeing him at his literal weakest and bringing him back to himself. I'd had to bathe him more times than I would ever admit. I spent so much time with him, more than anyone else, and that formed a bond that few could ever match, much to my chagrin.

"Hmm," he said, taking a sip of his coffee. "I miss cocaine."

I laughed and sat opposite him at the table, taking in his appearance. Once upon a time, he'd been twenty pounds skinnier and strung out on everything under the sun. When we'd taken him, Bear had shot him in the knee and it hadn't healed right. After he'd sobered up and gotten healthy enough for surgery, Selene had corrected the injury, and now he had a hard road to recovery. Every morning, one of the more forgiving Roses (usually me) came over to help him bathe and dress. After that, it was an hour of physical therapy exercises. Judging by the sleepy eyes and the fact he still had on my old robe, he hadn't done any of that yet. It seemed much easier to just kill him and be done with it, but what the hell did I know?

"Are you ready for a shower?" I asked, rubbing a hand over my face. Despite having taken my own prior to coming here, Verona hung heavy in the back of my nose, a tangy floral scent that refused to stop tormenting me. I'd been wasted, true, but I remembered all of it —and fuck, I wanted more. I wanted it when I was sober, when I could enjoy the whole thing with a clear head. But the regretful look she'd given me right before she left had me locking down my own desires. It didn't matter what I wanted. Clearly, that was a onetime thing for her.

"No pleasantries, huh?" Leo shook his head and tsked his teeth, taking another long sip of coffee. "Right to business, then." He assessed me with his curious stare, his long chestnut hair curling around his shoulders. He'd been given access to a razor to shave his face, but we hadn't offered a haircut. Objectively, I thought the longer locks suited him better, but I wouldn't tell him that. Leo was an attractive guy, and if he wasn't him and I wasn't me, I'd be into him, at least enough to try to hit it. Now that he'd put on some more weight, he'd started to fill out in all the right places. But there was no world in which I would ever sink so low as to fuck a Caputi. *Ew.* My dick might literally shrivel up and rot off.

"How's your knee this morning?" I went around the table to help him up, grabbing the crutch from across the room so he could lean on it as we walked down the hallway to the bathroom.

"It hurts," he said. "How's your chest?"

"It hurts." I grabbed the recently healed wound, clearing my throat as I ignored the awkward topic of conversation. The Roses had fucked up his knee, the Caputis had made Swiss cheese of my torso. On and on the cycle went.

When we got to the bathroom, I helped him out of his robe and grabbed the garbage bag we used to cover his leg wrappings. Once it was secure around his thigh, he used my shoulder to hop his weight into the tub before I leaned down to adjust the water temperature.

He didn't thank me, and I didn't stay for conversation. I left him alone, choosing to go to the living room while I waited until he was done. As I sat on the couch, I looked at the pictures lining the mantel and various surfaces. KC, Bear, and me on a fishing trip that some of the older brothers had planned. V and me in high school. One of Trojan and me when we were younger.

Another agonizing stab went through my torso as I tried to remember the sound of my brother's voice or the way he used to thunder down those stairs in the morning, bright-eyed and ready to drive me to school. I'd been almost ten years younger than Trojan, and he'd protected me from our piece of shit stepfather my entire life. Who the hell knew where our biological father was?

Trojan joined the army when he turned eighteen and went away for basic training. Without his favorite punching bag there to take the hits, our stepfather set in on me and my mom. I endured the beatings for four years after that. One night, the fucker knocked my mom out cold and left her bleeding on the kitchen floor.

I'd thought he'd killed her right in front of me, robbing me of the only real parent I had. I went to my bedroom and grabbed the shotgun my brother had given me for hunting. I loaded it, cocked it, and waltzed back into the kitchen, prepared to threaten him into never laying a hand on my mother again.

"Oh, look at you. Little tough man, huh? What are you going to do?" he teased, swallowing down another mouthful of Jack. "Shoot me?"

Hands trembling, I gulped and held firm. If I backed down, he'd never listen. He'd never leave us alone.

"Stop hurting my mom, or . . . or I'll kill you!" My voice had never shaken so hard before or since, but I forced my tiny body to stand firm.

My stepfather laughed harshly, walking forward like he didn't think I had the guts, and leaned down to grab the barrel, pointing it right at his forehead.

"Go on then, do it." He sneered, staring down the long, cool metal with soul-piercing eyes. "Do it."

Tension brewed between the two of us so thick and terrible that I coulda cut it with a knife. I shivered, my nerves trembling so hard, my teeth rattled. A child should never have to watch someone beat their mother, much less kill the abuser to stop the violence.

"You don't have the ball—"

Before he could finish, I took a step back, stumbled, and clenched down on the gun to steady myself. It went off. A loud bang reverberated through the tiny house and my stepfather's head exploded. Blood dripped from everything, the ceiling, the countertops, the breakfast table—the entire world covered in red. Warm specks of flesh and brain hit me in the face, and I stayed stock-still while his massive body hit the ground.

My mother had peeled herself off the floor, awakened by the gunshot, and once she'd understood what had happened, she let out a loud, high-pitched scream. It still haunted my nightmares.

"How are we supposed to live now?" She shook her head and grabbed the gun, complaining about the mess she'd have to clean up, worrying about what she was going to tell the cops when they came around looking for him. With resounding shock and horror, I realized she wasn't pissed I'd killed her husband. She'd been upset about the money.

In the end, she'd taken the fall. Her lawyers had advised her to blame it on me, that I'd get a lighter sentence since I was a kid, but she wouldn't steal my future. Which was why I kept sending her cash after she got twenty-five to life with the possibility of parole for good behavior.

That was the night I realized people could use their body to get what they wanted, that my mother had done that much of her life. People only saw her as an object, as something to play with and throw away, and she saw other people as a meal ticket, using her sexuality to feed both of us. She'd done what she had to do for survival. While a part of me hated her for failing to protect the fucker from beating on Trojan and me, I couldn't blame her for not knowing any better. Her parents had been pieces of shit, she was raised to be a piece of shit, and so was I.

Trojan had taken guardianship of me after Mom went away, and when he figured out what our stepfather had done to me in his absence, he'd wept for leaving.

*"I never thought he'd start on you,"* Trojan had said. *"I'm sorry I ever left you alone."*

We'd lived here in Madison County ever since . . . up until Trojan died, leaving me alone again.

"What about now?" I internally screamed at the heavens, praying it reached my brother in the afterlife. "What am I supposed to do without you?"

No response came. No response ever came. Trojan's widow, Marissa, had taken off shortly after he died, only contacting Selene to report she'd seen a woman who had betrayed the club at one of her local bars. Occasionally, I reached out to her, but she never took my calls, and eventually, I stopped trying.

"Hey!" shouted Leo from down the hall. "Hey, can you help me . . . please?"

Confused, I stood and walked back down the hallway, opening the door so I could grab the towel from the sink.

"Please? I get a please?" I smiled as I waited for him to dry off, purposely averting my gaze to give him what privacy I could. "So polite all of a sudden."

He let out a small laugh, and the sound nearly startled me. He'd been here six months, and I'd only heard him snicker once after a joke at my own expense. Did Leo Caputi, king of mafia assholes, have a sense of humor?

"What can I say?" Leo sighed and grabbed my shoulder so I could help him out of the tub. "You bring out the nicer side of me."

"I have that effect on people." I ignored the headache coming on and helped him limp across the hall to his bedroom, where the club had given him some clothes to wear from the lost and found. In all the years we'd been tailing this bastard, he'd always worn the nicest suits—Ferragamo, Tom Ford, Versace. Now, he had two pairs of jeans, one hoodie, and a few white T-shirts, all of it previously owned by people he considered enemies.

Oh, how the mighty had fallen.

## 7

## VERONA

I woke up to the sound of the television echoing down the hallway. Head splitting and still wearing the same clothes I went to the clubhouse in, I rolled out of bed and rubbed my eyes, deciding to change into something more comfy. As I slid underwear up my legs, I wondered where I put the panties I had on last night. My brain hadn't fully woken up enough yet to process that, so I hit the bathroom and stumbled down the hallway to the living room.

Castor sat on the couch next to Wheels, both of them spooning cereal into their mouths and watching cartoons. At least Wheels had an excuse. He lived here.

"What are you doing?" I grumbled to my brother.

"What's it look like?" Castor asked, wiping milk off his chin.

"Looks like you're eating my food and stealing my cable." I narrowed my eyes while I poured myself a cup of coffee. Thankfully, one of them had been thoughtful enough to leave some for me.

"What's yours is mine," Castor called. "That's the older brother code."

"Yeah, yeah, yeah." I poured cream and sugar into my delicious brew and trudged back to the living room, murmuring to myself at how much I'd had to drink last night.

"What's on your schedule for the day?" Wheels asked, taking a sip of water as he leaned back in his seat.

"You're looking at it." I shrugged, rubbing at the ache in the center of my chest. My scar always hurt in the morning, but especially after a night of drinking. I blamed dehydration and a lack of caffeine. "I was going to do yoga and meditate for a bit, but eventually, I have to go by the hospital to visit Pollux. I might as well hit the clubhouse to check on Dad."

"I'm heading to the hospital around noon when visiting hours start." Castor gulped down big swallows of his milk, reminding me of when we were kids. "We can go together."

"Sounds good." I rubbed at my eyes. "Fuck, why did I drink so much."

"Good question." Wheels flashed his devilish grin. "I have a better one. What were you doing in the side room with the door locked at four in the morning?"

Last night rushed back at me: playing poker with Hollywood, losing, making a bet to dominate him, losing again. And then . . . what came after . . .

*Holy shit.*

It had been one of the most intense experiences of my life, and it had happened with my big brother's best friend, the MC's heartbreaker, the one that rode through hang-arounds like the club rent-a-car.

"Uh-oh," Castor teased. "What's that look?"

I cleared my throat, my cheeks suddenly burning, the weight of my bad life choices suffocating me.

"There's no look," I said, my voice entirely too squeaky to be believable.

"Who were you in there with?" Wheels asked, his smile widening.

"It could have only been Lore or Hollywood," my brother added, narrowing his gaze at me. "But I saw Lore leaving with Cassie later in the night, so . . ."

"Hollywood is on a celibacy streak," I quickly added. "I kicked him out after he won the pot." My phone buzzed, drawing my attention, and thankfully, Ru's name appeared across the screen. "I have to take this." I got up and walked down the hallway to my room to answer it. "Hey, what's up?"

"Hey, any chance you came come by the Beacon later today? We're finally picking out marble, and I want to make sure I get the one you said to get last time."

"Sure." I clenched my eyes against the barrage of images assaulting my hungover brain. Hollywood whacking off. The sound of his deep moan. The way his lips formed around my panties.

I gasped. *My panties!*

He still had them. Either that or they were in the side room, lying on the clubhouse floor.

*Fuck,* this was a mess, an utter disaster. It could have been anyone in the club, and it had to be him?

"V?" Ru asked. "You still there?"

"Yeah." I brought my attention back to reality and finished the conversation with my friend before hanging up and leaning back against my door to slide down to the ground.

*Fuuuuccckkk . . .*

I didn't know what to do now. Should I text him? He hadn't reached out to me. Did he even remember? Did I want him to? I might be better off leaving well enough alone. If he didn't bring it up, I wouldn't . . . just like last time.

My cheeks flamed harder as I remembered the fifteen-year-old version of myself—young and naive and sheltered by three older brothers that hadn't let a boy so much as look at me, let alone date me. I'd gone to my first house party as a freshman. The juniors and seniors were already drunk by the time I got there, but I'd gone to school with most of these people all my life, so it wasn't the first time I'd seen them wasted.

I'd spotted Hollywood as soon as I walked in. At seventeen, he hadn't prospected for my father's MC yet, so he went by his given name, Matt Hudson. He was already the most attractive person anyone in Madison County had ever seen, so he got spoiled by any woman he met. No one said no to Matt Hudson, and anyone on his arm was a lucky bitch.

Of course, I knew better. He was my brother's best friend, the one that fucked girls with little abandon, the one that bragged about his exploits at our dining room table like it was celebrity gossip. I'd heard stories about the asses he'd fucked and the mouths he'd destroyed, and I wondered how much of it was hubris. But to see the way the most popular girls hung over him, he'd probably been telling the truth.

Sometime later in the night, after I'd had a lot to drink, I agreed to play Seven Minutes in Heaven. This was my first party, so I wasn't sure of the rules. In the first round, I ended up blindfolded and stuffed into a closet in one of the upstairs bedrooms with promises that Teddy, a boy I'd been crushing on since fifth grade, would arrive soon.

Time dragged agonizingly by, and my heart pounded while I waited for him to join me, panic ripping through my veins. Perhaps he didn't want to spend time with me. Perhaps he didn't even know who I was.

*Why did I agree to play this stupid game anyway?*

After what felt like a year in that tiny space, I decided they must have been playing a cruel joke on me. No one was coming. They were all standing out there laughing at me, the idiot freshman who fell for their—

The door opened and I gasped, straightening as I jumped back.

"She's already in there," someone said before shutting the entry.

Teddy's scent hit me next—deodorant, cologne, cigarettes, and whiskey. Musky. It wasn't what I associated with him, and up until that point, I didn't know he smoked.

"Are you here?" he whispered, and I thought I recognized the voice as his.

"I'm here," I whispered back, relieved he'd come at all.

A hand grabbed my shoulder, sliding down my arm to my palm, where rough, callused fingers intertwined with mine and lifted to his mouth. He kissed my knuckles, softly . . . tenderly . . . like he knew who I was and wanted to worship me. A tremble shot down my body as I raised my palms to his face, touching the cloth around his eyes. He, too, had been blindfolded, but he grabbed my hands and brought them back to his shoulders, taking a step closer to me, backing me up against the bare wall at the end.

"You're shaking," he murmured.

"I've never kissed anyone before," I blurted like word vomit. I hadn't meant to say it. Now he'd think I was some naive virgin who hadn't even had the nerve to kiss someone, let alone spend seven minutes in a closet with a blindfold over their eyes.

"Now, I know that's a lie." He chuckled, and the sultry laugh sounded familiar . . . too familiar. Not like Teddy, but perhaps deeper. I ignored those suspicions, trying not to psych myself out. "But it's okay. I'm good at that part."

With no other warning, he cupped my chin and connected his lips to mine. They were soft and demanding, and *oh,* a delicious sensation shot down the back of my legs and up my spine. I was fifteen and I had never really kissed anyone, so I had nothing to compare it to. Our connection escalated to making out, his big palms massaging my tits, and eventually, he kissed his way down my throat and over my chest, kneeling in front of me.

"If you've never been kissed on your mouth, I doubt anyone's kissed you here."

Quaking and hardly able to hold myself upright, I let him go down on me, licking and kissing over my sensitive parts, even going so far as to finger-fuck me. I rolled my head back on my shoulders at the twinge of pain mixing with pleasure. It was amazing, and I thought I'd never get another opportunity to be a normal girl with a normal boy doing normal teenager things without the prying eyes of my older brothers. I ran my hands through his hair, tugging and pulling in just the right ways to make him moan against me.

It had been the most erotic experience of my life until that point. Just as I was about to crest into the first ever climax given to me by another person, someone shouted on the other side of the door.

"Hudson! Anyone seen Hudson?"

"Fuck," Teddy growled. "Just when I was getting to the good part."

*What?*

"Teddy?" I whispered, shock dousing my arousal and impending orgasm like an avalanche. No . . . *No* . . .

"Shhh. It's okay, Becs." He pressed his lips to mine for one last kiss before whispering, "I don't have to tell you to keep this between us, right? If Jess found out . . . Fucking yikes." He disappeared and closed the door behind him, leaving me alone in the closet, confused and bewildered.

*Hudson? Becs? Jess?*

Oh. Fucking. No. He'd gone down on me. He'd almost made me come. He thought I was someone else. I thought he was someone else. He wasn't Teddy at all. It was fucking Hudson? Matt Hudson?

*All that time . . .*

My body revolted and I curled in on myself, suddenly too vulnerable to go back to the party. I'd let him do things to me I'd never let anyone do before. He'd handled my body like he had every right to. Ripping the blindfold off my eyes, I took steadying breaths to collect my wild emotions before pushing to my feet and storming out of the closet.

By the time I made it downstairs to look for him, he was already doing a beer shotgun with another group of seniors while Jess McCreedy wrapped her arms around his waist. I looked for Becs, Jess's best friend, and found her sitting on the couch at the far end of the room, shooting daggers at the lovebirds.

I didn't want to get involved. I wanted to pretend the whole thing had never happened, so I went home and that was exactly what I did. I never told Hollywood that story, and I wasn't sure I ever would.

He'd broken my hymen that night, and not that I'd ever given stock to the social construct of virginity, but I did believe in magic. My mother had believed in magic. He'd made me bleed, and he'd licked up the results, and for the next ten years, I told myself that had no power over me. It was a mistake, he didn't mean it, and neither did I. Wasn't it the *intention* behind the magic that mattered most?

After that, I'd made it my life mission to break him down. Women spoiled him. Men spoiled him. Because of his beauty and charm, he lived the type of life where he could publicly date one person and fuck their best friend on the side. I refused to let him get away with that shit.

So, when I tore him to pieces, I did so with the humiliation of that night in the back of my heart. I'd never let him forget not everyone wanted him and he couldn't have everything he wanted, either.

Coming back to the present, I sat in my bedroom and clutched my head, running my fingers back through my hair. Last night shouldn't have happened, and as I slumped against the door with my brother and bodyguard down the hall, I promised myself it wouldn't again. Besides, we hadn't really crossed any lines, right? Like he'd said, he could go online and watch the same thing anytime he wanted.

No, the taboo lay in his relationship to my brothers and my father, and how devoted he already was to them. I would expect the same devotion to me, and I wasn't sure either of us was ready for that kind of commitment.

*Nope. Don't think about it. Don't mention it.*

Deciding I could use my yoga session now, I grabbed my mat from my closet and unrolled it next to the bed, stretching into downward dog while I ignored the churn in my stomach.

*Inhale . . . Exhale . . . Go to your safe space . . .*

Once I was done, I'd say a prayer to the Goddess for direction, perhaps do a repairing spell to reset whatever Hollywood and I used to be. In the end, I suspected nothing was stronger than the blood we'd shared, and perhaps I had just been waiting for that to catch up to me all this time.

# 8

## VERONA

Pollux was in great spirits during our visit, literally counting down the days until they released him. The nurse who had given him her number had been working today, so he mostly ignored me and Castor in favor of flirting with her until her ears turned pink. I liked her, and I hoped my brother was worth risking her professionalism and reputation in the end.

Then Wheels accompanied me to the Beacon, where I helped Ru pick out a replacement for the counters in the bathroom that had been ruined in the explosion. By the time I got to the clubhouse to see my dad, it was nearing seven o'clock. Most of the members were already milling around, playing pool or drinking and bullshitting on the sofas. I swept my gaze over Hollywood, KC, and Bear seated around the bar, their backs to me. I normally would have walked up immediately to start shit with them, but I decided to seek out my father first.

He sat in the back with Aris and Coins, murmuring among each other, reminding me of the kings of old as they schemed and plotted against their enemies. Not much had changed since the medieval times, unfortunately. Humans were still intent on killing each other until the bad blood flowed so thick, the world drowned in it.

"There she is," Dad said when I wrapped my arms around him, giving him a hug. I regretted how much this war with the Caputis had drained him, physically and mentally. He'd aged so poorly in the years since I'd been gone. I'd left behind a man in his forties, only to come back to one that looked to be in his sixties. Gray streaked his long, thick, dark hair, and wrinkles marred a once youthful face. "Hey, V."

"How's it going?" I smiled up at him before giving a hug to Aris and Coins. Both had been officers in the MC as long as I'd been alive, my father's adopted brothers in every sense. They had become surrogate uncles to me somewhere along the way.

"Just talking shop." Dad kissed my temple. "How was your day? Did you go see Pollux?"

"He's excited to come home," I said.

"I swung by this morning," Dad said. "He told me the same."

We caught up for a few more moments before I headed over to the bar for a drink. Still feeling rocky from the previous night, I opted for a bottle of water, sliding the fridge door open so I could grab one from the bottom row.

My skin prickled like someone was watching me, and I didn't have to glance up to know who. Hollywood had tracked me the moment I'd walked over, his dark gaze raking down my body and back up again. When I glanced at him, he pulled his lips into a smile around the top of his beer, not bothering to hide his obvious perusal.

My pulse sped up, my stomach fluttering with butterflies as a tremble raced down my spine and back up again.

*No,* I reminded myself. *Off-limits. Danger, danger.*

"Hey, V," Bear said, raising an eyebrow in my direction. "Riddle me this . . . where'd you get twenty-five hundred dollars to blow on a few hours of Hollywood's time?"

"That's not a riddle," I said, twisting off the top of the bottle so I could take a drink of cool aqua and wash down the scalding shame of how I spent Valentine's Day.

"Answer the question," he said. "Imagine my surprise when I learned my baby sister got into a bidding war over my best friend."

Hollywood kept his casual stance, leaning on the bar with his elbow, his forearm raised so he could rest his cheek on his palm. Like that, he resembled a lazy male lion that had snoozed while the others caught his meal for him.

*Too bad I'm a lioness, Hollywood. I'll just claw back.*

"I'm not a baby," I reminded my brother. "And I thought we agreed we wouldn't talk about how I made my money."

Bear grimaced before taking another drink.

"Aww," KC cut in, reaching across the bar to chuck me on the chin, a proverbial older brother despite him being my cousin. "My little baby cam-star cousin, all grown up."

"Hmm." I took another drink, zeroing my gaze in on Hollywood, who had let this go on despite his part in what had happened last night. I couldn't help teasing him. "What about you, Hudson? Am I a baby to you, too?"

He smirked, pulling one side of his mouth into a grin. "You're definitely no baby, V."

"Hey!" Bear punched Hollywood's arm.

"What? She's hot." Hollywood balked and held up his hands, feigning innocence. "She knows she's hot, and she's not *my* sister, thank fucking fuck."

"Jesus fucking Christ." Bear rolled his eyes and shook his head. "You want to beat him now, KC, or wait until he's toasted?"

KC only shook his head and sighed. "Hollywood thinks everyone is hot, Bear. Let the man have some peace."

Hollywood winked at me, smiled, and finished the rest of his beer in a single gulp.

"Besides, I'm still a born-again virgin." He slammed the empty bottle down and threw his head back to let out a wolfish howl. "Eight months and counting, baby!"

I laughed, trying to keep up appearances as my skin burned and my heart pounded. We'd gotten too close last night, much too close, and I had to keep my guard up in order to make sure it didn't happen again.

"Aww, c'mon, Hollywood," Chelsea said, appearing out of

nowhere to wrap her arm around his shoulders and press her obnoxiously fake tits against his bicep. "It must be a throbbing mess by now. Let me kiss it better."

Time slowed as she raised her hand to bring it toward his lap, reaching down like she meant to grab his cock right there at the bar in front of the rest of us. A fiery stab went through me and I reacted before I could stop myself. I reached out and snatched her wrist in a vise grip, sinking my nails into her skin so hard I'd leave marks.

"Don't touch him," I snarled, leaning over the bar to get in her face. "Don't ever fucking touch him again. You understand?"

For a moment, everyone stared. Chelsea dropped her jaw, widening her eyes like she didn't know how to react. Most of the time, I ignored the hang-arounds. They came and went, and only if they married one of the brothers did I consider the idea that they might become family. But this bitch had touched Hollywood without his permission for the last time or I would tear her Goddamned throat out with my teeth.

"And who the fuck are you?" Chelsea finally said, trying to yank her arm away from me. "His mother?"

I cackled at her audacity, the heat of furious challenge rising inside my gut. "No, I'm the bitch that's gonna beat your face in for touching people without their consent."

At that, I jumped up on the bar to climb over it, not caring I kicked glasses and ashtrays out of my way. I needed to teach her a lesson. After I was done with her, she wouldn't touch anyone like that again, and she'd think twice before laying hands on Hollywood.

I'd just gotten on the other side, about to grab that disgusting mop on her head when a strong grip circled my waist and lifted me into the air.

"All right, that's enough," Hollywood said in my ear as I kicked and squirmed, trying to get out of his hold so I could scratch her eyes out. "C'mon, V."

His voice came out in broken chuckles, and that infuriated me more.

"Are you laughing?" I shoved against him while he carried me to a back room, putting me down long enough for me to struggle while he opened the door.

"Yeah," he said, shoving me inside before kicking the thing closed behind him, leaving us in the soft glow of moonlight trickling in through the window.

"Why?" I huffed, blowing hair out of my face and curling my hands into fists to keep myself from swinging on him instead.

"Because you're adorable." His grin nearly made me punch him, and he tilted his head to the side, seeming to admire my ire.

"Oh, fuck off." I shoved at his chest, growing more aggravated when he barely budged. At over a foot taller than me, he had me by at least a hundred pounds of muscle, if not more. I must have looked like a fussy little rodent to him. "I hate you."

He blew out a breath, narrowing his eyes into predatory slits. "Don't I know it."

Ice sizzled down my spine, turning my incinerating anger into a simmering and sultry desire. Last night came rushing back—the way he'd let me hold him in place with my boot, the way he'd taken my panties off with his teeth, how he'd moaned when he came. Christ, it had been so enticing.

And the worst part? I had enjoyed it.

Then, I realized we were in one of the bedrooms in the back, hardly more than a closet with a cot and a small bathroom on the side. The brothers used these rooms to fuck their old ladies or whatever hang-around they corralled that night.

I was trapped. He'd trapped me.

"Let me go, Hollywood."

"Not until you take a deep breath—" he stepped closer, invading my personal space to make me back up "—and tell me why you went after her like that."

"She's a bitch," I hissed. "She shouldn't touch you like that. They can't just touch you however they want."

"Hmm." He nodded, taking another step, forcing me back another pace. "Why do you care so much?"

I opened my mouth, but all that came out was, "No one should be touched without their permission."

"Is that all?" Hollywood raised his eyebrows, moving close enough that he'd pressed me up against the opposite wall, my spine straight against the cool plaster. His scent overwhelmed me, that damnable mix of leather and sandalwood and cologne. I didn't know how much longer I'd be able to put up the good fight to resist this.

"Of course, that's all," I snarled. "What else would it be?"

With nowhere to run, I stared up at him, prepared to bite and claw my way out this if I had to. My pulse beat through my body so fast, I heard it pounding in my chest. I clutched at the glass jar under my shirt, terrified he might see the outline despite it only being less than an inch in length. He couldn't know that I carried a piece of that night around with me, that I stared at it when I reached rock bottom.

"Well." He shrugged, rolling those pretty eyes at me. "I mean, after last night—"

"Last night was a mistake." I gulped against a painfully dry throat. "We were drunk. It won't happen again."

He smiled wider as he drew his massive frame mere centimeters from mine, wrapping his arms behind his back to be sure he didn't touch me. But the heat building in that small space was worse, a million little tingles of electricity from the near connection cascading over every part of my exposed skin.

"You sound sure of that," he said.

"I am." I nodded, my voice shaky despite how much I tried to force my confidence. "You're Bear's best friend. You're . . . *you.*"

At that, he straightened, staring down with a dark, playful gaze, letting my protests hang in the minuscule space between us. I trembled embarrassingly hard and tried to hide it, but he definitely saw it, and he knew why.

"That's right. I'm me." He leaned down and ghosted his lips over my ear, whispering a quiet, "I think that's the part you like the most. How wet do you get thinking about me on my knees for you? Does it get your little clit hard to imagine *me* sucking it?"

The last time Hollywood had me pressed against a wall to

whisper filthy things in my ear bounced through my mind, and I quaked so hard, my teeth nearly chattered. Hot steamy lust shot right down to my cunt, clenching in my lower stomach, forcing my thighs together.

"I want you to take the cat-o'-nine-tails to my back," he went on. "I want you to put clothespins on every part of my body and whip them off. I want you to bite your name into my skin hard enough to leave bruises and ride my face until you can't stand. Only then am I allowed to fuck you." He sank his teeth into the shell of my ear, making me gasp and let out a soft desperate moan as goose bumps erupted down that entire side of my body. "God, the thought of it has me so fucking turned on."

He bucked his hips into my stomach, a thick, decadent bulge proving his point. I almost broke down and agreed.

Then, he stepped back, cold air rushing into the void he'd left, smacking me out of my disillusionment. He put his hand in his back pocket, pulling out something black and lacy while he continued to move backward.

*Are those my undies?*

"Your move . . . *Mistress*." He put the fabric to his nose and inhaled, grinning like a villain as he twisted the door handle and whipped it open. He left me standing there alone and hating him even more.

I didn't stay much longer after that. I didn't want to see if Chelsea would try to sink her teeth into him again after I'd warned her not to.

Wheels took me home, and when we got there, he inspected the house before announcing he'd head to bed downstairs, the same room Thor had once occupied.

"You okay, V?" he asked, pausing at the door to the basement.

"Yeah, of course." I furrowed my brows, confused about his question. "Why do you ask?"

He shrugged. "You went after a hang-around. It seems beneath you."

"I bet she'll keep her hands to herself from now on." I flashed him a playful smile, one saying that was all it was.

"Yeah, okay." Wheels squinted his eyes into a knowing look before pursing his lips and opening the door to downstairs. "Have a nice night, V."

"You, too." I waved and wandered down the hallway to my room. But sleep did not come easily that night. After I did a wind-down yoga session and meditated to clear my mind, I lay in bed and stared at the ceiling, frustrated none of it worked. Hollywood's words spun in my head like a broken record.

*"How wet do you get thinking about me on my knees for you? Does it get your little clit hard to imagine me sucking it?"* I brushed my hand down the center of my body, pausing to clutch at the necklace hanging over my heart. *"I want you to take the cat-o'-nine-tails to my back. I want you to put clothespins on every part of my body and whip them off."* His voice rattled through my body, and I pushed my hand lower, ducking under my skirt and panties to find my clit. I hissed when I touched the sensitive skin, sucking in a breath that made me throw my head back. *"I want you to bite your name into my skin hard enough to leave bruises and ride my face until you can't stand. Only then am I allowed to fuck you."*

The fantasy it had me rubbing circles into myself. I was already dripping, and the forbidden thought of dominating Hollywood Hudson spurred me on. I should've stopped it before it started. I should have pulled my fingers right out of my panties and kept them above waist level.

But I didn't.

I moaned my way through an orgasm at the thought of his head between my legs and how all these years might have improved his skills. In the aftermath, I panted from the high and wondered if there was any way out of this now or if there ever had been.

I shouldn't want it. I should continue to shut him down whenever he brought it up. But after that night, there could only be one thing to do.

He'd told me it was my move, and I planned to make it worth my while.

# 9

## HOLLYWOOD

I pretended V going after Chelsea on behalf of my virtue wasn't the hottest thing I'd ever seen, and honestly, it took work. Like . . . a lot of work. When I'd peeled her off the hang-around, still squirming and cursing, I'd gotten harder than the night before. Yeah, I didn't like when the girls touched me like they owned me, but hadn't I earned the reputation? Hadn't I run through them like a raccoon at the local dump? Hadn't I taught them to treat my body like a fire sale? Grab what you can. Everything must go, go, go.

"You seem distracted today," Leo said, holding my arm as he lowered into a lunge, struggling to push back up again. "Not quite as talkative."

I swallowed and shook my head, knowing I should keep it to myself. As someone that normally bragged about their sexual exploits, whatever this was with V couldn't get out. Her brothers would kill me. Her father would cut my nuts off and shove them in my mouth before setting me on fire. I'd seen them do worse to enemies for less. Touching *the* princess, the only daughter of the MC's president, came with a death sentence, especially for someone with my history.

"What are you thinking about?" Leo raised his eyebrows and did another lunge, grimacing as he bent his injured knee.

There was no one else here, other than the prospects outside, and Leo had made it his SOP not to talk to anyone except for me. I didn't know why that was, nor did I ask him, but I figured why not take advantage of it? It wasn't like he knew V or would ever meet her. Even if Leo was an enemy, it might be nice to talk to someone about it, just to get it off my chest.

"There's a girl," I admitted.

He chuckled, going into the same exercise on the other side. "What about her?"

"She's my buddy's little sister," I said. "Not like . . . *little* little. She's only three years younger than me."

"Okay." Leo met my gaze, silently asking me to continue.

"I like her," I said, furrowing my brows. "She does things to me that no one else can do, that no one else has ever done."

"So she's a freak?" Leo let out another laugh.

A stinging rage shot through the center of my chest before I squashed it down. I didn't like anyone talking about V like that, least of all this piece of shit. But I'd learned at a young age to catch flies with honey instead of vinegar. No one liked an aggressive asshole.

"It's more than that," I said. "It's not even sexual." *Yet.*

"Ohhh," Leo said, nodding like he finally understood. "So you *want* it but can't have it because of your friend?"

I cleared my throat and straightened, ignoring the burst of dread in my gut. He'd hit the target dead on.

"She's the president's daughter," I said. "Her brother is my best friend. She's off-limits in a thousand different ways."

"And that makes you want it more, I imagine."

I scoffed and helped him upright, handing him the weights so he could start his deadlifts. They weren't more than ten pounds a piece, but he'd lost a lot of strength in the months we'd held him captive.

"Do you want my advice?" Leo pursed his lips and met my gaze with a friendly and sage one of his own, complete with an innocent smile.

My immediate reaction was to say no. Fuck this guy. He'd tried to have me killed a few times, and given the opportunity, I'd put money on him trying it again. But . . . who the hell else was I going to ask? No one in the MC could know. I'd thought about looping in Ru. Once upon a time, I'd been one of the few people who knew about her secret relationship with Saint. But she and V were best friends, and I figured if anyone deserved to confide in her, it should be V. So, I stared at my sworn enemy while he worked his hamstrings and offered a tentative white flag.

"Okay," I finally said.

"I think you should fuck this girl." He shrugged. "If it's as good as you think it will be, the risk is worth it."

I balked, my mouth hanging open while I processed what he'd said.

*No. No, no, no.*

I couldn't give myself permission for that . . . could I?

Laughter bubbled up my throat and over my tongue, pouring out of me in a wave of relief. No one had ever been that brutally honest with me, and definitely not about V. Hell, no one in the MC would *dare* talk about her like that, like she was just another fuck in a line of long fucks.

"Oh ho ho," Leo continued, "You've thought about it, huh? I bet you've been thinking about it for a while."

I swallowed against a parched throat, narrowing my gaze. "I'm not good enough for her."

"Isn't she the judge of that?" Leo winced as he straightened, setting down the weights so he could rub at his knee.

"Are you okay?" I started toward him, but he held up a hand, making me pause.

"Fine," he said. "Just aches is all."

"Do you need me to call Selene?"

"That sadist with the needles? Fuck no." He blew out a breath and sighed. "It's fine. I'll be fine. I just need to rest. Keep talking."

I sat down on the footstool in front of the recliner and ran my hands over my face. "We almost hooked up. It was great, but then she said it was a mistake, that it couldn't happen again. I told her what I wanted, and she acted like a deer in highlights." When I looked at Leo, mischief danced behind his dark eyes, indicating I already knew what I had to do.

If I wanted her, I had to go get her. Stop dancing around the fucking issue, no matter what her father thought. He'd respect me more for being honest about how I felt, despite the consequences, versus being a coward because I was afraid of them.

Trojan wouldn't have wanted me to do that. Trojan would have told me the same thing as Leo—go after her and make her mine.

"Life can't be easy for this girl," Leo said, his voice much softer now. "All those older brothers, a stubborn crow as a father, no mother to fight for her independence." Naturally, he knew as much about our family as we knew about his.

I cleared my throat and considered his point. Bear, Castor, Pollux, and KC (hell, even me) had scared off any boy she'd ever dared to bring around. In high school, there had been a kid named Teddy that took two steps inside the clubhouse, tucked tail, and bolted. I couldn't blame him; we were some terrifying motherfuckers, even back then.

No wonder she had run so far away as soon as she could.

"How do you know so much?" I resisted the urge to sneer at him, despite how helpful he had actually been. Let me not forget this was *Leo Fucking Caputi.*

"I have a little sister," Leo said with a hint of a smile. "I am arguably just as protective."

"Yeah?" I raised my eyebrows, instantly curious. Leo never talked about his life, and certainly not about his family. "And what would you do if she brought me home?"

Leo barked out a laugh. "Well, if you weren't a Rose and your loyalties lay closer to home, I might be all right with it."

I shook my head. "You don't know me very well."

"Do I not?" He put his arms out around him, gesturing to my old living room where pictures of my childhood and adolescence still sat on the mantel. "You seem like you've lived a wild life."

"I'm a bit of a slut." I pursed my lips. "I used to be. I've been taking a break."

"So you are capable of self-reflection." Leo tilted his head to the side. "This is not a bad thing in a partner."

Perhaps he had a point. Perhaps I had been too hard on myself.

"Who's the big guy?" he asked, pointing to one of a fishing trip Trojan had taken me on when I was in middle school.

"My brother, Trojan." I bit back the grief that usually came when I spoke about him. "He died last year. Benito killed him."

Leo paused, his eyes meeting mine with the slightest bit of regret dancing behind them. "I lost my brother last year, too."

I remembered that. KC had killed Julian Caputi when they'd snuck onto our land to steal from us. Selene had intercepted them but been taken hostage. When KC found them, he'd made mincemeat of anyone in his path.

"I'm sorry for your loss," I said, glancing down at the ground. "It's a hard thing, losing an older sibling."

Leo sighed. "I'm sorry, too. About Trojan."

It might not have seemed like much, but those few words softened my disgust for the Caputi bastard. Like me, he had a family he loved. Like me, he'd lost members of that family while trying to protect them. Perhaps we had more in common than I'd care to admit.

"I want to see my sister," Leo said, his tone much softer than he'd ever used before. "Julia."

I met his gaze, watching his features turn stoic and serious. He meant it.

"I've been thinking about what Crow offered," Leo went on. "This supposed peace between our families."

"Yeah?" This was a surprise, and I tried not to let my excitement show. I honestly hadn't thought it would work. I'd been sure a rogue Rose would have come through here to take care of the problem by now.

"I want to talk to my sister about it." Leo nodded before pushing to his feet, preparing for round two. "You bring Julia to me, and we'll decide where it goes from there."

"Why?" I asked, holding his arm while he went into his lunges again. "Why would you even consider this?"

He straightened and patted my shoulder, giving me a soft smile. "Maybe I agree with you. It's long past time this blood feud ended."

My heart dropped into my stomach, and I nodded.

"You could have killed me by now." He continued, purposely ignoring my startled look. "I could have killed you by now. The fact we have restrained ourselves shows that perhaps a Rose and a Caputi can get along . . . if the terms are reasonable."

*Yeah, or we've been stomping on thin ice with a spreading crack.*

"I'll ask Crow tonight," I said. "Thank you for considering it."

"Don't thank me yet." Leo blew a disbelieving laugh out through his nose and shook his head. "If you think I reek of Caputi filth, you haven't met *our* princess."

"THANK YOU ALL FOR COMING, BROTHERS," Crow said from the head of the table bearing the SRMC emblem: a rose with a dagger stabbing it through the middle. The vice president, Aris, sat to his right with the sergeant at arms, Thor, on his left. Aris was short for Aristotle, and he'd gotten his name because the surly motherfucker had a photographic memory, and he could rattle off facts about anything at any time. Thor, on the other hand, was a big Viking with long dirty blond hair and gray eyes who enjoyed beating our enemies' heads in with a sledgehammer. I cringed, remembering when he'd gotten his road name.

The road captain, Slip, sat down next to our enforcer, Doc, with Coins taking the other seat next to him. We had a full house, most of the members making it in to hear the latest update in the ongoing Caputi war. I stood in the back with Bear, Saint, and KC, taking a sip of my beer while I watched the president call the meeting to order. "I wanted to share the good news that Pollux has almost made a complete recovery. If all goes well, he should be out in a week or two."

Shouts and claps of approval came from around me, especially from Castor. I couldn't imagine what it must be like to have a twin, to know someone else out there shared the same DNA, the same face, the same everything. Admittedly, the world could only handle one Hollywood at a time, and that was a good thing.

"Which leads me right into updates on Gabriella Caputi," Crow continued, pushing his hands through his long salt-and-pepper hair. "Saint, what do we hear from the inside?"

"Gabriella is losing support from Caputi loyalists," Saint said from his spot next to me. "The carnage in Buffalo was a mess, and even her closest supporters are skeptical she can replace Benito."

"How so?" Thor asked.

"The Canadians have backed out of their deal," Saint continued. "We'll likely hear from them again soon."

"Good," Aris added. "Our bargain with the cartel is coming in handy."

Last year, Aris had gone to Mexico to make an arms deal with the controlling political group, suspecting Gabriella had tried to swipe our legs out from under us. Now, we waited for those that sided with her to come crawling back because she couldn't deliver on her promises. She had all of the demand, but no supply.

"What about Leo?" Crow asked, shifting his gaze to me.

"He's considering your proposal," I explained. "He wants to talk to his sister, Julia."

Crow's dark gaze shot to Saint for a moment, only a second, before coming back to me. But I'd seen it, and I suddenly wondered about the true identity of Saint's informant. Could the Caputi princess have been working with us this entire time? Could she have been the one to give up important intel for years?

"He said they'll make that decision together." I stuffed my hands in my pockets. "He seems grateful to have been spared, considering how they've treated our people they've taken." I glanced at my brother, Lore, who sat in one of the other corners with the eye patch over the evidence of my claim.

"Any objections?" Crow looked around at the group while they mumbled among themselves.

"It's a good idea," I continued. "I've gotten to know him over the last few months." At least as much as he'd let any of us get close enough. "There's always the chance he's playing us, but if he's not, he could be a good partner."

"I say let the two meet," Bear added. "I can be there to interpret, just in case they decide to switch to Italian midway through."

Crow looked around at the rest of the brothers, waiting for anyone else to add their opinion.

"What's the plan for Gabriella?" Doc asked, leaning forward on his elbows while he inhaled a cigarette. "We get Julia and Leo on our side, and then what? Lure her out? Make a trade?"

"That's a fair question." Crow nodded. "Thor?"

"We'll want to know how many allies we have on the inside," Thor said. "How many people would agree to a ceasefire should Leo take over."

"Are you thinking we stage a coup?" Slip asked.

Murmurs of agreement echoed around me, some liking that, some demanding more blood.

"If her support is dwindling and Leo is willing, now might be the time to strike." Doc pursed his lips, seeming to agree.

"They'll probably want a show of truce," Bear added, running a hand through his soft, curly locks. "Like a member exchange."

"Member exchange?" Slip asked, his blue eyes narrowing. "Is that what I think it is?"

"We'll send one of our guys there," Crow explained, "and they send one of their guys here."

Doc let out a sardonic laugh. "Who volunteers as tribute?"

I'd do it if they didn't find anyone else. Leo wasn't so bad, and if my time in the viper's den yielded good results for the club, it wouldn't be that much of a hardship.

"Let's see where this goes," Crow said, looking at me and Bear.

"Arrange the visit with Julia Caputi. Saint knows how to get in touch with her." Then, he glanced at Slip, Doc, and Thor. "I smell a siege. How can we choke her out with minimum damage? I've seen enough Caputi and Rose blood to last a lifetime."

Thor nodded. "I've got some ideas. I'll hash them out and report back."

"Good," Crow said. "We'll meet again in a week."

"Any other topics anyone wants to discuss?" Aris asked, glancing around with his ice-cold eyes. When no one said anything, he tapped his rings on the wooden table and announced the end of the session. "You better get your asses back here next week for the check-in. This shit with the Caputis is getting serious."

The doors to the front room opened and the members filed out, most heading outside to their bikes, while others mingled with the hang-arounds. I spotted Chelsea but ignored her in favor of throwing my arm over Bear's shoulder so I could lean in and whisper, "Have you ever met Julia Caputi?"

Bear shook his head. "No. You?"

"No." I remembered what Leo had said about his sister, that she reeked of Caputi stench more than him. "You think she's worse than Gabriella?"

My best friend laughed and shook his head. "How could anyone be worse than that?"

"Let's do some shots," Alba interrupted from the other side of the bar, lining up a row of miniature plastic cups before tilting a bottle over them. "V, Ru, get over here! We're shooting tequila."

KC walked to the other side of the bar to wrap his arms around his wife, leaning in to kiss her on the cheek while she made sure everyone had enough liquor in their cup. I cleared my throat when V came to stand next to me, squeezing into the space between me and her brother before grabbing a cup.

I took a deep breath and tried to ignore the citrus, floral scent wafting up from her skin, straightening as I backed away and put a few inches between us. I itched to run my fingers through her hair, tilt her head back, and claim her mouth for my own.

But I remembered our rules. No touching. Not like that. Not yet. Not until she told me I could. Like her, I did nothing without consent.

"What's wrong, Hollywood?" Verona teased. "You look like you're trying to solve the world's *hardest* problem."

I cleared my throat and forced a grin, flicking a gaze at Bear to see if he'd caught the innuendo. He furrowed his eyebrows into a scowl but didn't comment, only sniffed his shot and grimaced at its contents.

"Leave the boy alone," KC cut in. "If I had to spend my mornings with Leo Caputi, I'd have a lot on my mind, too."

"Exactly," Alba said, holding up her cup. "Cheers to family and alcohol."

We laughed at her toast, repeated it, and downed our shots. But I couldn't let a taunt like that from V go unanswered. So before she'd finished swallowing, I gulped mine down and placed the cup on the bar.

"You know, you're right, V," I said. "The things I've been thinking are just *dripping* with complexity."

Her bright gaze shot to me, insidious and laced with venom, and I sat on the edge of my proverbial seat as I waited for her to spit it at me.

*Go on, give me your worst.*

"The best solutions are the ones a person *erects* themselves, Hudson." V raised an eyebrow, daring me to continue. "Unless you're having trouble with that sort of thing . . . after all these months on your celibacy kick."

"What would you know about it?" I said, narrowing my gaze on my target, flashing a genuine smile. "Aren't you still *wet* behind the—"

"Hey!" Bear cut in, shoving my shoulder hard enough for me to stumble back a few steps. "What the fuck are you two doing?"

KC stared at me with wide eyes and a huge shit-eating grin on his face, his chin resting on Alba's shoulder from behind. His wife's features were also bright and entertained, clearly finding this tension between V and me amusing. Bear, on the other hand, looked like he was about to beat my face in. His cheeks had turned a violent shade of crimson that snaked down his neck and under his shirt. For as long as I'd known him, he'd always been the levelheaded of us three. KC could fly off into a rage at the drop of a hat, his temper consistent with the notorious Montgomery fury that Crow, Castor, and V had inherited. Bear had the right amount of both. He knew how to be calm, but he also knew when to light a fire under someone's ass.

Like . . . when his best friend started shamelessly flirting with his little sister right in front of him.

"Shut up, Bear," V said, shoving him back. "Didn't you see what I did to Chelsea yesterday? I paid twenty-five hundred dollars for his time, and until he pays up, that's my precious cargo." This time, she got in her brother's face, snarling as he winced and backed away from her. "If you break the merchandise, I'll break your hand."

"Damn, V," Bear said, frowning at her threat. "Back down. Fuck. I just don't like him talking to you like that."

"He can talk to me however he wants," V said, pointing to the spot on her chest where a ten-inch scar ran from sternum to stomach. "He earned it."

That shut everyone up. KC's jaw snapped closed and Alba's grin widened as she shifted her stare to Bear. He tilted his head, glanced from his sister to me and back again, then muttered a quiet, "Fine."

"Fine," she said, and that ended that. "Who wants to play pool?"

"I will." Alba broke loose from KC and walked around the bar to follow V toward the table, the brother closely trailing behind them and leaving me alone with Bear.

He stared at me, drilling holes into my head until I glanced up at him.

"What are you doing with my sister?" he asked, accusation and disapproval in his tone.

"I haven't touched her," I said, able to stare him in the eyes while I said it because it was the truth. I hadn't, not yet, and after V's display of . . . what was that? Jealousy? Chivalry? It didn't matter. It turned me on more than her hateful little mouth.

He didn't say anything else, just stared at me for a moment before dropping his gaze to the spot on my chest where I'd been shot, the middle of my left pec, four inches from my heart. The shock had knocked me unconscious, and when I woke up, I was struggling to breathe in an ambulance on my way to the hospital.

Of all the times I'd been injured for this club, that one had brought me the closest to death. No one knew that, no one except V. She'd been there when it happened. She'd stared into my lifeless eyes and believed I *had* died, that I'd given my life to protect her.

Bear cleared his throat, picked up his beer, and walked away, wrapping an arm over Saint's shoulders so they could talk about plans for Julia Caputi's visit.

I focused on V, raking my eyes down her cropped band tee and baggy black cargo pants, ending with her platform boots. Sure, she looked the part of the scary goth girl, the one that would deck a random hang-around for touching someone without their permission. But I remembered how hard she'd trembled when I had her cornered yesterday, how flustered she'd gotten when I told her all the twisted fantasies I had starring her.

She might have a diamond-coated exterior, but deep down inside, she was a pile of mush.

**10**

---

# VERONA

"Listen, the way I would leave those peasants behind for Elijah is shocking," Ru said, giggling while she stuffed popcorn into her mouth. We were crashing at her house for a girls' night, *The Vampire Diaries* already marathoning in the background.

"The whole premise is ridiculous," I said, shaking my head. "It's oddly compelling though." To be fair, I wasn't into this show when I should have been in high school. Now that I'd circled back around to it with my friends, I didn't mind it so much. I liked when the vampires ripped people's hearts out of their chests.

"I heard you got into it with a hang-around the other night," Selene said, raising an eyebrow in my direction. "What was that about?"

I took a deep breath, trying to keep my cool despite three pairs of eyes flicking to me. "She tried to grab Hollywood's junk." *Fucking disgusting.* "Is consent just a fleeting thought these days?"

"Hmm." She narrowed her eyes, considering. "Is she a problem?"

I snorted and raised an eyebrow. "Why? Are you offering to stab her in the neck with something fun?"

"I only do that for lecherous traitors." She sniffed, acting like it was no big deal she'd taken off after a hang-around turned snitch and killed her almost at the expense of her own life. "But I suppose I could make an exception if she doesn't knock it off."

A door sounded down the hallway by the kitchen and Hollywood appeared a moment later, wearing his cut over a black hoodie, a dark leather jacket, and matching dark jeans.

"Speak of the devil," Alba said, leaning her head over the back of the couch as he came closer.

"Now, Sunshine, I thought we agreed not to insult the devil by comparing him to me." Hollywood playfully winked at me and leaned down to plant a kiss on her temple. He did the same to Selene and Ru, but when he got to me, he paused to take a deep breath of my hair.

"Fucking sinful," he whispered before standing upright to put his hands on the back of the couch and glance up at the TV. "*Vampire Diaries?* Fuck yeah. Scoot over. I might blow off the guys to stay here instead."

"It's girls' night, Hollywood," Ru said, shoving his foot away when he tried to swing it over the back of the sofa in between me and her. "Hence why you're going out with the guys instead."

"Hrmph." He straightened and crossed his arms. "All I'm hearing is a bunch of stereotypical gender binary horseshit. What if I wanted to stay for girls' night?"

"Then, how would we talk about you, huh?" Alba gave him an innocent smile when he clutched his heart and pretended to be offended. "All good things."

"Yeah, like how V nearly knocked the teeth out of Chelsea's head for grabbing you." Selene nodded at me with a suspicious side-eye, and I pretended not to see the accusations lurking behind it.

"Fucking club girls, man." Hollywood blew out a breath and kicked his foot playfully on the ground. "They're gonna be the death of me."

"Well, that's what happens when you take candy away from children." Selene pursed her lips. "They'll cry until they get it back."

"Are you saying I'm sweet as sugar, Sel?" He gave her his most charming grin.

"No, I'm saying they treated you like junk and you deserve better."

"Damn, that's fucking cold," I cut in, grimacing on Hollywood's behalf as I stood to grab my winter coat, deciding to go outside for a cigarette.

"It's the truth," she called after me. "I call 'em like I see 'em."

Ru and Alba sided with me, arguing with the older MC princess about the proper time to roast someone in the name of love, but Hollywood took the hit with grace, bowing out of the conversation to follow me to the front porch. His expression flickered, a soft desperation echoing behind his eyes before he shut it down and returned to the same jovial Hollywood that everyone knew and loved.

*Your move, Mistress.*

Ignoring the shiver that snaked around my spine, I lit my smoke and handed the lighter to him so he could do the same. Then, we stood next to each other on Saint's tiny porch, staring up at the stars. This far out from the city, I could see the Milky Way, and it added a mystical ambience to the already confusing tether between him and me. Out here, we could be the only two people in the galaxy, like the stardust that made him was the same that made me and our silly affair had been written in the sky millions of years ago. Weren't we just particles of a dying sun in the end?

The smell of his cologne hit me next, reminding me of when he'd crawled between my legs and watched me masturbate with rapt attention. His dark eyes almost glowed in the moonlight, his features somehow softer and more delicate.

"You keep looking at me like that, V, and we might both have to bail on our parties tonight." He pulled his lips into a grin around his cigarette, which dangled from his lips in a charismatic James Dean way.

I scoffed, taking another deep inhale, letting the nicotine buzz go to my head. "You think stealing my panties and pinning me against a wall with some pretty words will work on me, Hudson?" Rolling my eyes, I let out a little sarcastic giggle. "You'll have to do better than that."

I'd said it to make him laugh, but he didn't react the way I'd hoped. He turned to face me, closing the distance between us to bring his lips to my temple, brushing his mouth so close to my skin, not touching me, but enough for a current of energy to spark in the void between us.

"I bet you haven't stopped thinking about it," he said, trailing his nose down the side of my face, ghosting his lips over my cheek. "I bet you rubbed yourself to sleep. Did you moan my name when you came?"

I gulped and stepped back, turning away from him so I could puff on the cigarette and get my nerves under control.

"You're right," I confessed, glancing up at him, watching as delight danced in his beautiful eyes and infectious smile. "I did, and I want the things you said."

"I fucking knew it." He laughed, stabbed the smoke out, and bit his bottom lip.

"But I respect your need for . . . celibacy or whatever it is." Finished with mine, I put the cigarette in the ashtray and turned to him again. "Kink doesn't need to be about sex."

"Oh, I know," he said. "I once had a Madam that liked to turn my ass purple before sending me on long motorcycle rides for fun."

"Don't give me ideas." I licked my lips and tried to ignore how much I would *love* to torture him like that.

He furrowed his brows, the surprise now gone as reality set in. "Are you really agreeing to this?"

"You want me to dominate you," I said. "I'd like to dominate you. It's an easy deal to make."

"What do you want in return?" He seemed confused, like he didn't understand why I would do this.

"Oh, I'm going to have a lot of fun stringing you up and—"

"Well, what do we have here?" came the voice from the darkness up ahead. The orange glow of a lit cigarette preceded KC with a wide grin on his face like he'd just discovered two thieves in the act.

"Mischief," he said to his buddy before glancing at me, "and Mayhem."

"Killer Cock," Hollywood said, smiling at his friend's nickname while KC stared at us.

"What are you two plotting out here by yourselves?" KC stabbed his cigarette out in the ashtray between Hollywood and me before stuffing his hands in his coat pocket, glancing to my accomplice.

"World domination," I said. "You know, the usual."

He laughed and clapped Hollywood on the shoulder. "I'm gonna run in and say hi to my wife. Then, we can go."

"Sounds good, brother," Hollywood said, pursing his lips as he looked down at me.

I waited until KC closed the door before speaking again.

"Think about why you want this . . . and why you want this *from me*," I said. "Something better than because it turns you on. A strong gust of wind could do that."

Hollywood let out a hollow chuckle. "Hilarious."

"Let's talk tomorrow at my place. Eight p.m."

He grinned that Cheshire smile, ear to ear, beaming with happiness. "You got it."

I nodded and went to move around him, but he caught my arm as I passed, pulling me in close enough for him to whisper again.

"Hey," he said, forcing me to glance up at him. Our faces were centimeters apart, his lips so close I could taste his breath. "Thank you."

It would have taken nothing for me to push up on my feet and close the distance, perhaps seal the deal with a kiss. His lips looked soft and mesmerizing. Instead, I nodded and turned away to go back inside, ignoring the suspicious stare from Selene still on the couch. Alba was in KC's arms, whispering sweet nothings to him while Ru did the same with Saint farther down the hallway. I went back to my spot on the sofa, grabbed the bucket of popcorn, and focused on the main character having another meltdown. When I couldn't stand it any longer, I glanced up at Sel.

"What?" I asked, the word hissing out of my mouth in a snarl.

She had a shit-eating grin on her face while she dropped popcorn kernels into her mouth. "Nothing." She shrugged. "Just curious what you and Hollywood had to talk about."

"A single lady on the porch with an eligible bachelor in this day and age?" I wailed in a dramatic southern accent and pretended to gasp, clutching my proverbial pearls. "What will my dear ole Pa think?"

"Stop." Selene shook her head and glanced at Alba to make sure she was still out of earshot before continuing. "I'm trying to look out for you. Be careful."

"What are you talking about?" I'd known Hollywood as long as her, if not longer, and arguably better. When I'd first gotten home from college, we'd been nearly inseparable because of his requirement to babysit me. I knew he fucked around, I knew he was a playboy, and I knew how much he was trying to change that reputation.

"Look, I love Hollywood like a brother, and I think it's hilarious how much he's going to have his hands full with you." She snickered and let out a deep sigh. "But I meant what I said about people thinking Hollywood is trash. Hell, he probably thinks it himself. He's been shot, what? Three times now?" She whistled and leaned forward, resting her elbows on her knees. "I know I'm one to talk about early graves, but that one . . . he'll be lucky to see thirty-five."

I sat back and ruminated on that. I hadn't thought about it before, but she was right. Hollywood had agreed to take care of Leo Caputi, even after everyone else swore him off. He had dived in front of a bullet for me, and two other times I knew about. Ru said he was spiraling, that he'd taken Trojan's death hard, and not that I blamed him, but it made his desperation to be dominated more understandable.

In a world that had suddenly spun out of his control, Hollywood wanted to relinquish that responsibility to someone he trusted, if only to ease the load for a short period of time. Warmth spread through my stomach, increasing the profound happiness that he'd come to me.

No one else in Madison County would treat Hollywood with the tender mix of gentleness and roughness he needed. No one else could understand how dominance and submission could make this fucked-up world seem livable.

I SPENT the next day thinking about what I wanted to do when I saw Hollywood later that night. I had an idea of what he'd be into based on what he'd whispered in my ear at the clubhouse. All that pondering did not prepare me for the conversation we would actually have or the shivers racing down my torso when I watched him walk into my house and close the door behind him, clicking the lock into place.

Wheels was on a run for the MC, and Hollywood assured my father he was up for babysitting me after spending the day with Leo. But that was a much more innocent way to describe what we would actually do.

I sat at the dining room table with a fuzzy black robe covering my matching leather outfit underneath. I didn't have to dress up to do a scene, but like an actor on a stage, having the right attire put me in a different mindset. Two glasses of water sat on the table next to the checklist I had for him to complete.

"Hiya, V," Hollywood said with his classic grin, stuffing his hands in his jacket pockets as he strolled forward. I understood why KC had called him mischief the other night, especially as it shimmered in his eyes while he took the seat opposite me.

"Hi, Hollywood," I said. "How was your day?"

He shrugged. "I spent my morning with a mass murderer that's kinda-sorta our enemy."

"Only kinda-sorta?" I pursed my lips and raised an eyebrow. "I thought any Caputi was an enemy."

"Yeah, I thought so, too." The sound of his soft chuckle made me smile. Then, he nodded to the piece of paper in front of him. "What's that?"

"A checklist." I pushed it closer to him and drummed my finger-nails on the table.

He picked it up and held it to his face so he could squint to see the writing.

*Did he need glasses?*

I'd have to remember to ask him that after this was over.

"Pegging?" He let out a loud disbelieving whistle. "Damn, V. There's some wild shit on here."

"If you think pegging is wild, you haven't gotten around nearly as much as I thought," I said with a small chuckle.

He shifted his dark gaze to mine, his features falling a little, just enough to hint at his trepidation. "You'll really do the stuff on here?"

"I have my own list." I pointed at the paper in front of me and kept my back straight, trying not to be intimidated by the fact this was *Hollywood,* a man I'd known since childhood, a person I'd always considered belonging to my brother. "I'd like to see how much our interests align before we go further. As for tonight, you gave me a wish list in the back room at the clubhouse. I have no limits with anything you mentioned."

He shifted his hips in the seat and ran a finger over his mouth while he considered the list. It had three columns full of activities with a Y M N for each—yes, maybe, or no.

"Do I have to fill it out before we begin?" He raised an eyebrow.

"That depends," I said. "Did you think about what I asked you?"

Clearing his throat, he kicked his boot across the floor and straightened his spine. "I did."

I waited, using the silence as my urge for him to continue.

"When Trojan died, I made a promise over his grave that I'd do the living for both of us, that I'd settle down and get my shit togeth-er." He shrugged and glanced at the floor, like looking me in the eye while he continued was too much, even for someone as playful and outgoing as him. "I went full time at the garage. I'm taking care of my mom and saving money so I can move out of Saint's house." Then, he paused and gazed back up at me, holding my stare while he said the next part. "I stopped fucking around. I want people to treat me a certain way for me, not because they want something from me."

"I'm happy for you, Hollywood," I continued, giving him an encouraging smile. "But that doesn't explain why you're sitting at my table, asking me to turn your ass pink."

His answering smile nearly blinded me, and I had to steel myself against the girlish tickle that twisted through my stomach. He was too damned cute.

"When I saw you up on stage at the Beacon"—he shook his head and blew out a breath, challenge sparkling behind his glittery gaze as he went on—"I'd never wanted to be bent over a spanking bench more in my life. You're magnificent, and I think we could make art. I think you have the right idea about what this is . . . and what it *isn't*."

Sure, I supposed that was accurate. The hang-arounds wanted to fuck him because of his reputation, because they thought of him like a piece of meat. Me, I didn't even like him. If I did this, it would be because he'd asked me to. I could understand that.

I held his stare for a moment more before allowing myself to smile and respond. "Okay."

"What about you?" he asked. "Why are you agreeing to do this . . . with me?"

I considered how to answer him, almost blurting out the first thing on my mind as the conversation with Selene rushed back to me. I wanted him to take better care of himself. I didn't want him to think of himself as trash, if he truly did. He'd saved my life, and I feared she might be right, that he might be on a martyr collision course with fate. Perhaps I could stop it. Perhaps I could take this bullet for him and remind him how it felt to be alive. Of course, I couldn't lead with that and scare him away.

"You deserve someone who knows what they're doing," I answered, which wasn't too far from the truth. "As you said, I know my way around a whip."

He chuckled, seemingly pleased with that answer.

"But you were right," I said, ignoring the burn in my cheeks. "It does turn me on to see you get on your knees, knowing I'm the one that put you there." It aroused me more than I would ever admit to anyone else. "What about your no-sex streak?"

"I only told the hang-arounds that so they'd leave me alone." He laughed through his nose. "It backfired on me though since now they're all in a pool about when I'll break."

"Fucking vultures." I hated them even more. "We'll keep it going tonight, but we can talk about ending it soon, if you want. When was the last time you had sex with someone else?"

He shifted again, clearing his throat before taking a sip of water. "Define sex."

"Someone else stimulating your cock, no matter the method."

"Eight months?" He winced while he thought about his answer. "The night before KC's wedding." His cheeks flushed, and he dropped his gaze to the floor, taking another drink of water. Admittedly, it had been longer for me, but I wouldn't tell him that. Like I said, kink didn't have to be about sex, and most of my clients were happy to take a beating from me and go to their partners for aftercare. I hadn't allowed anyone to penetrate me in over a year. "You?"

I took a deep breath before telling him the truth. "Since I was in Manhattan."

"Holy shit, really?" He whistled. "Why so long?"

"You've met my brothers, right?"

"Yeah, but you and Candy . . ."

"It was never about sex." I met his gaze, warmth dripping through my chest at how sincere he could be. Candy and I were friends, and she had agreed to be my submissive in order to put on a good show. But she didn't regularly participate in kink, and since that night, she'd found a girlfriend to do those things with instead of me. "You said you were with a Madam before, right? How long did that go on?"

He shrugged and shook his head, waving me off like it was nothing. "A few months. She was married, so when he found out, she ended it."

"I'm sorry," I said, hearing what he didn't say. He'd enjoyed himself, especially when she paddled him and sent him on a long bike ride, and he had been nothing more than a side piece for her. "That must have hurt."

His focus came to me, like he couldn't believe I'd said that. "Thank you."

"Speaking of my brothers," I went on, "this is none of their business."

Hollywood leaned his head back and nodded solemnly. "I agree."

"If they ask, that's what we'll tell them."

He hummed out a pleased noise, half moan, half laugh.

"And I don't share." I stood, preparing to head down to my dungeon to get into the right headspace. "Ever. Don't let me catch you with someone else, Hollywood, not while this is going on."

"That won't happen," he said. "I swear it."

I wanted to believe him, and perhaps that's why I agreed to this in the first place. But some small churning in my gut reminded me to keep my emotions at arm's length. This wasn't a relationship. This was kink. Period. End of story. With the tension of my sudden anticipation growing between us and nothing else to ask him, I glanced down at the paper again. "Get to work on that. I'll be back in a few moments."

Hollywood nodded, picked up the pen, and began writing down his limits. Now that we'd taken sex off the table for tonight, the real work of breaking him down could begin. Oh, he'd come, and I probably would, too. But I'd stay resolute on our No Fucking policy, at least until this felt more solid.

Right now, we were walking on cracked glass, hoping it didn't shatter, and I'd never been much of a risk-taker, at least not when it came to my stupid little heart.

**11**

---

# HOLLYWOOD

I scribbled through that checklist like my ass was on fire, marking maybe or yes to most of the stuff on it. I'd never been into scat or wet works, so those were firm limits, but anything else was on the table. I filled out the spot for safeword, writing "Full House" since that was the hand I'd been dealt that put us in this position. Then, I sat at the table and waited for V to return. She'd told me to stay put, so I didn't dare move. I just sipped at the water like a good boy and stared at the scratch in the middle of the wood, remembering when KC made it as a teenager.

My heart pounded down into my cock, already rock hard with expectation at what tonight might bring. I hadn't had a dominant since my ex and that had been more about her pissing off her husband than it was about building a relationship with me, but fuck it. I'd just wanted to get my ass spanked and dick sucked, and she'd been up for the job.

When the door opened down the hallway and the boom of V's shitkickers sauntered toward me, I bit my bottom lip and glanced up at her.

*Fucking. Fuck.*

She looked amazing, wearing a black leather bodysuit with a

halter crossing her chest that disappeared over her shoulders. She'd worn the same boots she had on the night at the clubhouse, and my blood pounded harder at the memory of her digging that heel into an old bullet wound.

I didn't realize my mouth was hanging open until she tucked the end of a riding crop under my chin to close it.

"Are you ready, pretty boy?" She leaned down so she could glance at my checklist, giving me a view straight down her cleavage. Fuck, I wanted to shove my face into that mound of flesh and breathe her in deep. I wanted to tuck my cock in between those magnificent tits and fuck the tip into her mouth until I came. "Hmm, so we like pegging after all."

"I like a dick in the ass as much as anyone." There was nothing quite like being held down and screwed so hard I saw stars. Not all guys would admit it; most wouldn't even try it. But with someone who knew what they were doing, my prostate ached for a good massage.

"Shut up." She brought the crop down on the table so hard, I jumped more than the glasses of water. "You can talk when I tell you."

Gulping, I nodded and swallowed the exhilaration shooting through my veins. She was the only one who talked to me like this, and it was so fucking mean, I loved it. I couldn't imagine anyone else doing what she could do. It was part of what made her so alluring in the first place.

"Safeword is 'full house,'" she said, fisting her fingers into my hair. "You may speak that at any time. Otherwise, the only words you'll say are 'Yes, Mistress.'"

"Yes, Mistress," I repeated, giving her another quick nod of approval. My hands trembled, and I clenched them into fists to keep myself from appearing so nervous. Why the hell was I shaking? This was V, a woman I'd known since childhood, a woman I trusted beyond reason.

"Good boy," she said, yanking my head back.

Another jerk rocketed through my cock at her words, and the praise slut inside me sat up at attention. I liked earning her affection. I liked when she handled me like this.

"Now, get up and walk down the hallway to my old room. When you get there, take off your clothes and kneel on the pillow on the floor." She let me go as I pushed to my feet, attempting to play it cool by not sprinting down the hallway to do her bidding. Her degrading giggle indicated I hadn't done a very good job.

I ripped my shirt over my head as soon as I got inside the room, kicking my boots off by the heels. I nearly lost my balance and fell over, but once I had those off, my jeans went next. I thought about leaving my boxers on. She had said we weren't going to break my streak, so I didn't want to be standing around with my dick hanging out. But she had told me to get naked, so I pushed my underwear to the ground and stepped out of them.

Then, I spotted the red cushion on the ground, perfectly sized for someone to kneel. Giving myself one last chance to bail out, I eyed the door and swallowed down my cowardice.

*I want this. It's gonna be fun.*

I dropped to my knees, rested my hands on my thighs, and waited for my Mistress to come do her worst. Heartbeats pounded in my chest like a bass drum as I looked around. A metal St. Andrew's Cross stood in the corner with padded cuffs at the end of each part of the *X*. A spanking bench sat next to that, the leather seemingly supple and unused though I knew better. I wondered how many asses that thing had seen. A rainbow display of ropes hung on the wall at my side and the dresser under that had all its drawers closed, but I could've guessed what treasures lay protected behind its wood. If she'd asked about pegging, she must have a strap, and my muscles quaked at the thought I might see it one day.

I took a deep breath to calm my anticipation. This was all part of the scene—drawing it out, making me wait, using my time against me. After all, the teasing was half the fun.

A fucking million years later, V finally walked down the hallway, the echoes of her boots thumping in time with my pulse. She rounded the door and slapped the crop in her other hand, raising a dark eyebrow as she assessed me.

"I have to say, Hudson," she started, taking a few steps toward me,

"I did not think you would be so obedient right away." Reaching the business end of her tool out to me again, she glided the cool leather down one side of my cheek before going to the other. "I thought I'd have to train you at least a little bit."

I swallowed, resisting the urge to talk back.

"Look at how beautiful you are on your knees for me." Mistress shook her head and squatted down so we were eye level, her gaze surprisingly gentle despite the horrors she must have planned for my ass.

I preened at the compliment, my cheeks burning, a hot flush going down my neck and over my chest. She reached out to trace a finger over the circular scar on my shoulder where I'd been shot two years ago. Chills erupted over my skin when she dragged it farther down to the one we shared, the one that meant I'd saved her life.

"You really are amazing," she murmured. "You know that?"

For one heart-shattering moment, I met her gaze and saw adoration behind it. This wasn't supposed to be that type of scene. She wasn't supposed to shower me with pretty words.

Then, she grabbed my chin between her index finger and her thumb, forcing my head to tilt up to face her. "So self-sacrificing. Such a fucking martyr." Her words had turned angry and vicious, *fuck yeah,* and the sneer in her eyes hinted it wasn't good I was those things. "Get up."

I shoved to my feet like my ass was on fire.

"Go stand in front of the cross." She nodded toward the metal apparatus, and I went, stretching my arms out and spreading my legs. My muscles trembled when she reached up to attach the restraints, circling the furry cuffs around my wrists before checking the tightness to make sure it wouldn't cut off my circulation. She squatted behind me to do the same to my legs, and I tightened my thighs to keep from shivering. "Are you cold? You can answer."

"No, Mistress," I said, although the winter draft coming in from the window breezed across my flesh and pebbled my nipples. Luckily, I was a grower *and* a shower, so I didn't have to worry about my dick shriveling up.

"Hmm." She dragged her fingertips up the back of my legs, over my ass, and across my spine, her nails adding to the prickling goose bumps. My shoulders shook, and I took a deep breath in through my nose to try to calm my nerves. "Now, I remember you saying something about a cat-o'-nine-tails and clothespins."

I cleared my throat and nodded, grabbing the top of the cross to brace myself. She hadn't told me to answer, so I stayed quiet as she walked to her dresser, seemingly exchanging the crop for something else. I couldn't help the moan that tumbled out when she came back and massaged my shoulders, rubbing her talented palms down my ribs and back up again. I melted into the contact, relishing in how good it felt to have someone else touching me.

The cool kiss of leather straps dangled over my deltoids, drifting from side to side as I firmed my stance.

"Tell me your safeword again." She leaned in to press her lips against the nape of my neck.

"Full house," I answered.

"Good boy. Keep it close, just in case." Cool air rushed in when she stepped back, making me quiver before the hiss of disrupted atmosphere preceded a loud crack. I jumped at the sharp zing on my ass, sucking in a breath because she'd gone zero to a hundred. No warm-up. No preamble. Just right into a five on the pain scale.

*Fuuuck me.*

The ache that came afterward made me sigh and melt into the X-frame.

"Oh, I think he likes it," she teased with a giggle.

My heart jumped at the sound of her lighthearted taunt, my balls seizing as she brought the leather straps down on my other cheek, harder this time, making me groan. God, I fucking loved it, and I wanted more. I arched my back, sticking my ass out in invitation, purposely showing her how much I ached for it.

She gave it to me. She alternated soft taps with hard zings that had me panting and sweating much quicker than I would have thought. My cock strained in front of me, leaking precum from the tip, and every time she said something degrading, I almost came all over myself.

"Look at how pink your cute little ass gets," she said, dragging her nails across my butt in deep scratches that would certainly leave marks. I leaned into it, which only made her laugh. Then, she spanked me. Hard. I gasped and collapsed against the cross, jostling my restraints. "Such a depraved pervert, aren't you? I bet I could make you come without touching you."

I blew a small chuckle through my nose, knowing I was moments away from that very thing happening. My dick throbbed painfully, desperate for attention she wouldn't give it. I'd never felt more out of control than that moment, like I'd have no say over whether I shot spunk all over the place. My fate, and my penis's, were in her capable hands, and there was no place I'd rather be.

"Let's see how you like this, huh?" Her boots sounded toward the dresser, and I glanced over my shoulder to see her pulling the top drawer out. She reached inside, returning with a handful of wooden clothespins and a long leather whip with a pink handle.

I gulped and tried not to get too excited, but that went out the door when she circled in front of me and grinned, her eyes sparkling so bright, I thought she might be the one to come in her pants unprompted. She held my stare while she fastened a pin to the skin over my ribs, just under my armpit.

"Ahh." The groan barreled over my lips, a surge of euphoric agony twisting down that side of my body, making me curl into the zing.

"Too much?" She raised her eyebrows and paused. "Do you need to say something?"

Swallowing against a dry throat, I shook my head and straightened. "No, Mistress."

"Good boy." She smiled and added another just under the first one. Then a second and a third. The pinch stung at first in a delicate, passionate way, but then dissipated when she went to the other side and did the same thing. She glanced down at my nipples, running her fingers over my chest before scratching the sensitive skin with her claws. I braced myself as she lifted the wood to the right and fixed it in place.

*Fuuuccckkk...*

It smarted in the best way possible, and my lower stomach twisted with arousal. I didn't know why the pain turned me on so much; I'd learned a long time ago not to look too closely at that. It was best to revel in my kinks without thinking about the reasons why they were there in the first place. I repeated this to myself when she put another clothespin on the other nipple before squatting down to put more on the insides of my thighs. I watched her while she worked, and when she stopped to focus on my balls, I sucked in a breath, thinking she planned to attach a few there as well.

Instead, she just looked up at me and stood, running her nails up my abs to my pecs and over my shoulders.

"Are you okay?" Her voice drizzled over me like honey, sweet and decadent and soothing.

I nodded. "Yes, Mistress."

She ran the back of her knuckles down the side of my face in a move too endearing for what she'd been thinking of doing to my nut sack only moments ago. "You're a good man, Hudson."

I hummed out an appreciative sigh while she circled around to my back, cracking the whip through the air to let me know what was coming. The spots where the clothespins pinched throbbed in time with my pulse, the initial sharpness having worn away. But I knew that wasn't the height of that agony. No, that would come when she finally wrenched them off.

The first time she brought the whip down on my back, I sucked in a harsh breath and sagged in relief. Pain erupted over my shoulders and down my spine, echoing into my legs and arms. But fuck, I loved the torture. My toes curled, my knees shook, and my cock wept, inching closer to the release that had been building all fucking day.

She worked me over, alternating desperate flogs with her soft palm, rubbing circles over my twitching muscles. When she brought the leather down on the left side of clothespins, ripping them off in one swipe, I cried out and curled in on myself. It burned in a wonderful display of ecstasy, cascading over my chest and up the back of my neck, and I prayed I had bruises in the morning. She did it to the other side and I clamped my eyes shut, fisting my fingers and pushing up on the balls of my feet.

"Fucking Christ," I whispered, trying my best to keep my voice low enough that she might not hear it. But she did. She stepped closer, grabbed my hair, and ripped my head back. My scalp prickled as I arched into the sharp pang.

"What was that?" she asked with a vicious snarl. "Did you call me Christ?"

I moaned, unable to say complete sentences though I knew she wanted an answer. My cock dripped, my hands tingled, and my balls were practically in my stomach. I ached to come. I needed release.

"No, Mistress." My lips could barely form the syllables.

"Oh, good," she said. "You know my name, pretty boy. That's the only one you need to call."

Carnal need hit me like a freight train, and I couldn't stop the shaking that came after it. Never in my life had I wanted someone more, and I wasn't sure if that was because of the eight months I'd spent whacking it or the beautiful woman who held my entire life in the palm of her hand. The world faded away. Suddenly, there was no more SRMC or Bear or long list of Montgomerys that would beat my face in if they found out. It was only me and V and the magic she created on my back.

She walked to my front again, staring up at me while she knocked the pins off my legs with the handle of the whip. I tugged against the cuffs and let out an exhale that weighed a ton. Now, I only had the ones on my nipples, and they were going to hurt the worst. I wanted them to.

My mind started to fog, all of the misery from her attention having launched me into a dopamine-filled haze much more potent than any bud I'd ever smoked or whiskey I'd ever drank. *Subspace.* Nothing compared to it. Nothing. And when she flicked the wooden clamp on the right, a harsh breath whooshed out of my lungs from the wicked heat that lanced down to my dick.

"I'm going to bite my name into your back, Hudson," she said. "And then I'm going to push you to your knees and ride your face."

The vicious wave of arousal that hit me in the nuts almost made me bust. I had to clench my eyes together to keep it from happening. She hadn't forbidden me to come, but I didn't want to embarrass myself during our first scene. Sure, we had said this didn't have to be sexual, and maybe if I hadn't responded like a teenager getting my cock wet for the first time, it might not have gone this way.

"Only then are you allowed to release," she continued, flicking the clothespin on the left. "Do you want to keep these on or rip them off now? Speak."

"Now, Mistress," I said, desperate to do what she described. Sparks of adrenaline-laced excruciation rushed through my torso when she ripped the first one off.

I groaned and sagged against the cuffs, my knees buckling. Then, she did it to the next one and I threw my head back, moaning at how much it turned me on. My cock jerked and I canted my hips, desperate for more friction to relieve the pressure but finding nothing.

"Hold still." She circled around to my back, rubbing the tender skin like one might do when approaching a skittish horse. Her body heat radiated into mine when she stepped closer, her soft corset cool against my overheated spine. Then, she sank her teeth into my trap muscle by my shoulder, sucking it long enough to leave a mark before ripping her mouth away. V moved lower, biting her way toward the center of my spine at the base of my back before doing the same toward my other shoulder.

Based on the stings and cool drips of saliva left behind, she'd made a huge V of hickeys, and if I wasn't close to losing it before, I would have been after that. It was territorial and possessive in a way no one had ever been over me, and I couldn't wait to check out the results in the mirror. Of all the marks she left, I hoped those lasted the longest.

"There we go." She ran her hands over it a few times, scratching her nails down the pattern to connect her teeth marks. "Now, if any of those bitches even thinks about touching you, they'll know who's going to come after them."

*Fucking. Hell.*

"Isn't that supposed to be my line?" I tried to say, confused when my lips wouldn't cooperate.

"Shhhhh," she said, planting delicate kisses over the skin she'd just destroyed while she unhooked the cuffs on my wrists. "Just enjoy this."

I curled my hands into fists as soon as I could bring them down and stepped away from the cross once she'd unhooked my ankles. Thank God she put one of my arms over her shoulders and helped me to the ground because the second I tried to walk, my legs shook harder than I could manage.

The world suddenly seemed softer, my life not quite as hectic. My body pulsed with agitation, every mark and bruise and scuff pounding in time with my heart. But even that added to the buzz behind my eyes.

I sat back on my heels, put my hands on my thighs, and stared up at my Mistress—beautiful, ethereal V. No one else could have given me this pleasure like this. Only she knew how to work me over and make me pay for it. And now, I got my reward.

"You can stroke yourself," she said, "but you're not allowed to come before you make me come. Understood?"

I nodded, but she grabbed my chin and forced my head up so I had to meet her gaze with the unfocused one of my own.

"Say yes," she said.

"Yes, Mistress," I said, grabbing at my straining cock, squeezing the tip enough to make me wince.

"Good." She pushed the bottom piece of her costume to the ground before stepping out of it. I licked my lips when she walked toward me, all long legs and fishnet stockings. I opened my mouth, stuck out my tongue, and stared up at her, waiting for her to rub that pretty little clit in between my lips.

When she got close enough, she grabbed my hair and dragged my face to her cunt. I sank in like a starved man, licking her from opening to tip, relishing in the deep noises that poured out of her throat. God, she tasted good—like strawberries and pussy and sweat. I wanted to roll around in her scent to mark myself with it. I wanted it buried in my skin so that anyone else that tried to get close to me would know she'd laid claim. I wanted to implant my own smell into her molecules so that no one would dare touch her again. I may have liked to be dominated in the bedroom, but out in the real world, I was six foot five inches and two hundred and fifty pounds of kick ass. No one would touch her without going through me first.

She dug her nails deeper into my thick locks and rocked against my face, moaning when I pulled her clit into my mouth and sucked it like a dick.

"Yes," she murmured. "Yes, right there."

"May I finger you, Mistress?" I traced my free hand up the inside of her thigh, cupping the skin close to her pussy without touching it.

"Do it," she said.

I nudged my digit inside her warm, wet pussy, slowly at first. Fuck, she was tight, and I sighed, imagining what it would feel like to get my cock inside her for the first time. The sex we'd have would probably rock my fucking world and leave me ruined for anyone else. But I didn't want to think about that. I squeezed my dick with one hand, fucked her with the other, and focused on lapping at her delicious, sensitive flesh.

"Fuck, I'm close," she said. "Keep doing that. Keep—"

I followed directions like a star student, licking and sucking and rolling her around in my mouth like the sweetest candy in the world. She clamped my hair harder, holding me in the spot she wanted while her body tightened, indicating her release. When it flooded my mouth, I lapped that up, too, sucking down whatever she'd give me, desperate to consume all of it. I'd never been so overjoyed to have a person come on my face, not once in my whole life.

Once she'd had her fill, she stepped back and ran her palms over my head while I focused on my own orgasm. It wouldn't take much. I brought the fingers that had been inside her to my mouth and sucked them clean, and as her decadent taste slid down the back of my throat, I burst open at the seams. Come flew out of my cock harder and faster than it ever had before, including the night at the clubhouse.

My vision darkened. My mind went blank. I fell forward on my free hand, panting and gasping and struggling to see straight as I fucked my own fist through it.

"There it is, huh?" Verona kneeled in front of me, cupping my cheeks while I broke apart. My orgasm hit me in the gut, knocking my entire soul out of my body before ripping it back home again.

When I could finally suck in a deep breath, I sat back on my heels and rubbed my face, trying to get my fucking shit together again.

"Are you okay, Hollywood?" V stroked my chest, down to my torso, and back up again, using touch to ground me in the present, to bring me back to reality.

"I'm fucking great." I smiled as I struggled to focus on her. She swam in my vision, blurry and shiny like Christmas lights in the snow. "You're amazing, you know that? You're the best thing that's ever happened to me."

"All right," she said with a laugh, pulling me into a hug with her arms wrapped around my neck, cradling my head like it was the most precious thing in the world. "You're a quick trigger for subspace. Good to know."

"I really like you, V," I muttered, my lips practically numb. Like she'd said, I'd fully submerged into my endorphins, letting them pull me into that liminal weightless feeling where the world became sparkly and none of my issues mattered anymore. "I would eat your pussy every morning if you'd let me."

That made her giggle harder as she kissed across my forehead to my temples and down my cheeks, peppering my skin with affection. When she got to my mouth, she held my chin in place so she could press her warm, soft lips to mine.

It was delicate and compassionate compared to what she'd done to my body, but it meant everything to me. She didn't see me as a piece of meat and she wouldn't wreck me only to leave me alone in subspace on the cold wooden floor. No, V stayed with me until it passed, kissing my mouth and my neck and my face, silently telling me she cared for me despite the damage she'd done.

Perhaps it was the buzz or perhaps it was fifteen years of friendship suddenly collapsing into something new, but when she pulled away to stare in my eyes, I saw my future in hers.

I saw kids and a house and a big wedding with her family. I saw her tying me up for the rest of my life and taking out all of her frustrations on my ass. I saw everything I'd ever wanted and *she* was the one who could give it me.

Or rather . . . I could give it to her. We could give it to each other.

I'd never been so sure about anything ever before.

## 12

## VERONA

Hollywood's smile blinded me as I hauled him to his feet and led him across the hall to the bathroom inside my room. It had a bigger tub and, after the carnage I'd created on his back, I thought warm water would help.

"You're so beautiful," he said, his eyes still hazy from the comedown. I sat him on the toilet while I adjusted the water, making sure it wasn't scalding.

"You're adorable, Hollywood." I walked back over to him and stood in between his legs, raking my nails through his hair to massage his scalp while he preened for me. "Let me see your back."

Grinning, he turned around so I could assess the damage. I'd broken the skin in a few places, but nothing serious and nothing that hadn't been done to him before. Once he got out of the bath, I planned to rub antiseptic on them to make sure they didn't get infected. I ghosted my fingers over the *V* I'd carved into his skin with my teeth, making him hiss in a breath and arch his away from me.

"I liked when you bit me the most," he murmured.

I took a deep breath and let it out on a sigh, ignoring the flutter in my heart when he said it. I had liked everything, including the bites, and after all the scenes I'd done and all the people I'd been with,

Hollywood had been my favorite. He responded to each touch, each brush of the whip, as if it would be the last thing he ever felt. After this, I couldn't deny how well we matched, how much I wanted to keep doing these things to him.

*Careful,* a part of me warned. Thoughts like that would lead down a very dangerous road, one neither of us wanted to walk. This wasn't a relationship. This wasn't even supposed to be about sex. This was about control and release, end of story. All these feelings rattling around in my brain were nothing more than a hormone release. It would pass. It *had* to pass.

When he moved on, when he decided he wanted someone else, I couldn't be attached. He had to stay at arm's length.

"Was it too hard?" I asked. "Do you want me to go harder next time?"

"Hmm." He gave me a dreamy smile and nodded. "Harder."

"All right." Once the water was high enough, I helped him stand and guided him to the tub, holding his body while he stepped in and sat down. He hissed in a breath when the water touched his back and his ass hit the ground, but then he relaxed against the porcelain and let out a deep sigh.

"Thank you, V," he said. "For all this."

"Yeah, Hudson. What are friends for?"

He laughed deep in his chest and raised an eyebrow. "Is that what we are? Friends?"

"Barely. With really good benefits." I kneeled by the tub and ran my hand through the water, letting it flow through my fingertips.

He grabbed it and intertwined his fingers in mine. "Get in with me."

Despite all we'd just done together, that seemed too personal, as if sharing a bath after I'd come in his mouth made this more intimate than it should be. Suddenly, I was too self-conscious to take my corset off. I had a big nasty scar going down the center of my chest, one that distorted the tattoo under my breasts. I didn't like the way I looked, at least not right there.

"Next time," I said, smiling. "This one is for you."

"C'mon, V." He tilted his head to the side and stuck his bottom lip out in a pout. "I just wanna cuddle."

"I don't like getting wet."

He rolled his eyes. "That's not true. You enjoyed being wet just a few minutes ago."

I splashed his face and scoffed. "Don't be crude."

"Dommes need aftercare, too. Get in with me, V. Please."

*Well, since he begged . . .*

"Okay." I stood and pulled at the laces on my top, loosening them enough to yank the suffocating thing off. Thankfully, I'd taken off the jar containing the bullet fragment before I changed so he wouldn't see it and start asking questions. Then, I tugged off my boots and slid my fishnets down to the ground so I could step out of them. He sat up so I could squeeze in behind him, my legs going to either side of his hips, his head planted between my breasts. I relaxed against the back of the tub and he let out a breath as he laid back on me.

"This is the best," he said, grabbing my calves. He slid his hands up and down in a soothing, massaging motion that had me nodding and agreeing with him. "When can we do it again?"

"Whenever you want," I said, tunneling my fingers through his hair. "I've got clients in the morning, but you could come over after that."

"Clients," he said, the word sounding sad in his mouth. "You do this to others."

"You knew that before we started." My heart pounded under his head, the postcoital high now almost gone as reality sank back in.

"You said you didn't share." His hands froze on the outsides of my thighs, holding me in place while he tried to coax out my response, and he looked up at me with his brows furrowed. His lips pulled into a thin line, like it hurt him for me to say it.

"I don't touch anyone else," I explained. "Most of it is talking them through their orgasm. You and Candy are the only people I've seen in person since I got home."

"Okay." He hummed appreciatively and relaxed again. "I'm okay with that."

"Good," I said. "And when the Beacon opens up again, I'm planning on resuming the general manager spot. I'll only put on shows with an eager pretty boy, if he's up to it . . . assuming this is still going on."

"Why wouldn't it be?" He narrowed his eyes up at me, but even that was likely a side effect of his comedown.

*Because you're you, and I'm me,* I wanted to say. Hollywood had a reputation for a reason, and even if he'd spent the last eight months soul searching, a tiger didn't change its stripes. I had a hard time trusting people, and if I let him in, he had the potential to hurt me more than anyone ever had.

"It's just a hypothetical," I said instead.

Hollywood grinned and arched up to kiss me, his lips warm and soft despite how rough around the edges he was. The sensation shot down the back of my legs and curled my toes, and I smiled into the connection, knowing he'd gone so long without doing this to anyone. Admittedly, I hadn't kissed anyone in a while, either, and hell, how I had missed it.

We talked a little more but eventually fell into comfortable silence. He grabbed the washcloth and lathered soap up my legs and feet. I took it from him and washed his torso and his back, taking my time to memorize the bumpy pattern of his scars, especially the one we'd gotten together. Then, he turned around and pushed up on his knees so he could do the same to me.

He paused when he dragged the cloth over my chest, over the permanent purple memory of that night, his gaze focused on the angry mark. Yes, it marked the fact that I had survived that night, but who wanted a scar right in the middle of what they once loved about themselves? Suddenly more self-conscious than I needed to be, I grabbed the rag from him and squeezed out the excess water.

"We're starting to prune," I said. "It's time for bed."

"Can I stay?" he asked, his expression too hopeful to refuse.

"Of course, Hollywood," I said. "You're welcome here anytime you want."

His answering grin twisted down my chest and squeezed my heart even harder. Fuck, I shouldn't be feeling this giddy around him, and I definitely shouldn't look forward to him sleeping in my bed. But I knew, as we let the water go down the drain and made our way into my bedroom, this was *my* favorite part. Yeah, it was nice to carve my name into his flesh and shove him to his knees to eat me out, but my deepest, darkest secret was I *liked* aftercare. I liked holding my partner until they fell asleep in my arms. I liked knowing the intimacy of our connection didn't end in the dungeon.

I hadn't trusted anyone with this side of me in a long time.

*Did I trust Hollywood?*

No. This was just my own hormone comedown, the domme version of subspace.

Naked and wrapped in a big fluffy towel, Hollywood crawled into my bed and shoved his long legs under the covers, his feet hanging off the edge because of how tall he was. I grabbed the antiseptic and a few cotton swabs before getting on the mattress with my knees and crawling over to him so I could straddle his ass.

He groaned and looked over his shoulder. "I don't need that shit, V."

"Hush," I said, dabbing some cream on the deepest gash. I hadn't meant to make him bleed, but now that I had, I needed to clean it up. "No one else takes care of you. So let me."

"Hmm." He didn't argue anymore, and by the time I'd finished, his breathing had evened out to a slow, steady pace. I climbed off him to throw the used swabs away and wash my hands. When I returned, I crawled under the covers next to him and turned off the lamp, letting my eyes adjust to the moonlight trickling in through the window.

Completely at peace like this, Hollywood looked even more beautiful. The fake face he put on for everyone else had dropped, making him nearly unrecognizable. He wasn't the cocky playboy I knew from high school, nor was he the lovable goofball that had patched into the SRMC. Like this, he'd been stripped of those personas, pulled apart at the seams, and put back together as his authentic self. He seemed so innocent, so endearingly fragile.

I ran a finger down the center of his forehead, over his nose, to his lips, memorizing the feel of his skin under mine and the way his features curved. I told myself not to get used to it. I didn't trust these emotions rumbling around in my chest or the thoughts drifting through my head.

But as I lay in that bed with nothing but the moon and the stars to confess to, I let myself admit maybe . . . just maybe . . . I could let him in . . . one day.

## 13

## HOLLYWOOD

"I didn't think you'd arrange it this fast," Leo said, stuffing his hands in the pockets of his hoodie. After Saint had gotten in contact with Julia Caputi, she'd wanted to meet Leo right away. I received a text from Bear this morning telling me to get my ass over to Leo's crash pad as soon as I could. I said goodbye to V, promised to come back over tonight, and headed out. Now that I was here, I couldn't help the skip in my step, nor the perpetual grin on my face.

"You said you wanted to see her," I explained. "She was in a hurry to see you, too."

Leo narrowed his dark eyes on me and ran the length of my body before meeting my gaze again. "You fucked your girl, didn't you?"

I gasped and clutched my imaginary pearls. "Leonardo Elizabeth Caputi. How dare you speak to me like that? I am a lady!"

He ignored my mock protest. "You did, didn't you?"

"We didn't fuck," I confessed, shifting my shoulders as the aches on my back pulled in a glorious stretch. I had an enormous *V* in bite bruises going from one shoulder to the other, and between me and God, I'd been thinking about getting them tattooed there permanently. I liked knowing she'd roughed me up. The filthy things she'd said to me played on a loop in my head, and my cock gave half a jump anytime I thought about it.

"But you fooled around." Leo crossed his arms and grinned. "Good for you."

I cleared my throat and shifted my weight, aware the only person I *could* talk to about this was him. No one else could find out about this, at least not until she and I were both okay with the news getting out. We agreed it wasn't anyone's business.

"How was it?" He raised his eyebrows, awaiting my response.

"Fucking amazing," I murmured.

Leo threw back his head and laughed, clapping. "Very nice, my friend. I'm happy for you. Are you going to see her again?"

Ignoring the way *friend* sounded coming out of his mouth, I nodded and smiled. "Tonight."

"This is a good thing for you," Leo said. "You look ten times lighter than yesterday."

Before I could respond, voices echoed from outside and footsteps pounded on the stairs leading to the door. I turned as Saint walked through, the quiet brother nodding before glancing at Leo, who was still seated in the living room.

A small brunette came in next, wearing expensive black trousers and a matching blouse, her feet shoved into six-inch red-bottomed stilettos despite the threat of snow today. Her long hair hung down to the middle of her back, and when her gaze shifted to me, I understood what Leo had meant. Her sneer could penetrate Fort Knox. She reeked of old money and privilege, and the way she assessed me then immediately dismissed me reminded me of pre-surgery Leo. I didn't need to know they were siblings to see the family resemblance. If he'd been born a woman, they might have been twins.

"Leo!" Julia gasped and rushed to her brother, throwing her designer purse on the sofa so she could wrap her arms around his neck.

Bear walked in behind her, closing the door before giving me a glare like the woman had done nothing but annoy him the entire drive here. I stuffed away the memories of what I'd done to his sister and what she'd done to me last night, focusing on the present. We were here to discuss the terms of a truce. Leo had wanted to get his sister's opinion before agreeing to anything, and if all went well here, the next step would be to get Crow on board with a compromise.

"How was the trip?" I asked Bear.

"Fucking terrible," he whispered. "She's more Caputi than he is, not in a good way."

I chuckled and patted him on the back. "You're here now."

"Yeah," he said, rubbing his hands over his face. "Let's just get this over with."

We walked into the living room while they were still catching up.

"Look at you," Julia said, cupping her brother's face. "You're a mess." She rambled in Italian while she fussed over her brother's hair before pointing at the wrappings on his knee. "What is that?" She turned to me and shoved my chest. "What did you do to him?"

I held up my hands and stepped back, making a show of solidarity.

"Hey!" Bear stepped in front of me, leaning down so he was in her face. "Your brother's lucky to be alive. Quite frankly, so are you."

She ranted in Italian, putting her hands on her hips and stepping closer to Bear, jutting her chin out to show she wasn't going to back down from him.

Bear let her spit venom for a few moments before clapping inches from her mouth, startling her enough to shut her up.

She gasped when he answered her in Italian, and whatever he said made her cheeks turn a bright shade of pink.

Saint met my gaze and raised his eyebrows, covering his mouth with his hand while Julia and Bear argued like the rest of us weren't here. I'd never seen anyone talk to Bear like that, and I couldn't even understand what she was saying.

Leo chuckled and raised his eyebrows, watching the dramatic display with delight.

"Ahh," Julia finally growled before turning to her brother. "Leo, please tell me it's okay to . . ." She muttered something else in Italian.

He grabbed her hand, brought it to his mouth so he could kiss her knuckles, and shook his head. "No, *mia sorella*. Take a deep breath. They've been kind to me, especially that one." Leo nodded to me. "You've wanted the war to end since Julian died. This is how we end it."

She sat on the footstool next to the recliner, holding Leo's hand while she seemingly got her emotions under control. "What does that mean?"

"Tell me about Gabriella," Leo said. "What has been going on while I've been here?"

Julia licked her lips and looked at us before clearing her throat. "Uncle Frankie is getting restless. He doesn't believe Gabriella has what it takes to lead the family."

I didn't know who Frankie was, but I kept my mouth shut to allow her freedom to continue. I assumed, based on what I knew about their family, Frankie must have been one of Benito's brothers. But who knew with the fucking Caputis; they bred like rabbits.

"Stefano wants to make a bid for himself, but everyone knows that will end in more bloodshed." Julia shook her head and brushed away a tear. "If you go down this route, you will surely have Bianca and Gia on your side, and perhaps some of the underbosses."

Leo balanced his chin on his thumb, rubbing his index finger over his lips while he considered this.

"And if we take out the others?" Bear asked, glancing between the two of them.

Julia opened her mouth before closing it and shaking her head. "I won't do that. Any drop of Caputi blood spilled is too much. They will not follow you if you take out any of our kin besides Gabriella."

"We'd be willing to make a show of allegiance," Bear cut in. "A member exchange or—"

"A marriage," Leo cut in. "I will not accept anything less."

"Marriage?" Julia and Bear said at the same time, causing them to look at each other before returning their attention to Leo.

Leo hummed a laugh. "Indeed."

"There's no need for that," Bear said. "We stand by our promises.

If you send one of your brothers here, we'll send one of ours to you. The Caputis and the Roses will be allies."

"No, no, no." Leo shook a finger at Bear and tsked through his teeth. "Haven't you been listening to my beautiful sister? The only way this ends is if we are family. Spilling our own blood is a sin. Unforgivable." He held up his hands like there was no other option. "If I am to trust the Roses will not come for me and mine again, I need to know that to do so would be against their own self-interests."

I ignored the stirring in my gut and the rising bile in the back of my throat. Deep down, I knew I'd volunteer for this. I would throw myself to the wolves for the sake of everyone else in the club. If this would end things, if this would make it right between us, I could swallow down a marriage to one of my mortal enemies and make the very fucking best of it.

*What about V?*

My heart twisted and my stomach churned at the thought of never being strapped to her cross again, of never feeling her whip come down on my back or her teeth sink into my skin.

*That fucking figures. It's just my luck.*

Of course I would find the girl of my dreams right in front of me and never be able to have her, not the way I wanted, not even in the future.

"Okay, fine," Bear said, rubbing a hand over his forehead. "I have to talk to my father, but we'll find a suitable match."

"Who is your heir?" Leo asked, raising his eyebrows. "Who will replace the old Crow when he steps down?"

Both Saint and I looked at Bear, who shifted uncomfortably on his feet and crossed his arms.

"That would be me," Bear said, looking at Julia for a moment before glancing back at Leo and tilting his head up, holding his chin high.

"Then, it will be you." Leo steepled his fingers over his mouth, giving Bear a nod. "You will marry Julia."

"What?" Julia balked, pushed to her feet, and shouted at him in her other language, waving her arms around like a child throwing a tantrum. "I won't agree to this."

At that, Leo stood, towering over his little sister, giving her a glare that silenced her. "Do you want to lose more of our family? Do you want to watch our home overflow with Caputi blood?"

Julia closed her mouth and dropped her gaze to the floor between them.

"When Crow steps down, Bear will be in charge and his wife, his *old lady*, will be a Caputi. For as long as he lives, he won't come after us because his family is our family and our family is his. This is how it's been done for thousands of years, *mia sorella*." He stepped closer to her and wrapped his arms around her shoulders, bringing her in for a hug. "If we left it up to Gabriella, you would marry an under-boss's son." He whispered something else in Italian, something hushed that made Julia wince, seemingly with regret.

She bit her bottom lip and looked at Bear, who ran his hands through his hair and blew out an exhausted sigh.

"What else?" Bear said. "What else will need to be done?"

"Who do we have on our side?" Leo said, taking a step back. "Who can we convince to turn on our dear *zia*?"

Leo and Julia talked about members of their family I didn't know and how they might be able to convince them that a decades old territory war needed to end, but I could only focus on Bear. He'd widened his eyes and stared at the two Caputis while they hashed out the future of our families, but I saw the signs of his quiet panic: the sweat beading on his forehead, the bite of fear at the corner of his eyes, his tensed muscles waiting to pounce. Whatever he'd hoped to do with the rest of his life had just gone right out the door. The only way for us to end this was for him to marry into the enemy's family and accept a stranger as his wife.

"You must come home, brother," Julia said, grabbing his hand. "No one will believe you are strong if you are not visible."

"No," he said, leaning forward to emphasize his point. "We play this one in the shadows. Tell only the people you trust. You will speak for me until my return."

"Leo." She shook her head, apparently struggling to form words. "I don't know if I can do this."

"Yes, you can," he whispered, cupping her jaw so she had to look up at him. "You are the strongest of us. You always have been."

She stood, taking a deep breath before turning to face me and Bear. She raked her gaze down to his boots and back up again before shrugging and giving one final nod.

"I'm ready to go home now." Then she grabbed her purse and headed to the back door. Saint smirked, clapped Bear on the shoulder, and followed her out, leaving the three of us to finalize the discussions.

"You can trust her," Leo said, looking at Bear. "She hates the Roses for killing our brother, but she hates Gabriella even more."

"Why?" I asked. "What could make her turn against your aunt?"

Leo pursed his lips, perhaps debating the best way to explain. "That is not my story to tell, but I will say if Gabriella had done to me what she did to Julia, I would have sliced her open from throat to belly button and left her for the scavengers."

I met Bear's gaze, and he returned it with a look that said he didn't like this but didn't see how we had another choice. We could kill Leo, maybe even kill Julia, but that would not give us the peace we wanted. It would only make things worse.

"We'll be in touch," Bear said, turning to follow Saint and Julia out of the house.

When it was just me and Leo, he smiled and held up his hands like this had been a victory.

"Bear doesn't like being backed into a corner," I said. "You could have told me you wanted to arrange a marriage."

"Where would be the fun in that?" Leo laughed. "To see the look on his face when I said it was vengeance enough for all you've taken from me."

"Hmm." I narrowed my eyes before turning to leave myself.

**14**

———

## VERONA

"You disgust me," I said to the masked man on my computer. "You and your pathetic cock, so vile. How can you stand to look at yourself in the mirror?"

My client yanked at his penis, crying into the computer while he jacked off. I saw him once a week for our sessions, and it usually ended with him sobbing and coming at the same time. As long as he kept paying me, I kept showing up.

"I'm sorry, Mistress," he whined, tears streaking down his face, his hand stroking faster.

"You should be," I continued. "But you can make it up to me."

"I can?" He played along with the game.

"Come for me, you pathetic worm," I said. "Come really hard, and I might think about giving you a compliment."

"Oh, thank you," he said, squeezing his eyes shut. "Thank you, thank you, thank you." He spurted all over himself and sat back against his chair to breathe down the high. "Jesus, that was good."

I smiled, letting the praise rush over me. "You're welcome."

"Same time next week?" He grinned and raised his eyebrows like a hopeful puppy.

"Sure," I said. "I want you to eat healthy foods and drink lots of water, okay? Today was a hard session."

"Yes, Mistress," he said. "I will."

"You better. If I find out you aren't hydrated for our next talk, I'll go easier on you."

"No," he said, widening his eyes. These masochists, they wanted it hard all the time. "I will. I'll drink my water and eat my protein."

"Good." I moved my mouse to the red button to end our session. "Take care of yourself."

I signed off and smiled at the three grand tip he'd sent me, knowing it was some of the easiest money I'd ever made. I didn't have any other clients for the rest of the day, so I'd just been about to sign off when a strange direct message came through my platform.

"Hey, gorgeous."

I smirked and clicked into it, certain it was a bot. None of my clients would dare to call me gorgeous unless I asked them to, and I didn't have my profile set to taking on new one on one sessions. I had my plate as full as I liked it, and after the Beacon reopened, I didn't know if I would retain anyone currently on my roster. I enjoyed the work, but last night with Hollywood had changed things even if he said he was okay with me keeping my day job.

I moved my cursor to block the newcomer, but paused when the next IM came through.

"I saw you at Crimson headquarters," the message said.

My blood ran cold and I sat up straighter. Alarms blared in the back of my head, skidding down my spine to churn in my gut.

*No, it couldn't be . . .*

"You look more beautiful than ever."

Chills erupted over my body, tensing my shoulders, and I almost closed my laptop to break the connection. I didn't want to confirm nor deny that whomever this person was had seen was me, but I also needed to know if they were who I thought they were.

I'd left my entire life in Manhattan behind because of him. I'd come home to the safety of my family because of what he'd done to me. How did he find me? He didn't know my real name or where I'd been from. He'd seen my face, that had been unavoidable, but I didn't know if that was enough to track me down.

"Tell your father I'm coming for you, Verona," the next message said. "Tell them all."

I exited the app and slammed my laptop shut, jumping out of my chair so fast it fell over behind me. My heart pounded and my hands trembled as I ran them over my face into my hair. Memories from my former life bombarded me: the look in Curtis's eyes when he shoved me around his apartment, the pain that erupted through my face when he'd smacked me to the ground, the way the knife had slipped and cut into my fingers when I'd hit the bone in his leg. I closed my eyes, and I wasn't in my room anymore. I was in his tiny apartment, weeping as he threatened to keep me as his forever.

Compared to some abusive relationships, it wasn't nearly as violent as it could have been. But I'd been terrified, and the thought he might pop up again to finish what he'd started had stayed with me since that night.

I'd thought I'd left him behind. I thought I'd gotten away.

*He'd found me.*

No. *No.*

*Get yourself together, Montgomery.*

I wouldn't be scared of him, not anymore, and I didn't even know if this *was* him. This could just be someone fucking with me. I'd ask my brother to look into it. Castor was a computer genius, and he could find any information about anyone.

But ... if this really was Curtis and he really was trying to find me, taking it to my brother would mean I'd involve the Roses. They would track him down and gut him alive, and I wanted to pretend the whole thing had never happened.

I texted Castor, asking where he was, and when he replied he was on his way to my house, I dressed in sweats and waited for him in the living room.

"I need a favor," I said when he came through the front door, carrying a paper bag that had better be full of the groceries he promised to replace.

He narrowed his dark eyes and raised an eyebrow. "A favor for my little sister? Hmm. That'll cost you." Laughing, he swept past me to the kitchen, unloading a box of cereal and a bag of chips before going to the fridge.

"This is serious," I told him. "I need you to do something for me and not tell anyone . . . not even Dad."

That got his attention, and he straightened before turning to face me and shutting the refrigerator door. "Verona Marie . . . do you have a secret?"

My cheeks burned as I punched him in the shoulder. "I have a billion secrets from you, idiot. Now, are you going to help me or not?"

"All right, all right, damn." He rubbed at his shoulder as he nodded to my laptop and sat down. "You hit harder than Pollux and Bear combined."

"I got a creepy message on my cam channel this morning." I opened the computer and signed in so he could see what I was talking about. "Would you be able to find out who this is? Or if they're just fucking with me?"

Castor pursed his lips and started typing on the keyboard, narrowing his eyes as he read over the asshole's words. "Jesus, V. Who the hell are you talking to on here?"

"I've vetted all my clients, Cas," I said. "I don't work with people I don't know."

"Do you have anyone from your past that would be looking for you?" He asked the question mindlessly as he continued to pound away on the laptop's keys, pulling up screens I'd never seen before.

I rubbed the back of my neck and kept silent, ignoring how hot my skin became. The stabbing pain in my chest snaked down my spine and the back of my legs, a stark reminder people want me dead, and some would do anything possible to get that outcome.

"Looks like they bounced off a VPN in Greece, but it was shitty work." Castor paused and looked up at me, raising an eyebrow while he waited for my response. "Who's after you, V?"

"An old client," I said. "Someone from Manhattan."

My brother gave me an incredulous look while he waited for me to elaborate.

"If I tell you, promise me you'll keep this between us." I couldn't have this getting back to my father, not after what happened to Pollux. The SRMC already had enough on their plate with Leo and the Caputis. Adding my drama would only complicate things.

Castor softened his features and held out his palm to spit in it before holding it out to me, a symbol of our youth. When we were kids, we'd seen the spit-shake in a movie and, to this day, there was no terms of agreement more sacred between me and the twins. I did the same and slapped our palms together, sealing the deal.

"One of my clients tried to abduct me… when I was in the city."

"Fucking hell, V." He sighed and ran his hands back through his dark, curly hair. "Tell me everything."

I did, explaining to him how Curtis followed me to the club, terrorized me outside of my house, and eventually trapped me with far worst intentions than what had actually happened. It was the reason I'd packed up my bags and come home.

"He had that look in his eye," I said, rubbing a hand over my scar.

"The soulless eyes? Like old man Robbers?" Castor asked, mentioning the recluse that lived down the street from our childhood home. He likely had been an aging widower who could no longer care for his house, but as the building deteriorated around him, our childish imaginations ran away with us and turned him into our own real-life version of Boo Radley.

"Yeah," I said. "Except he actually fucked me up, instead of just looking scary."

Castor shifted his focus to me. "Why don't you want Dad to know? We shoulda taken care of this fucker as soon as you got home."

"That's exactly why I don't want Dad involved." I sighed and went to the cabinet, retrieving bread so I could make lunch for both of us. "The Roses don't know the meaning of the word 'subtle.' I just want to forget it ever happened. I didn't think he knew who I was or where to find me."

"You're on the internet as a domme," he said. "Anyone can see anything they want." He didn't mean the words to be vicious or condescending, only truthful.

"No one knows my real name," I said. "No one sees my face. Ever. He shouldn't have been able to find me. He shouldn't know where Crimson headquarters is."

"Give me a few minutes." Castor went into hyper-focus, ignoring me while he worked. I made us both sandwiches and placed his down in front of him before pouring chips next to it. We ate in silence while I scrolled on social media, and I tried to hide my excitement when a text from Hollywood came through.

**Hollywood:** Are we still on for tonight?

I bit my lip and replied back.

**Me:** Yes.

**Hollywood:** I have to swing by the clubhouse. Will you be there?

"Are you heading to the clubhouse after this?" I asked my brother.

He furrowed his brows and muttered a quiet, "Yeah," while he typed on my laptop.

**Me:** Castor and I are heading over in a little bit.

It would have been easy for me to leave well enough alone and wait until I got to the clubhouse to mess with Hollywood, but where would be the fun in that?

**Me:** Were you a good boy today?

**Hollywood:** The best.

**Me:** Hmm, show me.

The response bubbles appeared . . . then disappeared. My heart sank. Had I stepped too far? Had I been too pushy? Just as I went to type a retraction, explaining he could show me later, a video came through. Not even thinking about it, I hit play. Hollywood's moans filled the kitchen, and I hastily clicked the power button to shut off my screen, my cheeks burning, my eyes wide. But it was too late; the damage had been done.

Castor stared at me, his eyebrows halfway up his forehead. "What the fuck was that?"

"Nothing," I said, shooting to my feet. "Let me know when you're leaving. I'll go with you."

"Okay, weirdo," he said with a laugh, returning to his mission with my laptop.

I walked to my bedroom, into my bathroom, as far away from my brother as I could get, and turned the volume down low on my phone. Then, I hit play again, my eyes glued to the screen as I watched Hollywood stroke his cock.

"This is what you do to me, Mistress," he moaned, his fist sliding over his velvet skin, yanking on the tip to scoop up his precum before going back to the shaft. "I can't wait for you. I need you." His moans grew louder as his fist worked his dick harder until finally, he let out a deep groan and spurted all over his hand. My lower stomach constricted and I twisted my legs together to soothe the ache, knowing I'd get a firsthand view of that tonight. Then, he flipped the view on his camera so I saw his face as he said, "It's all for you."

I took a deep breath to calm the arousal coursing through my veins. I'd certainly seen my fair share of men whacking off, but none had ever made me as instantly turned on as this one video. Growing up in a house with three brothers had desensitized me to cocks at an early age, which probably explained why I could do my line of work. But watching Hollywood come for me had been magical, and the heat in my cunt and the rush in my chest only made me want it more.

I hopped in the shower, preparing to head to the clubhouse, and when I rubbed one out to that video, recording myself so I could return the favor, I told myself it was because he was so beautiful . . . not because of the complete control he had over my reaction to him.

## 15

## HOLLYWOOD

When she didn't immediately reply back, I thought I'd fucked up. No one liked an unsolicited dick pic, even if said dick had been called aesthetically perfect. I walked into the clubhouse with a lump in my gut, wondering what retaliation would look like once she got here.

"Hey ya, Hollywood," Chelsea said, walking up to me so she could throw an arm around my waist.

"Hiya, Chels." I promptly detached myself from her and moved away. "You doing okay?"

"Better now that you're here." She gave me a big smile and batted her pretty doe eyes, the way she did when she wanted to drag me to one of the back rooms. Hollywood of yesteryear would have already had his pants halfway down to his ankles, but I'd learned there was something better out there, something more potent and powerful than an empty connection with her. I wanted that with V.

"Well, aren't you a charmer?" I smiled and walked toward the meeting room on the right. "See ya around."

"Hollywood," she whined, and I turned around to face her. "You're not really going along with that bitch, are you?"

"Bitch?" I raised my eyebrows and took a step toward her. "You mean V?"

She grinned and wrapped her index fingers in my belt loops, trying to pull my hips toward her. "Yeah. Who cares what she thinks anyway, right?"

Fire erupted in my gut at the fucked-up way Chelsea spoke about the MC princess. Even if I wasn't in this random situationship with her, she was still my best friend's sister. I wouldn't let anyone talk shit about her, especially not a jealous hang-around.

"I care," I said. "And the next time you talk about her like that will be the last time I talk to you."

Chelsea furrowed her brows, seemingly hurt. "Are you serious? What are you like . . . in love with the cunt or something?"

*That's it.*

I didn't say anything else, just rolled my eyes and headed toward the meeting room for church, taking up my spot in my normal corner. Had Chelsea always been such a self-righteous bitch? Or was this a new development based on the fact that I wasn't interested in her anymore? Hang-arounds didn't hold the same position in the club as the old ladies or the princesses. She was lucky I didn't have her banned from showing up here.

My phone buzzed, so I reached into my pocket to retrieve it, biting my bottom lip when I had a video response from V. I made sure the sound was turned all the way down before I pressed play.

*Holy fucking hell.*

She'd returned the favor. My pulse kicked up a notch when she ran her soapy tattooed fingers over her amazing tits, blood shooting down to my cock when she rubbed in between her legs. If I focused hard enough, I could almost taste her on my tongue, and when she threw her head back in a euphoric display of her orgasm, I damn near came in my pants like a teenager.

"You and V make out all right?" KC said, coming to stand next to me.

I quickly turned my screen off and glanced up at him with wide eyes, heat rushing through my face and into my neck.

"What?" I blurted much louder than I intended.

"Yesterday," KC said. "Wheels told me you volunteered for a shift to guard her again. Everything go okay?"

"Oh." I cleared my throat and nodded, swallowing down the rotten images of what V and I had *really* made out last night. "Yeah. It was fine."

KC furrowed his brows and lit a cigarette. "You okay?"

"Peachy keen, jelly bean."

If he was going to reply, he got distracted when Bear walked up to us and rubbed his hands over his face. KC looked about the same as he always did—a big smile for everyone, happiness radiating out of his pores, the attitude of a man that had married the epitome of sunshine. Bear, on the other hand, had deep purple bags under his eyes and the twinge of panic at the corner of his mouth while he lit a cigarette before letting the smoke out on a deep sigh. He never smoked, so to see him this stressed out yanked on my heart.

"Hey, brother," I said, grabbing his shoulder. "You all right?"

"Yeah, fucking great." He shook his head and inhaled deeper. "Just watching my whole fucking life go up in flames."

"Hey," KC cut in. "You don't know if your pops is going to go along with it."

"Yeah," I said. "Maybe he'll marry the Caputi wench instead."

Bear narrowed his eyes. "You think I want a stepmother that's only two years older than me?"

Damn, he knew how old Julia was? What other research did he do about her? He must have been thinking about this since it happened.

"It's fine," Bear said, shaking his head and stabbing out his cigarette in the ashtray next to us. "My life was never mine anyway."

"Don't be like that," I said, hating that my brother and best friend was hurting so much. I didn't want to say my next words, but when I patched myself into this club ten years ago, I'd sworn to do anything to protect it. If marrying Julia Caputi spared him this misery, I'd bend over backward to make it happen. "I'll do it, okay? Just tell Leo you're not available and—"

"No," Bear cut in. "No fucking way."

"What?" That surprised me. "Why?"

He let out a breath through his nose and gave my shoulder a firm, reassuring squeeze. "It's not your burden to bear, okay?"

I started to argue I would take on *any* burden if it meant he'd suffer less for it, but I never got the chance. Aris banged his rings on the table to open up the floor for session.

"All right, you motherfuckers. Listen up." The veep ran through the list of charity drives that were coming in the next few weeks, including the huge one on St. Patty's Day. "That also happens to be the time the Beacon will be completed, so keep an eye out for news there."

Slip spoke next, running down the schedule for the next few runs. "KC, Hollywood, Picasso, Lore, and Coins—you're with me down to Asheville in four days. The cartel is meeting us to drop off a big shipment. We need a lot of muscle to haul it back."

"Six people on a run?" Doc said after letting out a whistle. "That's like ringing the dinner bell, isn't it?"

"We don't have a choice," Slip said, rubbing over his bald head. "The cartel isn't like the Canadians. They're not interested in small transactions. They deal in millions, and I'm not taking any chances."

"It'll be fine," Aris added. "I guaranteed we'd bring backup as part of the deal when I made it."

Doc crossed his arms and sat back in his seat but didn't argue. He wasn't someone who kept his opinion to himself, so he must have felt okay with Aris's explanation. I swallowed against a dry throat, unsure if I found any comfort in it myself, but I was just a peon—what the fuck did I know?

"We have bigger things to discuss," Crow said, bringing everyone back on topic. Bear shifted his weight next to me as he waited for his father to drop the hammer. "Leo Caputi has offered a deal in exchange for truce."

The room fell silent, the rest of the brothers waiting to see what he wanted.

"I haven't spoken to him myself," the prez explained, "but if we agree, I'll head there as soon as I can to formalize everything."

"What's he want?" Wheels asked, his dark eyes serious as he glanced at Crow.

"A marriage," Bear said. "He wants to join our families."

"Aren't we already?" Castor said, nodding to KC. "Isn't Alba a—"

"Alba is a Montgomery," KC snapped, yanking down the neck of his shirt to show the Sunshine tattoo on his collarbone. "She claims no heritage from that piece of shit family and never will."

Two years ago, while KC and Alba were dating, she had learned her mother was Benito Caputi's daughter, long thought dead. Turned out Alba was the love child of Aris and Alessandra Caputi. After she found out she was pregnant, Alessandra faked her death, hid on Rose territory, and changed her name to Penny Wright. Even though one side of her family came from the Caputis, Alba didn't consider herself one of them. She was a Rose, end of story.

"If we want him to trust we're serious about ending this, then we need to show it." Bear cleared his throat and ran a hand back through his hair. "He wants me to marry his sister, Julia."

Crow winced and pinched the bridge of his nose, the added gray in his hair indicating how rough this year had been for him, for us all. As the patriarch of this found family, the crown would always lay heavier on his head.

"How does Julia feel about this?" Lore asked from a few feet to my left, itching at his eye patch.

"About as great as you'd expect," Saint explained. "But she hates her aunt more than that, so she'll agree."

"*I* haven't agreed," Crow snarled. "I don't like being told what to do, especially not by that Caputi piece of shit."

"Yeah, me neither," Bear added, shaking his head with his hands on his hips. "But what's our other choice? We could bomb one of their clubs to draw them out, maybe send them on a wild goose chase to God knows where."

Thor shifted at that, probably remembering when he'd had to follow Selene up to Buffalo to keep her from becoming Caputi cannon fodder. She'd killed a rat in the process, so it wasn't a complete loss, but she still had a limp from where she'd gotten shot in the leg, and probably always would.

"We could raid their houses," Doc said, leaning forward on his elbows. "Bring them to the barn, take care of them all in one night."

"You leave a void that big and something worse is going to fill it," Aris said, pursing his lips.

"We'll deal with that if it happens," Doc reasoned.

"No," Crow said. "I don't like it, but I also don't like the thought of my son living with one of those treacherous snakes for the rest of his life."

"Isn't that my choice?" Bear took a few steps forward, shoving his hands into his pockets as he glanced around at our brothers. "Don't I get a say in whether I put my future on the line for the club?"

"I won't lay that at your feet, son," Crow said.

Bear glanced at Slip. "Last year, you stepped in front of a bullet for me."

Slip adjusted his hips in his seat, crossing his arms before shifting his sky-blue eyes to the table. "It's my job."

"And you." Bear turned to Doc. "How many horrible things have you done for this club? How stained are your hands?"

"It's not permanent," Doc said. "I don't see it that way, and I never have."

"Hollywood," Bear shifted his attention to me. "How many times have you been shot defending our family?"

"Three," I said. "Three times."

"He almost died protecting my sister." Bear glanced back to his father. "Is my future not an adequate payment for his safety? If it means that this ends, that no other Caputi spills a drop of Rose blood, isn't it worth it?"

Crow took a deep breath and ran a hand over his mouth, staring up at his son with that infamous Montgomery fire behind his eyes.

"I won't ask you to do that," Crow said.

"No one is asking. I'm telling you." Bear let out a harsh sigh and shook his head, his dark curls glimmering in the overhead light. "If you expect me to take this club over one day, then I have to be willing to give up the same thing I'd ask from anyone else."

Whoops came from all the brothers, a round of hollers echoing over that.

"Besides," I said, "Julia Caputi's pretty hot."

"That's my future wife you're talking about there," Bear snapped, pointing an accusatory finger at me. "Watch your fucking mouth."

I clapped and howled like a wolf baying at the moon. The sound came from my soul, and others joined it with their own applause or shouts of excitement.

"All right, knock it off," Aris said, banging his rings on the table again to get our attention refocused.

"Let's pause this for now," Crow said, giving his son an indignant side-eye. "I want to hear updates about Gabriella. I'm not in favor of Doc's mass execution idea, but I also don't want her to blindside us again."

"She's struggling," Saint said. "Some of Benito's brothers are making things difficult. If there were a right time to invade from the inside, now is it."

"Will his brothers be a problem for Leo?" Slip asked.

"Julia seems to think she can win them over," Saint continued. "She said they don't want the power; they just don't think Gabriella is capable of maintaining order."

"How do we know we can trust Julia?" Lore spoke up. "If she's related to Leo, she's as much of a liability."

I understood why Lore thought so poorly of Leo and Julia, and I didn't blame him. I'd been shot by the bastard's cronies, so Lord knew, I sympathized. But this was bigger than an eye or a bullet to the chest. This was future generations of Roses and Caputis growing up and knowing peace. This was the end to a blood feud that had plagued us for decades.

Crow met Saint's gaze, and the quiet brother shrugged, as if suggesting he didn't have an opinion about whatever the president had silently asked him.

"Julia Caputi has been sending us information for over two years," Crow said. "She's Saint's leak."

The room went silent again, and this time, my heart pounded in my chest at the realization.

"It's a long story," Saint explained. "A few years back, I met her during one of my Christmas visits to the orphanage. I didn't know who she was at first, and she didn't use her real name, but we got to talking. She's a nice girl, even if she is a firecracker. If she didn't have such a shitty last name, we'd have no problem with her. Six months after that, I found her beamer in a ditch outside Fairfax. She was almost dead. Her boyfriend in the passenger seat had a bullet wound in his head. If it wasn't for me taking her to the hospital, she woulda died right then and there."

Leo's words went through my head.

*"She hates the Roses for killing our brother, but she hates Gabriella even more."*

I wondered if Gabriella had anything to do with her boyfriend's death.

"A couple months later," Saint continued, "it was me almost getting shot on Caputi territory when I was trying to get intel."

*Fuck, I remember that.*

"I was caught, trapped in a room, waiting for the fuckers to smoke me out. I shoulda died. She found me and made sure I got free." He ran a finger over his brow and blew out a disbelieving breath. "I can't say why fate put us in each other's paths so many times, but when the universe speaks, I listen." Saint waited for the murmurs from the crowd to die down before continuing. "Trust me on this, she wants Gabriella gone as much as us."

"Let's play this low-key," Crow said. "Take it slow, and keep me updated on anything new."

Saint nodded and retreated back to his corner.

"There's one more thing," Coins said, rubbing at his gray beard. "Detective Jordan has been poking around. I think I had a tail the other day."

"Yeah, me, too," Aris said. "I'm stepping in pig shit everywhere I go."

"Do we think she has anything?" Crow looked at Castor and Switch, our IT geniuses. They had the inside track to anything the Feds might secure. I didn't understand how they did it, and I never asked because I didn't *want* to understand it, but Castor and Switch usually knew what the pigs had before they did.

"I haven't seen anything new," Castor said. "But that doesn't mean they aren't searching."

"Keep an eye on them," Crow ordered before nodding at Aris.

"All right," Aris said, pushing to his feet. "That's all for tonight."

"Pollux is getting out in a few weeks," Castor said, holding up his hands. "When he does, we're heading to the Viper to celebrate. Everyone's invited. I'm letting you know now so you can clear your fucking schedules. You all better be there!"

"First round's on Castor!" I shouted over his voice, and everyone whooped in response.

"What the fuck, man?" Castor pretended to punch me in the gut, but I laughed and threw my arm over his shoulders, tugging him in for a playful hug. "Fuck off."

He shoved me away with a chuckle as we walked into the front room. I immediately caught V's gaze at the bar, where she talked with Ru, Alba, and Selene. She smiled and waved before returning to her conversation. Like a moth to a flame, I saddled up beside her and reached across the bar for a shot glass and the bottle of whiskey, pouring myself a drink.

"Hiya, Hollywood," she said and pursed her lips with a hint of mischief playing in her eyes.

"Hi, V." I mocked her teasing tone, hoping she got the message. I didn't want to stay at the clubhouse, especially with the way Chelsea burned holes into my back with her gaze. "Are you ready to get out of here?"

"Hmm," she said, looking at her friends. Alba, Ru, and Selene huddled together and giggled at a video on a phone, completely unaware of V's sudden shift in interest. "Do you think you've behaved enough to leave so soon?"

"Nope," I said, leaning into the role-play and bending down so I could whisper the next part next to her ear. "I've been so bad. I deserve to be punished."

She made a deep, wicked sound that sent chills down my spine and back up again.

"I want you to break my streak," I murmured low enough no one else would hear it. "I want you to break my streak tonight, and then I want to tell everyone about it tomorrow."

V met my gaze with a soft violet one of her own, seeming to verify I meant what I said.

"I don't . . ." She cleared her throat, and a sinking feeling ran through my gut. "I don't think we should say anything to anyone . . . not yet."

I furrowed my brows. "Why not?"

Did she not trust me?

"It's just so new," she said, giving me a small smile. "Can we keep it a secret a little longer?"

I swallowed down the shame that came with the thought that she still didn't want anyone to know about this amazing thing we created, but I relegated that to the recesses of my heart.

*It doesn't mean anything. This doesn't mean anything.*

"Okay," I agreed.

"Okay." She downed the rest of her shot, grabbed her jacket, and pushed off the stool. "See you ladies tomorrow." She gave her friends a goodbye wave before heading toward the door. Like the lost puppy I was, I followed closely behind.

I had a moment to make eye contact with a very curious Ru behind the bar before the door shut between us.

**16**

---

# VERONA

B y our agreed-upon definition, breaking his celibacy streak meant stimulating his cock until he came. But I wanted to be sure of the boundaries. Did he want me to fuck him? And if he did, was that something I wanted?

*Yes.*

Resoundingly and unequivocally, yes.

I would fuck him until the sun came up, and then I'd do whatever I could to keep him under me for the rest of the day. Then, I wondered how long I had wanted that. Had it been subconscious all this time, waiting to be uncovered? Or had the other night created an insatiable hunger in me? What did it matter anymore?

But telling the others still made me pause. What if we told them and this ended the way I thought it might? I could let Hollywood in, *really* let him in, and he could decide that I was only another notch on his belt, another lover in a long list of people that didn't make the cut for the long term. Despite what had happened between us, despite having a connection that seemed deeper than anything else, I still couldn't depend on this being real . . . that there was a future with him that lasted beyond the time it took for him to get bored with me and move on.

Hollywood had the potential to get closer than anyone ever had before. He could weasel his way inside my heart and I'd let myself love him. I'd let myself trust him, and he'd devastate me. Perhaps part of me wanted to throw caution to the wind, but that part who had lost her mother at nine, who had made out with him in a closet and watched him carry on with two other girls, who had a client try to kidnap her and abuse her, that part wanted to shove those mushy emotions way down inside. Keeping it to ourselves ensured a sense of distance that would lessen the backlash, if it came to that.

When we got to my house, Hollywood did a round to make sure it was secure before returning to me in the living room with a smirk that meant he was ready to play.

"Coast is clear," he said, pulling his mouth into a big smile.

I tilted my chin up to meet his playful gaze with a stern one of my own.

"When you said you wanted to break your streak"—I stepped closer, running my fingers up his stomach and over his chest to his shoulders—"what exactly did you have in mind?"

"Hmm." He grabbed my hips and jerked them forward so my lower stomach collided with his semi-erect dick. "What did you think I meant?"

"Do you want to fuck me?"

He raised his eyebrows, his grin growing bigger. "Is that on the table?"

"If you want."

The words barely left my lips before he responded. "Yes, fuck yes. Please."

"You're so pretty when you beg." I coasted my palm up the side of his face to cup his cheek before pushing on my toes so I could plant my lips on his. It was a soft, sweet kiss, nowhere near as commanding as what I had in store for him, but it conveyed my message loud and clear. I would have Hollywood because we both wanted it. I would break his streak because he knew I would treat him with respect and dignity, something his other partners had obviously neglected. He'd said as much the other night when I asked him why he wanted this in the first place.

"I'll beg all night if you let me," he muttered against my mouth.

Remembering the checklist he'd filled out, he was okay with fluid bonding, and I'd been on birth control for years. Deciding I very much wanted all of that, I stepped back and nodded to the hallway, gesturing toward the dungeon in the spare room. "Go on, then. Get ready. I want you naked and on your knees when I get there."

Biting his bottom lip, he turned and rushed down the hallway, ripping his shirt over his head while he walked. I laughed and followed him, turning into my room so I could put on my domme costume and get into the right headspace. Sure, Verona the person liked to make grown men sink to their knees, but it took a special part of my personality to keep up the charade for the whole scene.

I took off my shirt and stared at myself in the mirror, running my gaze along the scar between my breasts. The glass jar hung over the purple flesh, reminding me of how connected Hollywood and I really were. That night in high school had started it, but after this bullet went through his torso and into mine, Hollywood had bled into me for an eternity. If power existed in blood magic, it had certainly wormed its way into my molecules, my very being.

*"Do you believe in soulmates?"* Ru had asked me.

A year ago, I might have told her no. But the pull I felt toward the man in the other room couldn't be denied. I wouldn't go so far as to say I was in love with him. I'd never been in love with anyone. I'd never trusted anyone enough for that, and part of me still couldn't trust him completely. But what we had was more than friendship, more than a normal domme/sub relationship. Everything in my body compelled me toward him, and I feared it always would. I'd have to tell everyone some day, but I didn't want their opinions ruining what we might have if they kept their noses out of my business.

Deciding I'd done enough thinking for one night, I shut off that part of my brain, put on my corset and fishnets, and yanked on a floor-length skirt where the slits went up to my hips on either side. I

didn't wear boots, opting instead to stay barefoot since I would probably climb him like a tree before the night was through.

*All right. Get your head in the game, V. Break him down. Tear him up.*
*Make him squeal before you give him what he wants.*

When I walked out of my room, my dominant alter ego had taken
over. I wanted to mark him and turn his ass redder than I had the
other day. I wanted to make him yearn for my cunt before I'd give it to
him. I wanted—

*Fuck.*

The sight of him kneeling on the ground for me would live in my
mind until I died. At six five, his powerful body could crush mine
with barely any effort. Yet, he willingly made himself smaller for me
. . . because he wanted to give over that control to someone else . . .
because he had to maintain it every other part of the day and sometimes, it became too much.

I ignored the strange pitter-patter in my heart, opting instead to
circle around him and admire his perfection from all angles. His
enormous arms gave way to massive shoulders and a chiseled back
with vibrant bruises marking a big *V* across his skin. It sent a perverse
craving straight down to my pussy, clenching parts of me that longed
for him all day.

"Look at you," I said, tracing along his graceful neck. He leaned
his head to the side, allowing me more access to his sensitive skin,
and I couldn't help myself. I sank my nails into his trap muscle,
making him suck in a hiss through his teeth. "Aren't you just the most
adorable boy in the whole world?"

He laughed, and I liked the sound of it too much, so I slapped his
shoulder blade hard enough to make my fingers sting. A bright hand-
print reddened his flesh, and that, too, pleased me more than I
expected.

"Shut up," I snapped. "The only words I want to hear from you
are 'Yes, Mistress' and your safeword. Do you remember what it is?"

"Full house, Mistress," he said, glancing up at me with big,
adorable eyes.

"That's a good boy." I ran a knuckle along the curve of his cheek, admiring yet again how beautifully made he was. "Such a delicate face. I love fucking it."

He licked his lips before curling them into a big grin. "Yes, Mistress."

"Oh, you like the sound of that, huh?"

He nodded, his eyes shimmering like I'd just told him he could have free run of a candy store.

"Well, I guess I know what we're doing tonight." Ideas pummeling my mind's eye, I went to my dresser full of toys and grabbed the biggest cock cage I owned. Hollywood had a giant dick flaccid, made even more pronounced once he got aroused. But the man was a masochist, and judging by the greedy expression on his face, he enjoyed eating my pussy entirely too much. This would set him straight.

I walked back in front of him and kneeled to the ground, watching as he took in the metal contraption currently headed toward his cock. He stiffened and inhaled a deep breath, but his reaction made me pause.

"Do you have something to tell me, pretty boy?" I raised an eyebrow, waiting for him to say his safeword and mean it.

"No, Mistress." He gestured to his dick, currently half hard and jerking to life between us.

He had marked 'Y' to wearing a cage on his checklist, so I figured this was okay. But I'd never make a submissive do something they didn't want to, even if they'd originally agreed to it. I welcomed the revocation of consent at any time in my dungeon. It was the reason safewords existed.

"If that changes, you let me know." I raised an eyebrow as he nodded and canted his hips forward, encouraging me to continue. He melted when I grabbed him, almost falling forward as I maneuvered the cold metal around his flesh and locked it into place. "Hmm, look at your dick, so pitiful and sad locked up like that."

Hollywood blew out a harsh exhale and shook his head. "I've never worn one before."

"Really?" That delighted me in the worst way. Hollywood had

gotten around Madison County more times than the local bus. Not that I slut-shamed him, but I liked knowing I could surprise him, that I could do something entirely new with him. "You're going to like this."

He hummed an approving noise while I walked over to the queening chair in the corner, grabbing it and a mat before coming back to my submissive, still on his knees. He assessed the black box and the rolled-up cushion before glancing up at me with that same inquisitive gaze, excitement and anticipation mixing in his expression.

I unrolled the mat on the floor and patted it. "Lie down."

He scrambled to do what I asked, stretching out on his back with his hands by his sides.

"So eager," I said with a chuckle, and his smile shined brighter. "Arms up over your head."

Hollywood followed directions, and I put the padded box over his face, making sure his forearms were in the right spots so it fit correctly. The top of the box had bright red cushions for me to sit and an opening for him to put his face. When he leaned up into it, I paused to enjoy the shimmer behind his eyes and the grin on his lips. He looked happier than I'd seen him in months.

"You keep your arms there," I said. "Don't make me cuff you."

"Would you?" He lit up at the suggestion. "Please?"

"Such a naughty boy." I went back to my dresser to grab a length of silk fabric that I liked to tie around genitalia, but since he'd asked so nicely, how could I refuse? Hands trembling, I twisted it around his wrists, securing it with a bow worthy of any holiday present before standing up to admire my work. God, he looked so delicious like this —massive legs spread out on the floor, gorgeous face waiting for my cunt, strong arms locked into place, desperate cock straining against the metal. "Snap your fingers if you need a break."

I put one leg over the box and sat, ignoring my shaking legs as I slotted my clit right up against his mouth. The box kept me spread for him, and he wasted no time lapping me up.

"Fuck." The word barreled out of my mouth as he swirled my

pussy in his mouth, licking me from my entrance to my clit, sucking as hard as he could before licking me again. "There ya go. Just like that."

He listened to my cues, learning from my moans so he could make them louder and deeper. Heart pounding and ecstasy shooting through my veins, I rocked against his mouth, my blood singing as he coated my skin in euphoria. He struggled against the bindings, clenching his fingers before opening them like it took all his willpower to stay still, to not touch me the way he wanted. His cock bulged against the cage, his flesh bubbling around the small openings in a way that must have pained him. But he didn't let that stop him.

My molecules burned as I got closer to my release, my muscles tightening in response to how amazing and perfect his mouth was as he worked me over. I clenched around his tongue, sending a shock wave up my spine and down to my toes. Just when I was about to come, I pushed myself off him, amused when he leaned farther up to keep going.

"Tsk, tsk, tsk," I chided, falling forward to run my nails down his chest, leaving a trail of bright red marks. "So greedy."

"Yes, Mistress," he said. "Please."

"Hmm." I lay flush on his torso, bringing my face inches from his straining cock. Even from this angle, I could see the tip was wet with precum, the muscle agitated from being confined. Unable to resist temptation, I ran my tongue over the length of him, teasing his pretty dick in between the bars. He bucked upward and pushed his hips closer to my mouth, desperate for more friction.

Such a greedy boy, but I liked that about him, especially when he was tied up and helpless like this. I laughed and dug a forearm into his pelvis, shoving him back down to the ground so I could lick him again. His salty-sweet taste slid to back of the throat, and I swallowed it down before turning to face him. I grabbed his chin to hold him in place and leaned to swipe my tongue over his mouth, chin, and upper lip—anywhere that was wet with my arousal. The delicious mixture of the two of us thrilled me, and I tried not to think about how much it made me shiver. It could make me come on its own. I could devour our decadence for the rest of my life.

"Open your mouth. Stick out your tongue," I said, and when he complied, I dribbled spit in his mouth in a depraved display of marking him as mine. "Now get back to work."

I sat on him again, this time facing his outstretched hands, and I worked myself against him harder. He licked and flicked and sucked me, matching my pace, bringing me back up to outstanding levels of ecstasy faster than he had before. My muscles tightened as I fell forward, holding myself up with my palms on his forearms while I rocked my cunt on his face. I pushed up, panting and moaning as waves of pleasure yanked me under their grips. I crested just as my fingers interlocked with his, and the intimacy in that small connection had me gripping him tighter while stars erupted behind my eyelids.

"Fuck, yes, yes, yes," I groaned, relishing in the aftershocks of my climax as he kissed my sensitive flesh, bringing me back down to earth.

Worked over and rippling with the aftereffects of my release, I sat up straighter and pushed myself off the queening chair, straddling his chest so I could take it off him and peer into his excited eyes.

# 17

# HOLLYWOOD

For eight months, I'd whacked it to my greatest hits highlight reel. Despite being a healthy man in his twenties, I wasn't a fan of porn and fake orgasms. I'd rather use my imagination to bring me exactly what I wanted.

Nothing could have prepared me for this night with V. I would have stayed under that queening seat all night, eating her delicious pussy until she couldn't stand anymore. But I'd asked her to break my streak, so the feel of her hot, wet cunt on my chest as she slid down my torso sent my anticipation through the fucking roof. The metal bars around my cock ached in the best way, and every time my dick jerked, I winced against the confinement.

I could see how it would be comfortable to wear around during the day, and if she asked me to, I'd agree in a heartbeat. However, that wasn't what she wanted from this scene. She wanted me to get hard, and she wanted it to hurt—and I couldn't find it in me to disagree with her. The stabbing entrapment urged me on in a weird, ironic way, the pain adding to my pleasure.

Yeah, I was a sick fucking masochist and I loved it.

"How are your fingers? You can speak." She rubbed my palms,

massaging blood flow back into them despite not removing the silk restraint.

"Fine, Mistress." I opened and closed my fists to show her I was okay.

She smiled appreciatively, and I ran the length of her body, memorizing how she looked like this—sitting on top of me, completely in her element, controlling me like she owned me.

The thought of that sent a shockwave straight down to my balls, making me grimace when my cock jerked against the metal.

*Did I want her to own me?*

It happened again, and I moaned, closing my eyes as I turned my head to the side, wincing against the agony between my legs.

"Do you want me to play with your dick, pretty boy?" Her voice rolled like velvet over my stretched sweaty skin.

"Yes, please." It came out in a rushed whisper, but fuck, I couldn't stand it. I wanted the cage off. I wanted to be buried deep inside her. I wanted to never leave this Goddamned room again.

"You're so sweet after a good face fucking," she said, leaning to plant a gentle kiss on my lips. Then she scooted farther down my body, leaving a trail of wetness across my stomach from her pussy. I prayed it never dried. I loved the way she smelled—like strawberries and vanilla and woman. I would bury myself between her legs every morning just so I could wear her scent as cologne. Did that make me a special brand of deviant? Probably, but I stopped caring about that when I agreed to this in the first place.

"Fuck," I murmured as she unlocked the cage, carefully pulling it away from my skin so it didn't hurt me more than it already had.

"Oh, look at that," she said, and I picked up my head to glance down my body. My cock stood ramrod straight, the grid from the cage imprinted in my skin. It throbbed and leaked, but I loved the sensation. "It looks like art. Would you get this design tattooed here if I asked?"

"On my dick?" I barked out the words before I thought about them, and she slapped the insides of my thighs hard enough to have me buckling in the middle. "Fuck. Yes, Mistress. Yes, I'll do whatever you want."

She chuckled and leaned down to drag her soft tongue along the length of me. The warmth of her lips enveloped my cock and I groaned, relaxing against the mat underneath me.

"Fuuuccckkk." For the first time in so long, my cock was inside another person, inside a scalding, inviting mouth. The heavens parted. Angels sang from the sky above. God Herself could walk in on us and I wouldn't stop this. V grabbed the base of my cock with both hands and teased the slit with her tongue before focusing on the base of the head. I surged my hips up, trying to get deeper, desperate to slot down her throat.

"Patience, pretty boy," she said, squeezing my dick. My blood burned and surges of pure pleasure skated through my nerves, turning my brain to mush, making me incoherent.

I mumbled something about needing to be down her throat, and she accommodated by swallowing me, gagging around my thick length, choking on me in the best display of throat fucking.

"Jesus fucking Christ, don't stop. Please don't stop. Please." I didn't even know what I was saying, just blurting out anything my stupid brain came up with. It had been so long since anyone had sucked my cock that I felt the pressure building far too quickly. "Shit, shit, shit."

It was coming . . . It was happening . . . And just as I was about to embarrass myself with my utter lack of stamina, she pulled away from me, letting my dick flop down on my stomach like a fish.

"Ahh." I threw my head back and cried out from the ruined climax, my balls tightening up into my body, my cock pulsing like it might explode and not in the way I wanted. "Fucking hell!"

"Aww, it doesn't sound like you appreciated what I did for you." V pouted and climbed up my body, resting her warm pussy over my abused dick, sliding the aching muscle through her folds. The contrast of the cool air to her burning flesh made my legs tremble, and I tried to hide my shaking muscles, but with her on top of me, I was sure she felt it anyway. "Do I need to gag you, Hudson?"

*That's an option?*

No. No, I wanted to be able to talk and tell her how much I loved it. Gagging me sounded fun, but I wanted to save that for another night.

"Please, Mistress," I croaked, my throat suddenly dry and scratchy.

"Please what?" She leaned on top of me, covering my chest with hers so she could sink her teeth into my chin. "Tell me what you need."

"Please fuck me." The words sounded despairing, even to me. "I need it. Please. Please."

"Okay, pretty boy," she said, lifting her hips as she reached between us. "I'll take mercy on you."

She positioned my tip at her entrance before sliding down slowly. So. Fucking. Slowly. I sucked in air as the sheer joy of being connected to her rushed through my nerve endings, fogging my brain, thumping my heart louder.

"Jesus Christ," I muttered.

"Nope," she said, giggling. "Just me."

I laughed as she sheathed my cock completely, all the way down to the hilt. A moan slid over my tongue, deep and agonizing, and I pushed my pelvis up, trying to get farther in, but I was already as connected to her as I could be. She raked her talons down my stomach and over the indents on my hips, digging her nails in so she had leverage to rock against me. When my cock brushed up against the soft, wet decadence inside her, I was a goner.

This was perfection. I had a big dick, and most girls could only fit most of me inside them without complaining. Only a few exceptions had ever been able to sit completely on me.

V fit like a glove, like we were made for each other, like there was no other pussy in the world that would devour me so entirely.

I never wanted to leave.

I never wanted this to end.

"Fucking hell, Hudson," she said, throwing her head back, revealing the column of her pale throat. She rolled against me again, moving her hips in whatever way would bring her the euphoria she sought. Just being inside her was enough for me, and I knew . . . fuck, I knew I wasn't going to last much longer. "You're amazing."

*Shit. There she goes with the praise.*

If there was one thing in this world that got me off more than her beautiful mouth dragging my shit through the mud, it was when she praised me. Verona didn't like most people, and she wouldn't spare a second thought before cutting down grown men twice her size. It was one of the things I liked the most about her. But when she chose to shower compliments . . . oh fuck, there was nothing hotter in the world.

"You do something to me," she said, riding me in earnest now, moving her hips up and down, back and forth. "You're such a beautiful little slut, *my* little slut. Say it."

"I'm your little slut." I damn near tripped over my own tongue to get the words out. "I'm yours. Only yours. Fuck, that's great, Mistress. Please."

"Yes, yes," she muttered, tensing her muscles around me, clawing her nails deeper into my skin. She reached another orgasm, twisting her features into pure bliss. She opened her mouth, closed her eyes, and slowed her pace. But I knew what she needed, so I kept surging up into her, maintaining the same pace so she could enjoy the way she felt.

Seeing her break apart set off my own climax, and I couldn't stop it. Tingles of release shot down my spine, tightening my muscles, clenching my toes and fingers. As the height of my bliss took me, she leaned over me again to grab my chin, holding my head in place.

"Open your eyes," she commanded, and I did. "Look at me. Look at me while you come inside me. I want you to see who did this to you, who brought you here after so long without."

Her dirty words fueled the deliciously horrendous flood, spurting from my cock in thick, heavy waves. I couldn't stop. For what seemed like an eternity, I groaned and stared into those deep purple irises as I emptied myself inside her welcoming body.

*Fuuuccckkk . . .*

I had never experienced anything so amazing, so fulfilling, so absolutely heavenly.

In the aftermath, I couldn't speak. I couldn't move. I couldn't even see straight, the weight of everything crushing my brain into sludge.

"Hollywood," she murmured, running the backs of her fingers down the side of my face. "Are you okay?"

I hummed and nodded, not trusting my voice. If I tried to talk, I'd tell her how much I cared for her and how much I never wanted to do this with anyone else again. I'd ask her to let me move in so we could play like this every night. I'd sell my fucking soul to keep her.

Once upon a time, the thought would have terrified me. At the first hint of commitment, I would have gone screaming for the hills. Old Hollywood didn't keep partners. He didn't have time for girlfriends or boyfriends or their jealous attitudes. Seven billion people on the planet, and that version of me wanted to fuck at least half of them.

But now . . . now, I just wanted this one girl.

I sucked in a breath when she ran her fingers over a particularly sensitive area on my stomach.

"I got you good here." She leaned down to kiss into the marred skin. "Let me go get some antiseptic."

"No," I tried to say. "No need. It's fine."

"Stop that." Cool air hit my cock as she stood, and I brought my hands down to it for the first time since she'd tied me up. My fingers tingled and my legs quivered like jelly, and if I tried to get to my feet, I'd fall flat on my face. I couldn't move, and never in my life had I been so absolutely okay with that.

When V came back, she straddled me again and rubbed cream into the scratches she'd left on my stomach. Once satisfied, she untied my hands and massaged the area that had been restrained, digging her thumbs into my palms before kissing each knuckle tenderly.

"You're too good to me," I muttered, surprised when I could actually form coherent syllables.

"No, Hollywood," she said. "We're good to each other."

## 18

VERONA

Days turned into a week, and a week turned into three. Hollywood spent most nights in my bed and most mornings between my legs. There was nothing like getting him off before he left for work, and if I could go about my day with the feel of his mouth still on mine, I considered myself one lucky bitch. But I still held a piece of my heart back, a piece that wasn't ready to let him all the way in. I could really care for Hollywood if I let myself. I could see myself falling in love with him and having a future, and even though he swore not to see anyone else while we were doing whatever this was, I wasn't sure he felt the same.

If I let him closer, if I let him in fully, he would have the power to ruin me, and I swore to myself that I would never let that happen. This life was dangerous. He was in a motorcycle club, and like Selene had pointed out, he'd been shot three times already. If he didn't leave me out of boredom, he'd find an early grave. I wasn't sure which would hurt worse.

When I woke up the morning that Pollux was released from the hospital, Hollywood wasn't in bed next to me. He'd had to go check in on Leo before heading to the garage. This did not stop him from being the first person on my mind. I sent him a good morning text as soon as I rolled out of bed, fighting the big smile on my face when he replied.

**Hollywood:** Good morning, beautiful.

A rush of deep abiding affection went through me at the compliment, and I told myself I had no business feeling that way. Loads of men had called me beautiful in my lifetime, but I became a pile of blushing hormones when *he* said it.

*Ugh.*

I ignored the flutter in my stomach and the skip in my heart as I showered and dressed for Pollux's release day, telling myself it was just stupid hormones. Nothing personal. Nothing emotional.

When I went out to the kitchen, I found Wheels and Castor sitting at the kitchen table. Wheels looked hungover, judging by the glassy eyes and growly disposition. My brother, on the other hand, had my laptop open in front of him while he sucked back his coffee.

"Morning," I said, leaning down to give my brother a kiss on the cheek before doing the same to Wheels. "How are you two?"

Castor lifted his head and narrowed his eyes. "What's got your tits in a tizzy?"

Wheels stammered out a laugh. "*Someone* got laid last night."

I gasped, pretending to be offended. "Wheels! How dare you? Roommates are supposed to keep secrets for each other."

"I saw Hollywood sneaking out two hours ago," Castor added, raising an eyebrow but not bothering to look at me. "You tell Bear about that yet?"

"It's not any of his business. Nor is it yours. It's not . . ." I cleared my throat and added cream to my mug, wishing my cheeks didn't burn as hard as they did. "It's not anything. Don't read too much into it."

Castor made a noise that said he agreed before nodding down to my computer. "I finally found your stalker."

He'd been working on it diligently since it happened.

"She has a stalker?" That got Wheels's attention, and he raised his brows halfway up his forehead. "Who?"

"It's not Curtis," Castor said. "That motherfucker is currently doing five to ten for attempted rape."

"Wait . . . what?" I couldn't keep up with only two sips of caffeine.

"He's not harassing anyone anymore, unless he's holding someone's pocket." Castor pointed to the screen in front of him. "Whoever sent you those messages is in Madison County, right under our noses. It took me fucking forever to find him. He's good . . . but I'm better."

"Great." I rubbed a palm over my face. "That makes me feel really awesome."

"You've got a whole motorcycle club looking out for you," Castor said. "I'll keep working on a location. Once I know where he's logging in, I can hack his system and see who it is through the webcam."

"Cas," I said, alarm shooting down the center of my chest. I rubbed a hand over my sternum, trying to alleviate the pressure in my scar. "Don't get yourself hurt."

"Who said anything about *me* getting hurt?" Castor balked and raised his eyebrows. "I'm going to line the back forty with this asshole's guts."

My phone buzzed with a message from Pollux.

**Ugly Twin:** Y'all coming or what?

"Our brother is ready for us to pick him up." Excitement replaced the dread in my stomach at the thought Pollux was *finally* leaving the hospital. They'd given him strict instructions not to do anything strenuous for the first few weeks since he was barely out of the wheelchair. But Pollux wanted to go out to celebrate, and after these months trapped in a medical prison, I couldn't fault him for aching to have a bit of fun.

Castor closed my laptop and nodded to Wheels, who set down his coffee and stood.

"You should have told me you had a stalker," Wheels said while we walked outside to his pickup. "It's my job to protect you."

"I thought it was a bot," I said. "But I promise to keep you in the loop from now on." He was right. He couldn't keep me safe if I wasn't honest with him about these things. It was stupid of me to keep it from him.

Wheels agreed, and the rest of the trip to the hospital passed in amicable small talk. I'd always liked the jovial Rose, and when Dad assigned him to babysit me, I didn't put up much of a fight because of that.

When we got there, Dad and Pollux were already at the discharge desk, getting the rundown of medications and release recommendations.

"Don't forget to make the appointment with your physical therapist," the pretty nurse said. She'd been the one that had given Pollux her number with a blush a few weeks ago.

"Anything for you, gorgeous." Pollux shot her a wink before grabbing his crutches and tucking them under his arms. "Are we still on for Tuesday night?"

She rolled her eyes, her pink cheeks and girlish smile hinting at her amusement. "Stop it, Montgomery."

"All right," Dad said, shaking his salt-and-pepper head at my idiot brother. "That's enough harassing the nice nurse. C'mon, son."

Pollux laughed and waved goodbye to the staff that had healed him before turning to face the barrage of family there to take him home.

"Look at you," Castor said, holding his arms out to hug his twin. "All that surgery and you're still uglier than hell."

"At least I don't look like fresh ground shit." Pollux punched Castor in the gut before turning to me. "Hey, little sis. You keeping these fuckers in line?"

"You know that's a full-time job, and I'm a part-time gal." I turned to Dad and pulled him into a hug, too. "Hi, Dad."

"Hey, V." His growly voice sounded the same as normal, but I saw through the mask. Dad had been stressed for the last year and a half, ever since KC shot Benito Caputi and escalated things with the crime family. They were trying to work out a peace with Leo Caputi, but the constant threat of violence was enough to keep anyone up at night. I wished I could do something, anything, to make it easier on him. But Dad had chosen this mantle himself. He'd wanted to be the president, the patriarch that kept the family together, and with that power came the burden of maintaining it.

We took Pollux back to Castor's place, where he showered and dressed before announcing he wanted to head to the clubhouse to see everyone. Some of the brothers were still at work as it was only three in the afternoon, but the ole ladies showered him with kisses and the hang-arounds lined up a row of shots to do in his honor.

"Look at what the mangy cat dragged in!" Doc clapped Pollux on the back and shook his head. "Honestly, my dude. I didn't think you were gonna make it."

"That woulda been music to your ears, huh?" Pollux teased, joking with the MC's enforcer.

"One less idiot to keep in line," Doc said, hugging both Castor and me before nodding at Dad.

"There you are," Ru said, walking up to throw an arm over my shoulder and guide me toward the bar. "I've been looking for you."

Alba stood on the other side with her curly blond hair up in a bun, her glasses high on her nose. Ru had let her dark hair fall around her shoulders, but that didn't lessen the intensity in her bright blue stare.

"I thought you'd be at the Beacon." I furrowed my brows, looking for Saint and KC down at the other end of the clubhouse.

"We took off early to celebrate Pollux coming home." Alba gave me one of her genuine smiles, radiating happiness and joy like KC's nickname for her.

"Oh, great," I said.

"So . . ." Ru leaned over the bar, balancing on her elbows, and crossed her hands in front of her, focusing her scrutinizing gaze on me. "You and Hollywood have been spending a lot of time together."

I glanced up at her, refusing to neither confirm nor deny her allegations, and looked to Alba, who had an equally interested expression on her face.

I wasn't ready to tell anyone, and I wasn't sure when I would be. I was a secretive person, in general, but when it came to this whatever it was with Hollywood, I didn't want anyone else's judgment to taint it before it could even get off the ground. I didn't want to see the pity in their eyes when he left me like everyone else did.

"And?" I raised my eyebrows as if to suggest there was nothing wrong with it. Because there wasn't. "We're just hanging out."

"Are you two together?" Alba kept her tone polite and nonchalant, but I could hear the anticipation brewing at the edge of her words.

"How is that your business?" I dodged her question by asking my own.

"It's not," Ru cut in. "We're just . . . curious."

"He's been helping babysit me while Wheels has the occasional off night. Is that a problem?" I looked between the two of them, waiting for the other shoe to drop.

"It's just—" Alba started, scratching the back of her head before trailing off.

I waited to see what she planned to say. I didn't want to get defensive with these two. I generally liked them, as far as having female friends went. But digging into my personal life was a hard line, one Ru should know all about. Hadn't she kept her relationship with Saint a secret for like ten years or some shit?

"I think you two would be really good together," Ru said in a matter-of-fact tone. "You'd make him more serious, and he'd loosen you up."

I cleared my throat and rubbed the pain in the center of my chest, now throbbing with her accurate assessment. "Well, you don't have to worry about that. I still hate him, and he still lives to annoy the hell out of me."

It wasn't necessarily a lie, and truthfully, if I dug a little deeper on why I didn't want anyone else to know about it, I'd probably be able to fund a therapist's bills for a year. Was it because it was *Hollywood*? And if it was, what did that say about me and my willingness to have this situationship with him in the first place? Hadn't I avoided falling into his trap this past decade for a reason? Had he really changed that much in eight months of celibacy? There were too many unknowns, too many reasons to keep it to myself.

He would hurt me, and I wanted to shelter the fallout from that as much as possible.

Alba and Ru moved on to a different topic of conversation, but I caught Chelsea's gaze from across the room where she'd been eavesdropping. She'd curled her lips into a grimace, her eyes burning with jealousy and perhaps a bit of hatred, too. She had probably made the same assumptions as Ru and Alba. But I didn't give a shit.

*Let her look.*

I smirked at her and grabbed the shot glass Ru had placed in front of me, shooting it back and swallowing against the burn.

By the time we got to the Viper, the place was already packed with Madison County's finest blue collar shitheads and drunken biker assholes. The run-down dive bar used to be a motorcycle hangout in the '70s, but time had not been good to the ole girl. It reeked like rancid booze, stale cigarettes, and degraded leather, a homey patina that had taken over fifty years to accumulate.

"I wish the Beacon was reopened," I groaned.

"You and me both," Ru said, winking as she headed to the circular booth in the back. Some of the brothers had already arrived, KC, Bear, and Coins having taken up their spot on either side of the table. Alba sat on KC's lap while Bear talked in a low voice to Coins, the seriousness on his face hinting at whatever had made my brother miss Pollux's release.

Like my father, Bear had been stressed about the situation with the Caputis. I'd seen him at his worst, and this was more severe than that. He stabbed out a cigarette, only to immediately light another one. In the twenty-three years I'd been alive, Bear had never been a smoker, save for one or two when he'd been drinking. To see him chain-puffing like that meant this was bad.

*Should I be worried?*

*Yeah. All of this should worry me.*

I had a babysitter 24/7, someone on the internet was trying to scare the shit out of me, and my family belonged to a dangerous motorcycle club that had a decades long blood feud with the DC mob. Hadn't this been why I'd gone to college four states away? Hadn't I tried to remove myself from all this before?

It didn't matter. For someone like me, the world would be dangerous no matter where I went or what I did. The sins of my family would find me regardless, and when combined with my own debauchery, I was a time bomb waiting to explode.

The scar on my chest ached, and I rubbed my hand across it, trying to soothe it, before I grabbed my jar necklace for comfort and walked over to the booth.

"There she is!" Pollux shouted, limping over to the table with Hollywood trailing behind him, carrying a tray full of shots. Pollux stopped to grab one and hand it to me. "Hey, V, guess what time it is."

I brought the shot to my nose for a deep inhale, wincing when the sharp scent of a very specific liquor shot up my nostrils. "Tequila thirty?"

"Tequila thirty!" Pollux agreed, grabbing another one for himself. Castor came to stand on the other side of me, followed by Saint and Ru. Once most of the MC had a glass in their hand, we held them up in the center.

"Cheers to a healthy Pollux," KC said.

"And cheers to hot nurses!" Pollux added, throwing a free arm over the woman next to him, who I realized was the same person from the hospital.

"Cheers to hot nurses!" everyone echoed, clinking our shots together in the middle. I tipped it over my head and gulped it down, ignoring the burn in the best way possible.

I'd just put my glass down to turn my attention to Hollywood when Alba suddenly jumped off her husband's lap.

"Oh my God, I love this song. V, come dance with me." She grabbed my arm and dragged me out onto the dance floor before I could stop her, hustling Ru into it as we passed her. The DJ blared Bad Company while we jammed, and even though dancing in big crowds like this wasn't behavior I normally condoned, I enjoyed

Alba's and Ru's company. Selene eventually joined us, wrapping her arms around Ru before doing the same to me.

Sure, I looked scary in my chunky black platforms and dark eyeliner, but I liked shaking my ass. When I caught Hollywood's stare from across the room, I bit my bottom lip and went harder. My heart raced and my knees shook, but I kept going, turning a girls' group into a show for him.

Some of the other women hopped on to the bar to take off their shirts and flash the crowd while they danced, but I wasn't into that—especially not with the heinous scar between my tits. No one wanted to see that. No one needed the reminder that bad things could and did happen.

"Hollywood's staring you down," Alba said, leaning in to whisper in my ear. "Should we start a game of truth or dare?"

"No!" I grabbed her arm and shook my head, remembering the last time we'd played that game at the Viper. Ru had gotten on stage to rile up Saint, who carried her out of the bar over his shoulder. I'd gotten into a fight with a group of randos that had tried to grope me. Hollywood had to pull me off them, kicking and screaming. Truth or dare with this group always ended in bad life choices.

"Don't be a sourpuss," Ru said. "C'mon, it'll be fun."

Selene narrowed her eyes. "I don't know that I'd use the word *fun,* especially when we're more likely to end up in jail at the end of the night."

"Stop being such a negative Nancy." Alba grinned and headed to the bar so she could order another round of shots. Ru went back to the table to tell the others what we were playing, and I headed to the bathroom.

Walking down the hallway, I passed an older man I didn't know wearing an MC cut that I didn't recognize from South Carolina. *The Hell's Knights.* I got a good look at it because he was leaning against the wall with his forearm, crowding a much younger woman. If I had to guess, he was probably in his late forties, early fifties—my dad's age. She had to be as young as me, if not younger.

I didn't think much of it when I went into the bathroom and did my business. I didn't judge women who slept with older men any more than I judged older women that slept with younger men. But when I came out of the bathroom, she was crying. She shoved at his shoulders and pleaded with him.

"Please, I'm here with my friends. Just leave me alone. Please."

"Oh, aren't you the little cocktease," he growled. "Rubbing your ass all over me only to leave me hanging?"

"It's not like that," she said, sniffling.

If there was one thing I learned in my twenty-three years on this earth, it was that girl code didn't give a shit about strangers. There was no place where that was stronger than in a rowdy MC bar with a bunch of drunk motherfuckers lingering around.

"Hey, there you are," I said, intruding on the conversation like I already knew her, like I was one of the friends she mentioned. "We've been looking for you. Are you crying? What's wrong?"

I got closer to her, wrapping an arm over her shoulder so I was now in between her and the old greasy dude.

"Fuck off, bitch. We're talking here," Old Dude said.

I read the name on his cut—Hoss.

"Yeah, it sounds like you're making my friend cry." I hugged the girl closer to me. "Why don't *you* back off?"

"Who the fuck are you?" Hoss growled, narrowing his intense gaze on me. "No one asked for your opinion, you ugly fucking freak. Go wash your face before I rearrange it for you."

I rolled my eyes at his posturing. I'd grown up with three older brothers and learned to defend myself by the time I was six. This ancient piece of shit didn't scare me. My entire family was out in the other room.

"Oh yeah, real big man, huh . . . *Hoss?*" I laughed as loud as I could, right in his face. "You gotta intimidate women into sleeping with you? Make fun of their friends?"

"Listen here, bitch—" He grabbed my arm to yank me away from the girl, but I grabbed his wrist with my other hand and twisted, breaking his hold on me.

"You put your hands on me again"—I got up in his face, my platforms making me nearly as tall as him—"and I promise you, it'll be the last time your fingers work."

"I'm not scared of you." He grabbed both of my arms and tried to haul me away from the woman, still cowering in the hallway with her hands over her ears. But I kneed him in the nuts, causing him to groan and take a step back from me.

Taking advantage of his distraction, I wrapped my arm over her shoulder again and walked her back toward the main bar area.

"Are you okay?" I asked.

"Thank you so much," she said, holding her face while she cried. "I don't know who that guy is and he wouldn't leave me alone."

"Don't worry about it." I glanced over the crowd. "Where are your friends? I want to make sure you get back to them."

"I—I don't know." The poor girl shook in my arms, her voice starting to slur. "I'm not really sure where I am . . . I feel really fucked-up, much more than I should be after only one drink."

That infuriated me even more, and once I found this girl's group, I was going to shove my six-inch shitkicker right up that fucker's—

"Hey, you cunt," came a loud roar before a hand landed firmly on my shoulder to flip me around. "I wasn't done with you."

**19**

———

# HOLLYWOOD

I lost track of V as she walked into the hallway, sashaying that miniskirt like a homing beacon, keeping my eyes glued to the hemline. I had to grip the table to keep from going after her.

"So . . . what's going on with you and V?" Ru eyed me from across the booth as she sipped from the tequila shot in front of her.

I cleared my throat and shifted my hips in my seat, remembering that V didn't want me to tell anyone . . . not yet. It still ached to think of myself as her dirty little secret, but if that was the price I had to pay to have what piece of her I could get, so be it.

"Nothing," I forced myself to say. "Why? What did she say?"

"That she still hates you and you still live to annoy her." Ru asked.

I laughed and took a sip of my beer. "Well, that will never change."

Even though we were still on the down low, a small bite of fear went through my sternum at what her brothers might do when they got wind of it. True, it wasn't anyone's business, but I'd been afraid to start anything with her for a reason.

My little-sister-from-a-different-mister narrowed her eyes, seeming to assess every bit of me that she could see. "You like her."

"Don't be ridiculous," I said. "She's a pain in my ass."

*Literally most nights.*

"No, there's something else. I can smell it."

"Now, now, baby girl," Saint said from the other side of her, shaking his head and grinning like a monster. It was just the three of us at the table, the rest of our family either out on the dance floor or helping Alba get shots for truth or dare. "Let the boy have his secrets. You had your reasons for keeping yours."

"Yeah, but he knew about mine," Ru cut in. "At least tell me if you're okay." Ru took another sip and leaned forward, clearly done with me dancing around the issue. "Is she doing her sexy domme thing on you? Does she turn your ass pink every night?"

I cleared my throat, nervously glancing at Saint before looking back at Ru, trying to disguise how close she'd hit the mark. "I . . . I plead the fifth."

"Plead the fifth?" Saint cut in with a small laugh. "How are you pleading the fifth to fucking the president's daughter?"

"It's complicated," I said, drinking my beer, "and I've never been a lady with loose lips, so unless you want to draw her wrath to you—"

"Hey." Ru held up her hands in a show of solidarity. "I'm not judging. I'm just curious. I love you both, and I want happiness for you."

I smiled at just how much joy V had actually brought into my life in the last few weeks—hell, in the ten months since she'd come home from college. There was no one who gave me shit as well as she could, and I loved bantering with her.

"Wow, I don't think I've ever seen you smile that big," Ru said, blowing out a disbelieving breath, "and that's saying something. What about your celibacy streak?"

"Thank you for suggesting it in the first place," I said, recalling the conversation she and I had outside the clubhouse last June, the one where she made me realize I needed to start treating myself better if I wanted better. "You helped me, Ru. More than you know."

"Hey, you cunt," came a loud roar over the crowd. "I wasn't done with you."

"You're done with me now," shouted a familiar voice in return. "Back the fuck up or I'll stomp your face in, you old greasy pervert!"

"Say that again," he growled, but I was already out of my seat.

I knew that raging feminine war cry. I'd pulled V off enough fuckers in this bar to recognize it over the thumping bass and loud-ass bikers. By the time I got to her, she'd already swung on the guy, nailing him in the cheek with her right hook. She raised her hand to do it again, but I wrapped an arm around her elbow to hold her back. My heart hammered in my chest, fury racing through my blood at the thought of whatever this guy could have done to warrant this reaction out of her.

I saw red, and I knew only one thing as I pulled her away—I'd protect this woman with my life.

"You fucking piece of shit!" She kicked out at him, nailing him in the chest with her heel. "Don't you ever touch me again! Don't ever touch me!"

Slicing hot rage rushed through my veins, and I didn't think, just reacted. I shoved the guy back and got between him and my girl.

"What the fuck's your problem, huh?" I pushed at the angry fucker whose name tag said Hoss as he was trying to get to V again. "You wanna fight?"

"Is that your bitch?" Hoss nodded to V, wiping at his busted bottom lip. "Put a leash on her before I have to fucking teach her a lesson."

V wouldn't have started shit with a stranger for no reason. If she was in this guy's face, he did something to deserve it, and I'd bet it had to do with the weeping woman standing next to her.

"Lesson?" I raised my eyebrows and laughed. "You're a real dumb motherfucker, aren't you?" Just seeing his hands on her was enough to make me want to kill him, but hearing him refer to her like that set me off. I swung on the dude before he had a chance to say anything else, knocking his ass back. He lost his footing and fell to the ground, where I grabbed his shirt, holding him up so I could hit him again.

Wrath rolled through me, incinerating whatever restraint I had left. I collided my fist with his face, over and over again, until I felt he'd learned *his* lesson. MCs on our territory were here as guests. End of story. He didn't get to come to Madison County and touch our women, regardless of what club he belonged to.

"Maybe that's how you talk to your old ladies," I snarled, grabbing his bloody shirt to hold him up so I could spit in his face. "But here, you treat people with respect or you get your face stomped in."

"Hollywood!" someone shouted. Massive arms wrapped around my elbow, hauling me up, and another set circle around my waist. "He's done, man! He's done."

It was Saint, KC, and Bear, each of them grabbing a piece of me to pull me back. At my height and weight, it took three of them to get me off him and Verona cupping my face to get me to stop huffing fury.

"Get him out of here!" Thor shouted, coming over to assess the guy on the ground. "V, take him home."

"He started it," V snarled, pointing at the girl to her right. "He practically groped her in the hallway."

"Go!" Thor pointed to the door and growled before returning the bloody bastard on the ground.

I spit at him, disgusted with men who thought they could treat women like shit just because they were older or bigger. I was the biggest person in this fucking club, so by that reasoning, I could own them all. I had to consciously rein in my anger so I could turn my back on the mess we'd made.

"C'mon," V said, tugging my shirt toward the entrance. I went willingly, rubbing my busted knuckles as I passed the girl she'd saved in the first place. Reunited with her friends, she hung on to one of them while they consoled her. It didn't fucking matter anymore. I didn't need to know the situation to make mincemeat of that bastard's face. No one put their hands on V like that, regardless of whether I was fucking her or not.

"Jesus, Hollywood," she said. "I had it handled."

"Yeah, it sure looked like it." I grunted, shifting my shoulders to work out some of the tension from the fight. "You and that Montgomery temper."

She laughed, shaking her head. If there was one thing that ran in that family, it was their hot-blooded reaction when things didn't go their way. KC had been known to fly off the handle anytime Alba so much as got a paper cut, and I'd seen Castor tear through people with his bare hands. Crow was the worst of them. For as much as he was the calm and collected patriarch, he'd gotten the title of president for a reason. The things I'd heard about what he'd done to a former SRMC member-turned-traitor still haunted my nightmares.

When we got to my truck, she stopped and turned to face me, leaning up against the driver's side door while she pulled me closer by the belt loops. Grinning up at me, she pushed up on her toes to plant a kiss right on my lips.

"That was hot," she said. "If I didn't want you before, I certainly do now."

"Yeah?" The fever from the confrontation drained out of me, replaced by an entirely new warmth that had me arching my hips toward her, seeking friction for a greedy cock that wanted to sink itself deep inside her. "How bad do you want me?"

She bit her bottom lip and wrapped her arms around my neck, pulling me down so she could whisper in my ear.

"I'll let you sit on my face tonight," she murmured. "Would you like that?"

The visual sent shivers down my spine, and I scrambled to find my keys.

"Fucking hell, V," I said. "Let's go."

She giggled and grabbed the keys from me. "I saw the way you were shooting back tequila. I'll drive."

Not willing to argue with a sober queen, I circled around to the other side and climbed in, buckling my seat belt like a good passenger princess. She held the wheel with one hand and my trembling knee with the other, and I swore to myself that I would never do anything to tear this apart.

BY THE TIME we got to her house, the adrenaline from the fight had worn off and I needed a shower to get the guy's blood off me. V nodded to her bedroom, indicating I should use the one in the primary, before she turned to the fridge to search for drunken munchies. I heard her mumbling something about frozen pizza as I headed in that direction.

Once I was squeaky clean and ready to preen, I dressed in my boxers and white T-shirt before heading back out to the living room. The smell of something cooking in the oven made my stomach grumble, but I stopped dead in my tracks at the sight of her in the living room.

She'd washed her makeup off, looking so much more like her father without all the black around her eyes, and she'd put on loose gym shorts and a tight black crop top. I'd seen her in leather, I'd seen her naked, but those baggy clothes and that fresh, clean face turned me on more than anything ever had before.

"Fuck yeah," I said, plopping down on the couch next to her. Sure, there was an entire wraparound of cushions to choose from, but I wanted her to touch me and remind me *this* was real, that I had her with me tonight and maybe for as long as she wanted me. "Is that the stuffed crust?"

She nodded and handed me a bottle of water, twisting off the cap for me before I brought it to my lips for a deep drink.

"You're so good to me," I said.

"Thank you for that . . . with the guy." She grabbed my hand and brought it to her lips, tenderly kissing each bruised knuckle.

"Of course, V," I said. "I'll always protect you. Always."

She brought her gaze to up to meet mine, curling her lips into a sweet smile, one I so rarely saw her wear. Affection spread through my chest at the thought that *no one* got to see this expression, no one got to see her so relaxed. No, it was just for me and me alone.

*Well, doesn't that just make a guy swoon?*

I brushed a stray piece of hair behind her ear and leaned in to kiss her, trying to convey how much adoration I had for her with that one gesture. She moaned into the contact, cupping my jaw so she could take as much as she wanted.

"I'm sorry I ruined your truth or dare," she said, reaching to the side table to retrieve a bottle of whiskey. "We can play our own version if you want."

I narrowed my eyes on her and took the liquor, twisting off the cap so I could take a swig. "Okay, Little Montgomery. You first. Truth or dare."

"Truth," she said.

"Hmm." I narrowed my eyes at her taking the easy way out. "Why did you become a domme?"

"I was hurting for cash in Manhattan. It's a really expensive place to live." She explained how she'd found the club through her roommate, and eventually the rich investment banker that liked being financially dominated. "I thought it sounded like easy money, getting paid to say things to men that I already liked to say."

I laughed and handed the bottle to her so she could take a swig. "Fair enough."

"When did you find out you liked to be submissive?" She pulled on the liquor and swallowed, making me remember what it felt like to be shoved down that throat while her muscles worked. I ignored the twitch between my legs.

"You have to ask me truth or dare first." I smiled at her side-eye glare, but she played along.

"Fine," she said. "Truth or dare."

"Dare." I'd answer her question anyway, but I wanted to see what she would come up with.

"Okay, I dare you to get down on your knees and tell me exactly how you feel about our *situation*."

I damn near sprang off the couch to heed her command, falling to the ground so I could crawl in between her legs. Her thighs were silky smooth, and the devotion pouring out of her violet gaze created a burn in my cheeks that cascaded down my neck and into my chest.

"Verona Montgomery," I started. "Mistress Mayhem, I love the way you command my body. I started this celibacy streak because I was trying to make something outta myself, and the way you wreck me is unmatched by anyone else on this great planet."

She flashed a playful smile, and I slid my hands higher, spreading my fingers up over her shorts so I could cup her hips. V leaned into the touch, curving her pelvis off the couch as if to bring it closer to me. From this vantage point, I saw up her crop top, to those beautiful perky breasts I wanted to bite and mark. The edge of her scar poked out from under the hem, and I caught sight of something shiny lying over it.

"My turn," V said, handing the bottle to me, distracting me from her necklace.

I sat back on my haunches and took a drink. "Truth or dare, V."

"Truth." This time, she licked her lips and drew my attention to the soft, delectable skin. I lived to kiss V. I ached to have her devour my mouth the way only she could. I'd never thought I'd say that about anyone.

"Truth?" I groaned and rolled my eyes. "Again? You're no fun."

"That's not true," she argued, lifting a perfectly pedicured foot to my chest so she could press her toes into my pec and hold me still. "You had a lot of fun last night."

"That's right, I did." We both did. More fun than I'd had in a long time. I grabbed her foot and massaged it, running my hands up her calf and back down again. "Why did you agree to do this with me, V?"

"Have sex with you?"

I nodded as I dug my fingers into her muscles, working my way up to her knee and over her thigh.

"Well"—she rolled her big eyes in jest—"you are very pretty."

"That doesn't count." Lots of people were pretty, and she didn't go around dominating everyone.

"I don't know, Hudson. Maybe I thought I could we could treat each other right."

"We do," I said. "That's true."

"When you told me it turned you on when I hated you . . ." She blew out a breath as I went to the other foot, lifting it to my chest and working my way down her leg again. "I'd never wanted anyone more in my life. I knew I could be rough with you, that you wanted it that way. But I also knew you needed someone to be gentle, too. Someone to take care of you."

My stomach lurched and my heart pounded behind my ribs as I shifted my gaze to hers. No one had ever talked about me like that. Most people I hooked up with were selfish, only wanting a ride just to say they'd done it. Chelsea didn't know me like V, and she couldn't treat me the way V did, couldn't even understand why I would want such a thing. Those were superficial encounters, nothing more. But this . . . Whew, this blew my fucking mind.

"Can we forgo the game?" V said, taking the bottle from me so she could take a sip. "I just want to talk to you."

"Of course," I said, giving her a smile. I'd do anything V wanted, absolutely anything.

"Why did you want me?" V asked. "Why did me hating you turn you on so much?"

"I think we both know you never *really* hated me." If she did, she wouldn't have so easily agreed to this relationship. "No one talks to me like you do. No one even tries. All they see is—this." I gestured to my face and my body, both of which I had no control over. Yeah, I worked a physically demanding job and I went to the gym to take care of my mental health, but most of it was genetics. Plain and simple. I couldn't help the way I looked any more than anyone else could.

"Aww, poor wittle beautiful boy." V pretended to pout, clearly mocking me to lighten the mood.

But I wouldn't just take her mockery, not outside the bedroom, so I lurched forward and dug my fingers into her waist, right where she was ticklish. She squirmed and shouted, trying to twist away from me, but I outweighed her by a lot. She couldn't go far.

"Nooooo!" Laughing, she flopped her body down on the couch, trying to scoot backward, but all it did was scrunch her crop top under her body, giving me a clear view of her perky bitable breasts and the ten-inch purple scar between them.

But now, my focus froze on the necklace lying on top of it.

Attached to a long piece of black leather hung a tiny glass jar, and inside it—

*Is that a chunk of metal?*

*No, it's a bullet fragment.*

I reached up to touch it but V shoved her shirt over the evidence, quickly hiding it as she tried to wiggle out from under me. I wouldn't let her. Her wide eyes and blank features indicated I wasn't supposed to see it, and if I did, I wasn't supposed to mention it.

"What is that?" I asked, now even more curious.

"It's nothing." She crossed her arms, trying to hide it.

"What?" I chuckled in disbelief. "C'mon. I'm being honest with you. Show me."

V tucked her bottom lip between her teeth and hesitantly met my gaze, seeming to search for any signs of cruelty. If there were anyone in this world she could be authentically herself around, it was me. I knew all her dark, twisted kinks. I reveled in them with her.

"Promise you won't make fun of me?" She sounded much too small to be the V I'd come to adore.

"Of course, V. Why would I—" I cut off when she pulled her shirt up again, revealing the glass jar with the lumpy, uneven chunk of metal inside. "What is it?"

"It's . . ." She cleared her throat and clenched her eyes shut. "It's a piece of the bullet they pulled out of my chest."

"What?" My brain went blank. I couldn't understand what she was saying. A piece of the bullet? From the night we'd gotten shot together? From the night we'd almost died?

"I . . . uh . . . I asked Selene to see if she could get it." V still didn't look at me while she talked, as if meeting my stare would reveal something she had no desire for me to know. "She called in a few favors at the hospital. Some of her old surgeon buddies, I guess."

"Okay." That made sense. "Why are you wearing it around?"

V opened her eyes and took a deep breath, gliding her fingers up my torso to the spot four inches above my heart where that very bullet had gone through me and into her.

"It reminds me . . ." She sighed and gave me a look full of vulnerability and deep abiding affection. "It reminds me there are people out there who would sacrifice themselves for me, that I'm not alone, even when I feel like it."

My soul shattered. There was nothing she could have said that would have broken me so easily and completely. My heart clenched and I leaned down to bring my lips to hers, unable to resist the temptation of her mouth any longer.

"It reminds me you care for me, Hudson," she whispered. "That we're connected by more than family or relationships or whatever we're doing here. You and I share a life debt. You saved me, and I'll never be able to repay you for that."

She clenched her eyes shut again and tears slid down either side of her face.

"V," I said, blinking my own burning eyes as I cupped her face and swiped my thumbs across her cheeks to clear away her sadness. "It was my honor to save you, and I'd do it again. In a heartbeat. You don't need to repay anything."

She wrapped her fingers in my shirt and pulled me close, leaning up to kiss me, nudging her tongue against my mouth so she could get inside. I let her, melting against the contact as she devoured me whole.

Sure, our relationship was built on kink, and I loved when she tied me up to make me beg and bleed for her alone. But this was different, and it rocked my fucking world.

"Can I be inside you?" I whimpered in between breaths, running my hands along the side of her body so I could tuck my fingers under the waistband of her pants.

"Please," she said. "Please."

I yanked her shorts down to her ankles and shoved mine down to my knees, lining myself up at her entrance before surging home in one thrust. She gasped and arched into it, and my arms shook under my weight as I tried to hold myself up. But fuck. After her confession, my pulse hammered through my veins and my muscles trembled so hard that I could barely see straight, much less keep from crushing her.

She wrapped her fingers around my neck and pulled me down, linking her feet together at the small of my back to urge me on.

"Fuck," I said as sparks of joy lit up my bloodstream, coursing through my body like I was being set on fire. Even though this was vanilla-ass missionary, sex had never been so mesmerizing. I pushed farther inside her like I was trying to get my soul in there, too. And she rocked against me, inhaling my exhales, groaning in answer to my moans, like she knew what I was trying to do and wanted our very existences to merge.

We were magic. Together . . . like this . . . even without the leather and the whips and the honorifics. She slid her hand up my stomach and planted it over the spot where I'd been shot, where my life had nearly ended to save her. As I connected our bodies harder and deeper, I found her scar with my fingers, covering it the same way she did to me.

"Promise me you'll stay safe, Matty," she said. "Promise me you won't leave me."

The only person in my life who called me by my Christian name these days was my mother, but hearing it fall from her lips in that precious moment stunned me more than anything else she could have done. We were stripped down of our societal roles, of the MC and what it meant to be a part of it. There in that room, it was just me and V and our skin and our souls and our blood and how desperately connected we were.

"I won't," I said, grabbing her hand from my chest to intertwine our fingers. I rested my forehead against hers as my climax started to rise, surging up the back of my knees and into my spine. "I promise, I won't."

"Fuck, I'm close." She closed her lips over mine, sealing my oath with a kiss, before she tightened her internal muscles down on me, spasming with the height of her euphoria. It set me off, and I jerked into her two more times before my orgasm dragged me under.

The world stopped, and everything in it hung suspended for that one perfect moment. We were together. We were safe.

I lay on top of her and panted down the high while she idly ran her fingers up and down my back. We didn't say anything for a long time because what words could possibly top what we'd just experienced? Eventually, she tunneled her fingers into my hair and pet my scalp, causing me to tilt my chin so I looked in her eyes.

"I have a confession to make," she murmured. "And I'm not sure how you're going to take it."

*Uh-oh.*

I tried not to jump to conclusions, especially when her features dropped.

"When we were in high school, we both went to this party, and they were playing a round of Seven Minutes in Heaven." As she talked, I put the pieces together in my mind, remembering the night in question. I'd thought I'd been hooking up with Becs, but when I brought it up later in the night, she'd looked at me like I'd grown a second head. When no one confronted me about it, I figured she must have been drunk and forgotten.

"That was you?" I pushed myself back on my haunches and smiled down at her.

She grimaced. "I should have told you before. I'm sorry about that."

"Sorry?" I couldn't help myself from digging into her ticklish spots again, making her giggle and squirm and try to get away. "The only thing you have to be sorry for is keeping the best-tasting pussy I've ever had away from me for a decade."

"You weren't ready for me, Hollywood. Not yet." She smiled and I leaned down to kiss her one last time, conceding the fact we'd gotten together when it was right and not a moment before.

# 20

## HOLLYWOOD

"What's got you smiling like a stripper at a stiletto convention?" Leo narrowed his eyes while he ran a towel through his wet hair and limped into the living room.

I rubbed my mouth and read V's message again.

**Verona:** Tonight, it's my turn to fuck you. You better be ready.

After that came a picture of her huge purple dildo hanging from a strap on her wall. I'd marked *yes, very much yes,* to pegging, and if that was what she meant by fucking me, then I'd do whatever I could to dip out of work early. I'd been eating my fiber bars, and I'd gotten myself extra clean in preparation for this.

"Nothing," I said, clicking my phone off so Leo couldn't read it over my shoulder.

"Is it the girl?" He grinned and sat down on the other couch to sip his coffee and antagonize me.

"Yeah." I couldn't think about her without smiling, especially after what we'd done last night. It had been magical, making me question everything I'd ever felt for anyone, and it paled in comparison to this steady heat in my chest whenever she came up in conversation.

"Look at you," he said, holding out his hand to gesture to all of me. "If I didn't know any better, I'd say you were in love."

Everything in my brain came to a skidding halt. The train wheels squeaked, the brakes froze, the back end came rearing toward the front.

"What?" I balked. "Love? No, I'm not—"

*Wait ... am I?*

I didn't know. I'd never been in love with anyone before, certainly not an MC princess who would rather paddle my ass raw than admit to having mushy-gushy feelings for anyone in her life.

"Holy shit, you are." Leo laughed and clapped, seeming to congratulate me. "Good for you, Hollywood."

"No, it's not like that." Confused, I shook my head and touched the scar on my chest, the one that marked the time I'd saved her life.

*"You and I share a life debt. You saved me, and I'll never be able to repay you for that."*

"But, let's say that it *might* be like that. How would I know?"

Leo raised his eyebrows. "You don't know what it's like to be in love?"

I shook my head.

He took a deep breath and leaned forward to put his elbows on his knees. "It's like—" Leo clenched his eyes shut, seeming to reminisce about someone and covered his mouth with his palm. "It's like your world revolves around them, like you'd do anything for them. You'd put your life on the line if it meant their happiness. It's like a piece of you had been missing until you met them, and all of a sudden, the world makes sense."

"Damn, Leo." I blew out a breath at his words as the rightness of his sentiment settled in my gut. V had become everything to me. I'd gladly lay my entire world down for her in a way I wouldn't for anyone else. Was that love? Was that being *in* love?

Because I'd admit I loved my brothers. I loved KC and Bear like family, and I'd kill for them. I'd step in front of a bullet for them any day. But for V—hell, I'd move mountains. I'd survive death and come back to haunt her. I never wanted to leave her . . . ever. Was a few weeks enough to change our relationship dynamic?

"Were you ever in love?" I asked, running my palm over the back of my neck as heat snaked into my cheeks and down my chest.

Leo snorted out a breath and nodded. "Many times, my friend."

"Really?" Could a person fall in love again and again over the course of their life? And if so, why had it only happened once for me? Was I in love before and didn't know?

*No.*

This ache I had for V was unique to her.

Leo didn't answer, just shook his head and smirked. "It's been two weeks. Have you heard from my sister?"

I shrugged because I didn't know. Leo didn't have a phone or a way to contact the outside world. If Julia were going to accept our terms, she would have to go through Saint to do it.

"We're regrouping tomorrow," I said. "I'll find out more then."

Leo nodded, but my phone vibrated, distracting me. At the sight of the unavailable number, I got up and walked outside, reaching into my coat for my cigarettes so I could light one and inhale.

"Will you accept the call from Allegheny Correctional Facility?" said the robotic voice.

"I will." I waited while the line connected me to my mother.

"Matty?" came her exhausted voice.

"Hiya, Momma." It was good to hear from her, even if it had only been a few days. I'd transferred the money to her, like she'd asked, and if I knew my mother, this call would be about needing more. Jails were notoriously expensive, and she didn't make shit at that slave-trade sewing job she had during the day. "How are you?"

"Oh, I'm good, my baby. How are you?" She coughed a wet sound like she needed a doctor.

"I'm okay," I answered. "Are you sick? Do you have to go to the nurse?"

"No, it's the flu going around. I'll be fine." She sniffed and coughed again. "Tell me about you. What are you doing these days?"

I told her about work and the Beacon reopening soon. "I'm seeing someone new."

"Oh?" Momma laughed. "Who are they?"

She knew I was pansexual, and she didn't care. While she was in prison, she'd had a few girlfriends of her own, even so much as married a woman named Daisy a year ago. Who had time for bigotry when there were so many people in the world worthy of love?

"Would you believe me if I said it was Verona?" I chuckled out a disbelieving sound. "I think . . . I think I'm in love with her, Momma."

"Matty," she said, her voice surprisingly light and joyous. "That's so wonderful to hear. Isn't Bear's little sister called Verona?"

"Yeah, it's her," I said. "How do I know if I'm in love?"

She sighed and hacked again, clearing her throat and sniffling before continuing. "I didn't think I could love anyone except you and Troy, God rest his soul." Troy had been Trojan's name before he joined the SRMC. The only person who ever called him that was our mother. "Not until I met Daisy here at Allegheny."

"You weren't in love with our father?"

"No, baby," she said. "And your stepfather—"

"Don't mention him," I cut in. "Don't talk about him . . . not on this line." All the phone calls at the prison were recorded, and if she even so much as breathed his name, the DA would be on her ass for more information to use against her. "How do you know you love Daisy?"

"You just know, Matty." There was a wistfulness to her voice I hadn't heard before, maybe not since I was a kid. "It's in your heart when you think about them. It's in your eyes when you see them. There's no greater feeling in the world than being in love."

My eyes burned and I shut them to blink back the tears forming at the corners. I knew it, just like Momma was saying. It was new and fresh and delicate, but my affection and abiding love for Verona Montgomery went deeper than the sex we claimed it to be. She was my first thought when I woke up and the last face I wanted to see before I went to sleep. Maybe it wouldn't last forever like those sappy rom-coms (which I secretly loved), but it was something and that was a start. Even if she didn't feel the same way about me, I was proud of myself for experiencing it at all. If I had kept walking down the path I'd been treading two years ago, I would have never gotten the opportunity to be a part of something so amazing. She never would have given me the time of day, and honestly, I never would have wanted her to.

"Thank you," I said. "That makes sense."

"Of course," she said. "I know being in the pen means I can't be there for you the way you need, but I'm still your momma. I always will be. I'm always here for you."

I coughed back a sob and nodded, even though she couldn't see me.

"Do you need money?" I asked. "I transferred some a few days ago, but I can always send more."

"No, baby," she answered, kindness in her tone. "I just wanted to hear your voice. I miss you so much."

"I miss you, too," I said.

We talked about Trojan's memory for a few moments, laughing about when we were younger and we'd spent the winters in that tiny trailer in the shittiest part of town. We didn't have much, but we had each other, and that felt like enough to my childhood self. At the end of the call, I promised to come visit her soon and she promised to call me in a few days.

"Bring Verona with you," she said, "when you visit. I'd like to meet the girl that has my boy talking like this."

"I will," I said. "I love you."

"I love you," came her tender reply.

When we hung up, I finished my cigarette and flicked it into the ashtray, ruminating about when I'd actually be able to make the three-hour drive up to see her. It had been too long, but I didn't get much free time these days. That was no excuse. She was my mother, the one who had taken a life sentence for me when I'd made the worst mistake of my life. If I were to do some of Alba's psycho-therapy shit on myself, I might admit she was the reason I threw myself in front of so many bullets, why I considered myself so indebted to the club.

What was my life compared to V's? What was my life compared to Bear's or KC's?

Nothing. Insignificant. And if I had to die knowing they could live, well, that was still the easiest choice I'd ever make.

By the time I got to the garage, Bear and KC already had the music blasting and a few cars up on the lifts for tire rotations. Selene and Thor flirted with each other in the office, their marriage fresh off the press so they still had that honeymoon gleam in their eyes. I said good morning and made my way to the mechanic's bay, ignoring the skeptical way Bear watched me as I moved.

"You have a good night?" KC asked. "How's your hand?"

I flexed my right fist, giving him a nonchalant shrug. "I've done worse."

"Uh-huh," Bear said, tossing his oily rag over his shoulder before putting his palms on his hips and eyeing me from my toes to my head and back down again. "And what about my sister?"

I raised my eyebrows and matched his stance, recognizing both a taunt and a tease in Bear's tone. "What about her?"

"Are you fucking V or what, man?" Bear grabbed a tire iron from his mechanic's chest and swung it around before landing the business end in his other fist.

I narrowed my eyes on his weapon before glancing at KC, who hid his obvious smile behind his fingers. Like anytime I fought with Bear, KC wouldn't get involved, but he'd certainly enjoy watching. V said she wasn't ready for anyone to know about this, but after last night, how could we still keep it a secret? Hell, Bear already knew. Ru suspected. Anyone with eyes could tell there was something more going on. I knew I should have kept my mouth shut, but I'd just realized I was in love with her. I was ready to scream it from the rooftops.

"What if I am?" I said. "You gonna beat my face in?" I nodded toward the long metal rod before reaching over to grab one of his socket wrenches, the ones he specifically told me to stop using.

"I might have something to say about it." Bear stepped closer, his cheeks turning scarlet, the tips of his ears matching.

"Shouldn't you be concerned with your own upcoming nuptials?" I took a step back, giving Bear room to advance while also making sure I had an escape route just in case this got physical. I had about an inch on the brother, but he was bulkier through the chest. We'd been wrestling and giving each other shit since we were teenagers. I didn't take any of his threats seriously. Of course, I'd also never fucked his little sister before, which could change things.

"Don't make this about me." Bear pointed at me with the tire iron, raising his eyebrows up his forehead. "If I find out you're dicking her around like you do with your club slu—"

"Don't talk about them like that," I cut in, holding the wrench up like a makeshift sword. "It makes you sound like a slut-shaming prick. No wonder no one wants to fuck you."

"Hey!" Bear smacked the wrench away with his free hand, batting at me with the iron. I jumped out of the way just in time to miss the blow. "I get laid."

"Yeah," KC cut in with a chuckle. "Bear gets laid . . . sometimes . . . like two years ago."

"Fuck off, KC!" Bear and I both shouted at the same time, making him hold up his hands and take a step away from us.

"I'm not dicking her around," I said. "I care about her. She cares about me."

Bear narrowed his eyes and furrowed his brows, shifting his stance like the very idea was outrageous. "What do you mean?"

"We're together, Bear. Like . . . actually for real together." Or, at least, that was what I assumed. We hadn't put a label on this and it was still new, but we were exclusive. One of these days, I'd take her on a legitimate date, like a real boyfriend.

Bear looked even more confused.

"What do you mean?" he asked again.

Honestly, I understood I'd been a manwhore back in the day, but this shit was insulting. I'd never treated any of my partners with disrespect. They all knew what they were getting into at the beginning. It was the reason everyone still liked me, despite what we might have done in between the sheets.

"I care about your sister, man." I smacked his tire iron away with the wrench. "I'd never hurt her. Never. *If* I'm fucking her, it's because she likes it. And brother . . ." I blew out an obnoxious whistle. "She likes it. A lot."

Okay, maybe I didn't need to add that last little bit on there, but it had the effect I wanted. Bear's face got even more blushed, that classic Montgomery temper rising to the forefront.

"That's it." He threw down the tire iron and took off after me. I, of course, already knew what was coming, so I beat-fucking-feet to the exit, throwing open the door so I could race out behind the garage, dodging and weaving through the antique cars Thor said he'd get around to restoring one of these days. "You're a dead man, Hollywood!"

I laughed as loud as I could, showing him I knew he was joking and I wasn't scared of his empty threats. I had longer legs than him, but I was heavier. He caught up to me in an embarrassing amount of time, tackling me to the ground so he could wrap an arm around my neck and put me in a headlock. I elbowed him in the sides, not hard enough to hurt him, just enough to make him groan and let me go.

When he did, we lay in the grass and stared up at the bright blue sky, breathing down the race out here.

"You treat her right or I'll fucking kill you," Bear finally said, looking at me.

I smiled and nodded. "She'll beat you to it, brother."

He hummed in agreement before pushing to his feet, turning, and holding a hand out for me. I took it and let him pull me upright. He patted my shoulder and nodded.

"What about you?" I asked, raising my eyebrows as we walked back inside. "What did your old man say about Julia Caputi?"

Bear sighed and ran his hands back through his hair. "We're still discussing it."

"Seems like there isn't much choice." I reached into my pockets for my cigarettes, taking one out to give to Bear before biting one between my teeth to light it. "If you don't do this, Leo isn't going to partner with us. We might as well kill him."

"Yeah, I know. I just . . ." He shook his head and inhaled deep on the smoke. "I thought when I got married, it would be because I loved the person. Not because the club needed me to do it to secure an alliance."

"That motherfucking crown weighs a ton, doesn't it?" This time, I gave Bear the pat of support.

# 21

# VERONA

I brought the wooden paddle down on Hollywood's bare ass and smiled when he bucked against the restraints. A perfect "SLUT" appeared on his flesh due to the outline of the letters carved into the paddle. I had the prettiest man in the MC bent over my spanking bench with a rubber gag in his mouth and bright red imprints all over his bottom and legs.

"Don't you mark up like a rag doll?" I teased, running my fingertips down the back of his thighs, making him suck in a harsh breath through his nose. He liked the degradation. He liked the bruises. And when he saw this, he'd thank me until the sun rose.

Of course, I had bigger plans for him tonight. He'd been begging me for the strap for weeks now, ever since I had him fill out that checklist and he realized it was an option. Hollywood had been pansexual since I'd known him, and with people who owned a penis, he liked to bottom as much as he liked to top. I understood. There was nothing like being fucked by someone who knew what they were doing, and I definitely did.

I raised the paddle in the air and brought it down again on the fleshy part of his ass, making sure to dig the corner into the softest bits so he'd feel it in the morning. He let out a cry, part joy, part agony, and yanked on the restraints again.

The power gave me a rush. I loved seeing him like this. I loved being the one he trusted to wreak havoc on his body. Never had I felt more like my domme name than when he handed over control.

Mayhem. The thought made me laugh, and I decided when the Beacon reopened, Hollywood would be my beautiful submissive, Matty Mischief. Together, we'd make a complete set.

Dragging my nails up Hollywood's bruised back, I walked to the front of the spanking bench, where he lifted his head to look at me when I squatted. His eyes were hazed over, indicating how zoned out he'd become during the spanking, and drool dripped over his open mouth, sliding down his chin to make a big puddle on the floor.

"Aww, look at my little slut." I smeared my fingers under his bottom lip, gathering the sloppy evidence of his rough handling so I could spread it all over his face. "Did you like that?"

He eagerly nodded, widening his eyes at the anticipation of more to come. But I had a surprise for him. I ordinarily wouldn't do this in the middle of a scene, but I thought he'd appreciate it more that way. He was the one who wanted this arrangement, and now I had the urge to make the D/s part of it official. I didn't do this to all my submissives, but I was exclusive with Hollywood, at least physically. I wanted him to know how much that meant to me.

I undid the straps around his wrists and unhooked the gag from the back of his head, guiding him up so he could stand. Then, we went across the hallway to my bedroom. I liked to keep scene activities to the dungeon. It separated the part of me that was the mistress from the part that was Verona, but with Hollywood, the two lines had blurred. We liked playing, but we were also something more than that, something that had slowly crept up on me while we spent so much time together.

If I believed in that corny soulmate shit like Ru, I'd say Hollywood and I were as close as any two people might get. He matched me in ways I couldn't have predicted, and when I thought about the future, more recently I had started to envision him in it.

But that was getting ahead of myself. We had a long road to walk if that was the direction we planned to go. Right now, I focused on sitting him down on the edge of my bed, swallowing back a giggle when he winced at his sore ass.

"I got you a present," I told him, turning to my dresser so I could retrieve the long piece of metal chain and padlock. When I came back to face him, he flashed a big grin, his eyes lighting up like an excited puppy.

"Is that what I think it is?" He sat up straighter, seeming to hold his neck out.

"It is." I stood between his knees so I could place the chain-collar around his windpipe and stick the top of the padlock through two loops to secure it in place. It hung down to the scar above his heart, and I tenderly ran a finger along the side of it when I straightened. "I know we didn't talk about this beforehand, but you marked yes to being collared on your checklist. I hope this is okay."

"I love it," he said, running his hands down my arms to gather my hands so he could bring them to his lips. He delicately kissed each knuckle before looking back up at me. "Thank you."

"Thank *you*, Hollywood." In that moment, those words were about more than him acquiescing to whatever I wanted to do to him. It was about him taking a bullet for me. It was about his continued protection, even after he didn't have to anymore. It was about his friendship and the way he made me laugh and how much he loved my family and everyone in it. Even me . . . *especially* me.

*Holy shit.*

Chills danced down my spine as realization sank like an anvil in my chest. Hollywood loved me, and maybe . . . maybe I loved him. Blinking against the sudden burn in my eyes, I cleared my throat and remembered all the times he'd shown it, even before we started hooking up. He'd pulled me off more strangers at the bar than anyone else. He'd volunteered to look out for me when even my own brothers hadn't. He'd been there for me time and time again without fail because that was who he was.

I cupped his jaw and tilted his face up so I could press my lips against his, devouring his mouth like it had been made for me. Perhaps it had, just like I'd been made for him. We were perfect together, and in that perfection, we had found the easiest, simplest joy.

"You don't have to wear it all the time," I said, coming back to the present, "and definitely not at the garage or around other people, but when we're in scene—"

"I'll wear it for you, V." He leaned up to kiss me one more time before scooting back on the bed so we could get the rest of the scene going. I knew what he wanted, and he knew what I wanted, and together, we were going to make fucking magic in this bedroom.

I went to my dresser to retrieve the strap-on and the lube, hooking the belt into place. I'd already attached the silicone dildo to the front, where it hung between my legs, ready to be used.

"Remember your safeword," I told him. "If you want me to stop—"

"I've been dreaming about this since we decided to do it." Hollywood bit his bottom lip and grinned.

"Hmm." I crawled onto the bed, leaning over him to so I could give him another kiss before working my mouth down his torso. I dug my teeth into his chest, biting my way to his stomach, relishing the subsequent groan and arch into the touch. When I got to his cock, I met his rapturous gaze while I dribbled spit onto the tip.

He sucked in a breath through his teeth, hissing when I grabbed it between my hands and worked him up and down, squeezing the way that made him moan.

"Do you like that, pretty boy?" Pure unfiltered passion sparked through my blood when he groaned and nodded.

"Yes, Mistress," he said. "Yes, please."

"I love when you beg." Continuing to massage his cock with one hand, I lowered the other to his balls, fondling them enough to make him throw his head back. Then, I went farther back, running a finger over his entrance.

He opened his legs and whimpered, and I loved how responsive he was. I wouldn't lie and say I'd never done this before. It surprised me to learn how many people enjoyed a good pegging, but I would have never guessed Hollywood Hudson would be spread eagle in my bed one day, desperate for my big purple cock.

I grabbed the lube and dribbled some down his shaft before squirting it in my hand, dousing my fingers and rubbing them over the dildo. Then, I went back to Hollywood, swirling my index digit around his hole, making him spread farther for me.

"There we go. Does that feel good?" I watched in amazement as he nodded and met my eyes.

"More," he said. "Please, more."

"You ask so sweetly." I worked a finger inside him, squirting more lube on my hand so I could get the liquid where it needed to be. Most people thought a little spit on a cock would work before shoving it inside a person's ass, but this skin was sensitive. It needed coaxing and patience and a heavy hand when it came to lubrication.

I paid special attention to his reactions, replacing one finger with two, finding that special soft spot inside that had him moaning and covering his face with his hands. I kept pumping his cock, working both in time with each other, watching as he rocked into the movement.

"Oh, that's it, isn't it?" I teased, rubbing over it again.

He bucked his hips, begging for attention. Obviously, I'd been born without a penis, but I imagined someone massaging the prostate while milking the tip was like getting my G-spot pounded while someone played with my clit. So I kept at it, spreading my fingers apart so I could prepare him properly.

"Fuck me, V," he said, breaking out of our scene in his desperate euphoria. I didn't mind the slip. His lack of concentration due to my ministrations turned me on. I lined the dildo up at his entrance and pushed inside slowly, easing my way in at a glacial pace. Fucking someone in the ass wasn't the same as a pussy. One needed to pay attention to their lover, to know when they went too far or too fast, to always have an open line of communication.

Of course, Hollywood had been railed by people with an actual dick, so I wasn't sure how much caution I really needed to use. Still, once I was flush to his pelvis, I paused to let him adjust.

"Fuckkking hell," he said, digging his palms into his eyes. But I didn't like that. I nudged his chin with my nose, forcing him to pull his hands away so I could see his expression.

"Are you okay?" I asked.

"I'm fucking fabulous," he said, leaning forward to kiss me. "Keep going. Please keep going."

Smiling, I sat back on my haunches and lifted his legs in the air so I'd have a better angle to hit his erogenous spot with every thrust. Holding his calves, I pulled out only to surge back in again, reveling in how hard his cock jumped at the intrusion. I loved the way the strap rubbed my clit, amplifying the wanton sensations ricocheting up my spine. I wanted more, so much more.

"Grab your cock, Hudson," I said. "Get yourself off."

"I'm not going to last long. I'm sorry." He wrapped his grip around his dick, squeezing the tip so hard it turned a deeper shade of red.

"Don't be sorry," I said. "I'm riding your face after this, no matter what."

"Oh, shit"—he groaned and curled into himself, slowing his pace —"don't say things like that."

"Hmm, don't tell me what to do," I said, fucking him faster, finding that magic zone and curling my hips into it so I hit it with every rut.

"Fuck, fuck, fuck." He stroked himself faster, twisting his features into euphoria. He tightened his muscles around me, curling his toes, arching his back. He threw his head down on the pillow, the veins in his neck protruding while he reached his climax. "I love you, V. Fuck, yes, I love you. I love you." He repeated those three words while he spurted all over me and himself, and I memorized every last moment: the bead of sweat sliding down the side of his head, the tension in his body as he released, the way he gasped for air like I'd literally stolen the oxygen out of his lungs.

It mesmerized me.

And then, I realized what he'd been confessing.

*He loved me?*

Of course he loved me. I'd recognized it earlier. And I loved him, too. I did. I had loved him my entire life, and now, I was fairly certain I was *in* love with him. I sat there with my dildo in his ass while he panted and stared up at me with adoration radiating out of his eyes—like I was in living color and he'd only ever seen black and white.

It was intoxicating, having a powerful man stare at me like this, and if I didn't know any better, I'd say it was subspace taking him over.

Except, I did know better, and it was real.

"I love you, too," I said, leaning over him to plant a kiss on his perfect mouth.

"I want to move in," he mumbled, his speech slightly slurred as he fought off the comedown.

I laughed and gave him another kiss, easing myself out of him before grabbing the towel on the nightstand to wipe him clean. "Don't get ahead of yourself."

"I'm here almost every night anyway." Hollywood bit his bottom lip. "Wheels can move out and get on with his life."

"Wheels is happy to get out of his mother's house, I assure you." I made a half-hearted chuckle. "Besides, I like it just being you and me for right now."

His features dropped, and he licked his lips like he had something terrible on his mind, and not in a good way.

"Bear found out about us," Hollywood said, and suddenly, everything warm and gushy about this moment came to a screeching halt. "I admitted it to him."

"What?" My chest tightened and my stomach churned. It wasn't like I was worried about Bear's reaction, especially if Hollywood had made it out of the conversation alive. No, something more sinister and shameful brewed deep in my gut. I didn't want people to know because, despite how much I loved Hollywood, despite how much fun I was having, I still didn't trust that this wouldn't implode around me one day . . . that I'd wake up and find him gone for good.

"He already knew," Hollywood said, pushing up on his elbows to look down his body at me. "Ru suspects, too. After the Viper, everyone's got an idea. We wouldn't have been able to keep it quiet for much longer."

I pushed off the bed and clenched my hands into fists, trying to swallow down the rising tide of my temper. "I didn't know we were at a place where we were telling people."

"They already knew. Honestly, we haven't been that great about being discreet, or have you forgotten how you got up in Chelsea's face at the clubhouse?" He furrowed his brows and narrowed his eyes, gripping his hand over the padlock on his chest. "What's the big deal? I thought . . . I thought you were in this with me."

"I am," I said, wincing as I went to the bathroom to wash my hands. Hollywood climbed off the bed to follow me.

"I love you. You love me, too." He sounded more wounded than frustrated, like I'd reached inside his chest and clamped my fingers around his heart. He only waited for me to yank it out and eat it in front of him.

"I do, Hollywood." I turned to face him and brushed my hair out of my face, trying to figure out how to best explain the sudden tightness inside my body. It wasn't that I didn't care for him, and I certainly didn't want to hurt him (not like this), but I had a hard time admitting to myself that this would last, that he was in it for the long haul. He held my emotions so tenderly in his hands, and he could squash me like a bug. I feared that if he did, if I put too much emphasis on him and *this* only for it to blow up in my face, I could relapse into a deep depression again. Hollywood had the power to ruin me in ways he likely didn't realize. "It's just . . . I'm not sure where this is going, and until I am . . ."

He dropped his jaw and took a step back, rubbing a hand over the back of his head. "What the fuck is that supposed to mean?"

"You *do* have a history of leaving a trail of broken hearts behind you," I said, grimacing as it came out more demeaning than I'd meant it. "And I don't trust anyone. I don't like people knowing my private life. Anyone who gets close to me either destroys me or ends up in a grave."

"Oh, and you suppose I'll either leave you or die, is that it?" His voice grew louder, and it was the first time in all the years I'd known him that I'd ever seen Hollywood so upset. Normally, he faced everything with a smile. He had a laugh and a joke on his lips for every situation. To see his eyes redden with tears, to hear the sudden heartache and disappointment in his voice, it plucked at my self-loathing and made me feel worse.

"No, that's not what I mean," I said, the scar on my chest burning to life as he backed away from me and grabbed his boxers from the floor, shoving his legs into them before yanking them up his hips. It was like seeing a train wreck happening in front of me and knowing someone had to pump the brakes, but my foot was lodged on the gas.

"I thought we treated each other the way we deserved," he said, his voice breaking. "I thought you wanted me. Or was that all just horseshit?"

"No, it wasn't," I said, trying to smooth this over. "But Christ, we've only been doing this for a few weeks."

"Fine." He nodded his head and grabbed his jeans off the floor, sliding them on. Then he slipped his shirt over his arms and head. "Look, I have to go do a run for the club. I'll be gone most of the day tomorrow. Think about what you want . . . what you *really* want . . . and we'll talk when I get back."

In a rare twist of how we'd started this, Hollywood threw my own words in my face. He moved toward the door, but I caught his arm, trying to pull him back, trying to stop the damage I'd already done.

*No, no, no.* In my desperation to save myself, I'd probably ruined one of the best things I'd ever had. My eyes burned as tears streamed over them, dripping down my cheeks. I didn't want to rush things with him, I didn't want him to hurt me, but likewise, I didn't want this to end. "Are you breaking this off with me?"

"No, V," he said, his voice softening as he ran the back of his knuckles down my cheeks, wiping away the visible signs of my idiotic words. "But I'm not gonna be someone's dirty little secret. Not anymore. Being with you . . . it makes me want more than that. I thought you wanted that, too."

"And how am I supposed to know you're not going to hurt me?" I could barely form the words, the thought of losing this new amazing thing too overwhelming.

"Well, that's on you," he said, leaning forward to gently kiss my forehead. "I guess you're gonna have to learn to trust *me*."

With that, he grabbed his boots and he walked out of my house, the quiet snick of the door behind him rattling through my body.

## 22

## HOLLYWOOD

"It's good to see you again, my friend," Rico said, holding his hand out to Slip when we'd made it to the rendezvous spot for the run to Asheville. The cartel had met us here on time, not a minute later, and Rico immediately welcomed Slip like an old comrade.

I agreed with Doc that having this many guys on a run at one time smelled like a trap, but I didn't argue, especially not when we got to the pickup point and a trailer full of goodies waited for us. Picasso had driven the truck since he was well into his sixties and riding a bike for hours at a time flared his sciatica. Now that he'd attached the hitch, we were ready to head out.

Which was fucking good because after what happened with V, I itched in more ways than one. Hearing her tell me she didn't trust me . . . didn't trust *this* . . . ached more than I thought it would. Sure, she had a point. We'd only been doing this a few weeks, barely a month, but I'd known her for over a decade. She was my *sort of* friend before we hooked up, and now that we'd confessed our love, I didn't understand how she couldn't be in this one hundred percent like I was.

*I'm not sure where this is going, and until I am . . .*

Where else could it go? I'd never told anyone I loved them before.

I'd never been this vulnerable with anyone. Even if we'd only been doing this for a short amount of time, I couldn't resist the way I'd felt about her. The fact that she didn't want anyone to know because she harbored *shame* about me cut like a fucking knife.

Hearing her saying she was in love with me had rattled around in my head since the words left her pretty lips, flooding my chest with warmth and emotions I'd never thought I'd feel. It had happened quickly between us, but that didn't make it any less real. And then she'd gone and torn my heart out, clenching it in her beautiful bloody little fists.

*Calm down. I'll go home and talk it out with her. She still loves me. She still wants me. It was just an argument. We were bound to have one sooner or later.*

Her heartbreaking "are you breaking up with me?" yanked at my soul, giving me hope that this was far from over.

*I won't let her end it. She's mine in ways no one else ever has been. I'll make her see she can really trust me. I'll fight for her. I will.*

I didn't like leaving her like that, but we both needed space to think. My ass ached from the fifty "sluts" bruised into it, and I still felt her strap deep inside me. But I rode a little easier knowing Castor and Wheels were looking out for her and the rest of the MC princesses while we were here, even if we were in a rocky place.

"I don't know how you do it," I said to KC while Slip and Rico finished the deal.

"Do what?" KC pulled on a cigarette while he leaned back against his bike.

"Leave Alba alone all fucking day while you do these runs." I ran a hand back through my hair, letting my breath out on a sigh. "V and I got into a fight yesterday and I'm twitchy as hell being this far away from her."

KC pat me on the shoulder, and I bit back a wince from where V had sunk her teeth into my trap muscle earlier that morning.

"It doesn't get easier, brother," KC said. "But the Roses are there, and Selene won't let anything happen to V."

That was the only thing easing my anxiety. We were three hours south of Madison County, so if the shit hit the fan, it would be at least that long until I could get there to fix it. My stomach churned and my heart pounded, making my hands sweaty.

"What did you two fight about?" KC asked, narrowing his eyes in a sympathetic glance.

"She didn't want people to know about us. She still thinks I'm gonna leave her . . . or fucking die."

KC snorted and shook his head. "Well, you can't blame her for that, huh? Her mother died when she was a kid. Her brother nearly got blown up last year. And how many times have you been shot?"

I swallowed down the truth in that. "I just wished she trusted me."

"I've known V her whole life. My little cousin's not scared of much, but when it comes to the heavy emotions, she's terrified of getting hurt." KC smiled, a nostalgic glint in his eyes like he was envisioning the younger version of Verona. "If she's pulling away, it means she loves you. If you want her, you need to pull harder."

"Thanks, KC." I nodded, more resolute in what I had to do when I got home.

"Y'all are good together. I'm happy for you, Hollywood. Truly."

I wouldn't let her keep me at arm's length. What we had was too good for that. Assuming, of course, that I made it home. Something about this run didn't feel right, and it had nothing to do with the cartel or the arms we'd just picked up. It ached like a glass splinter, like I knew it was there, but I couldn't find it no matter what I tried.

"All right," Slip said, turning to us and circling his finger in the air, indicating we should round up to head out. I mounted my bike and kicked it to life, following Slip and KC when they led the way down the road. Picasso followed in the truck with the trailer behind him, the rest of my brothers bringing up the rear.

Twenty minutes into the trip home, tension flared in my chest again, like I should know better than to be here instead of with V, but I couldn't put my finger on why.

*It's just another run,* I told myself. *Nothing to worry about.*

That shitty affirmation did not stop me from checking over my shoulder every ten minutes to make sure we weren't being followed.

The guys in the back would handle it if we were, but still, my suspicion ached like a phantom limb.

Another two hours went by, and once we got into Virginia, Slip took us off the main highway and led us the back way. I figured it was because we were carrying *extra accessories*. We'd just turned onto a winding country road when my stomach sank into my knees. Up ahead, dark SUVs blocked the path, causing our group to slow to a stop. I glanced behind us only to see more vehicles pull out of the woods to keep us from backing up.

I grabbed my pistol and unholstered it, holding it out as the doors to the Range Rovers in front of us opened. I knew we were fucked when expensive loafers hit the ground and I heard Slip's voice in the headset of my helmet.

"It's the Caputis. Everyone remain calm," he said, dismounting his bike.

KC glanced at me from the side, his eyes wide with growing panic. The men got out of the SUVs behind us, at least twenty to our mere six.

"We're fucked," Lore murmured, knowing everyone would pick it up in their earpieces.

"Stay calm," Picasso repeated from the truck. "If anything happens, leave the guns and fucking scatter. We'll regroup back at the clubhouse."

"What the fuck is this?" Slip said, walking up to the eight Caputis in front of him like his life wasn't literally on the line. "Y'all got a death wish?"

One of the taller Caputis walked forward, a smirk on his face like Slip had said the funniest thing in the world.

"Heard you made a deal with our good buddy, Rico." The Caputi shifted his shoulders, making the gaudy jewelry on his neck gleam in the afternoon sun. "We couldn't let that stand."

"Sounds like you got a problem with Rico, not us." Slip pointed at the Range Rovers. "Now move your shit so we can get through."

"Can't do that," the Caputi replied, pushing his coat jacket back to reveal the guns strapped to either side.

*Shit, this is bad. This is really bad.*

"What are you going to do with that, huh? Shoot all of us right here in broad daylight?" Slip shook his head. "You really are some dumb mother—"

He never got the word out. One of the other Caputis pulled their gun and fired it at Slip's head, exploding through his skull and out the other side. He dropped like a bag of bricks, and all hell broke loose.

Shock coiled through my veins, scalding hot and angry. I fired two rounds into the Caputi that shot the road captain as KC went on the attack next to me, the sounds of his firing gun nearly deafening the ear on that side of my head. Despite Picasso's plan, I kept shooting, trying to take down as many of these fuckers as I could. A burning blast nailed me in the chest, making me stumble back, but I ignored it, choosing instead to keep firing until my clip ran empty.

"Fuck!" came the shout from next to me, and KC went down on his right, holding his leg as a bright crimson spot spread over his jeans.

"Fuck, no, no, no." Dismissing the ache in the center of my chest, I rounded our bikes and rushed to his side, grabbing him by the cut so I could drag him out of the center of the chaos.

"Let me see," I said, glancing down at his thigh. The bullet appeared to have gone clean through, but KC couldn't walk like this. I whipped my belt off my jeans and wrapped it around his leg, pulling it so tight he groaned.

"Fuck, Hollywood!" he growled. "Leave me be." His bloody hands grabbed my shirt, hauling me in close. "Go. Get our girls. Make sure they're safe."

"Shut the fuck up," I said. "I'm not leaving you."

KC winced and wiped at my chest, coming away with fresh blood on his fingers. "Fuck, man. Are you . . ." He dropped his gaze to my shirt, and when I followed his line of sight, I realized I'd been shot. Again.

"Fuck." I pulled my neckline away to see a huge dent in the padlock V had just put on me last night. But that only distracted from the flesh wound on my ribs. Luckily, it was nothing more than a cut, but it looked deep enough to need stitches, and it still fucking hurt.

I tried to push to my feet, only to collapse under the weight of my own massive form. Fuck, the bullet had probably broken a rib, too.

Slip was still in the middle of the fray, clearly dead, and Picasso was slumped over the steering wheel of the truck. Lore lay on his back up against the trailer, both arms out straight in front of him, his pistols in hand while he stared down the Caputis surrounding him. I couldn't see Coins from my position on this side of the trailer, but judging by the way his bike flopped on its side, I assumed he had also ducked for cover.

*This is it. This is the end. They're gonna walk up and shoot us all in the head.*

"Fuck." My heart sank into my torso like lead, a sob barreling up my throat as I realized I'd never get to have that future with V like I'd imagined. I'd never get to make up with her, and she'd been right. I hoped she moved on. I hoped she found someone better, someone that would love her and take care of her the way she deserved, the way I tried to.

Her bright violet gaze flickered through my mind, followed by the sound of her laugh, and I collapsed onto the tree next to KC, relegating myself to my inevitable demise. When I'd joined the MC, I figured this would be the way it would end, especially after Trojan died this way two years ago.

These fucking Caputi fucks would take everything from me: my brother, my freedom, and now my life.

I reached into my pocket to get my cell phone, sending a quick SOS to Thor. I wanted to say goodbye to V, to roll over her name and tell her I loved her again, to apologize for the way I'd left things. But the world had started to go wonky, and I didn't think I'd be able to see the letters.

*I tried,* I said to Trojan, wherever he was. *I tried to keep my promise.*

"Don't you fucking do that to me," KC growled, slapping me in the face. "You get your shit together, Hudson. You don't get to check out. Not here. Not today."

The sharp shock of pain brought me back to myself, and I gasped, sucking in air. My vision sharpened, and I shook my head, reaching for my hunting knife just in case these bastards came closer to us.

"Now, now," said a Caputi prick as he walked toward me. "There's no need for more violence. At least, not yet."

I swallowed down sweat and panic, scooting closer to KC to protect him with my body, to do anything to keep my brother safe so he could get home to his Sunshine.

"What the fuck do you want?" I snarled.

The Caputi only smiled and squatted down in front of us, his grin turning evil as a sinister look appeared in his eyes.

**23**

———

# VERONA

"Would you relax?" Selene said, gesturing to the empty spot on the couch. She'd brought a damn arsenal with her, literally decorating my coffee table (which used to be her coffee table) with her guns and ammo. She ran a brush through the barrel of her rifle while Ru typed on her laptop and Alba went through a binder full of financial reports from the last year at Crimson.

"Something's wrong." I rubbed at the center of my chest while I paced in front of the window. "I can feel it."

Selene cracked her neck and stared up at me. "You're making me nervous."

"You should be," I said.

"Hush." Ru pushed to her feet so she could grab my shoulders and stop my pacing. "Everything is fine."

I didn't think so. Hollywood and I hadn't left things on good terms, and since he walked out yesterday, I hadn't heard from him. Maybe I needed space to figure things out, to figure out what I wanted, but something still felt off. My blood sang with danger, as if the few pieces of Hollywood that were inside me and the pieces of me in him recognized that all was not well and had been trying to alert me.

"He'll let you know when he's back," Castor said from his spot at my dining room table.

"He's with Slip and Coins, and they do this run all the time. It'll be okay," Alba said, smiling in that sunshine way of hers.

"We got into a fight," I admitted, causing both Alba and Ru to glance up at me with identical raised eyebrows. "He wanted to go public, to tell everyone about us."

"So there *is* something going on?" Ru said, her eyes wide with hopeful anticipation. "I knew it."

"Yes," I said, rubbing my hands over my face. "But I fucked it up."

I told them the situation, trying to keep my voice down so Wheels and Castor didn't hear from the kitchen, but screw it. They were here most days anyway, and based on the conversation a few days ago, they already knew. Apparently, everyone already knew. I was the world's worst secret keeper, even when it was my own.

"He's changed," Ru said, as Alba nodded in approval.

"He wants to be better," Alba added. "To do better."

"I've never seen him this smitten with someone," Ru said.

"If he told you he loved you," Selene said, "that's pretty big. I don't think I've ever heard him admit that about someone before."

"Ugh, I know," I groaned. "I got scared. I didn't want people to know just in case this ends badly. This could hurt . . . *he* could hurt me."

"That's the risk you take by letting someone in," Alba said, her voice gentle like she was trying to coax a wild animal. "In order to love him, *really* love him, you have to trust that he won't do that."

"How did you know that about KC?" I glanced at her, hoping for some resounding life changing advice.

"I pushed him away, at first," she said, her eyes clouding with a wistful gaze. "When I thought Benito would come after me, I pushed him away to keep him safe." Alba let out a small giggle. "Fat lot of good that did. He just held on tighter."

"That's the thing about these alpha assholes," Selene said. "You run, they chase. You give an inch, they take a mile."

I sighed, letting that wash over me. I had to make up with Hollywood as soon as he got back. I didn't mean to hurt his feelings, and if there were anyone in the world I could trust, who I could bring into my life, it would be him. He'd already gotten a lot closer than anyone ever had before.

"Hey, V," Castor called. "I've got something to show you. Come here."

He'd been trying to find whoever sent me those strange messages for the last few weeks. When he'd gotten here earlier, he'd said he was close. I walked to the spot behind him so I could peer over his shoulder, watching as he pulled up a video feed of a bar with a group of bikers milling around. It reminded me of the clubhouse, but dirtier and smaller with different ole-timers and uglier hang-arounds.

"What is this?" I narrowed my gaze to see if I recognized any of the people. "I've never been there. I thought you said they were in Madison County?"

"I thought so, too," Castor said, leaning back in his seat as Selene, Alba, and Ru came to stand next to me. "Whoever it is bounced their VPN off a thousand different servers. They're good."

"Holy shit," Selene said. "How are you doing this? Are you spying on them?"

"Someone's fucking with V," Wheels explained, joining the group to watch the other club mill around. "Is it the Kings of Carnage?"

Selene straightened from her spot next to me. She'd had a run-in with the New York MC chapter late last year, but they'd sworn they didn't want any trouble with us.

"I don't know." Castor shook his head. "This is where they are right now, not necessarily where they were when they sent those messages to you."

"Wait . . ." Alba pointed to a person wearing a cut in the top right of the screen. "That doesn't say Kings of Carnage. What is that?"

I squinted and leaned in, just barely making out the same design as the one I'd seen on the guy who'd put his hands on me at the Viper.

"Is that the Hell's Knights?" I asked.

"That guy whose ass you kicked at the Viper," Wheels said. "Wasn't he from the same club?"

"It sure was," I said. "Do you see him there? Was he after me this whole time?"

Fuck, to have one stalker in my life was bad enough. To have two? I had the worst luck.

"I don't see him," Castor said, pressing something on his keyboard to shift the camera view to another angle. "Plus, he didn't seem like he was interested in you. He had his sights on that other girl."

The one he'd drugged. The one he'd tried to lure away and harass in the hallway.

"I don't understand." I shook my head, trying to rationalize what had happened that night. "Is the person who sent me those creepy messages someone else from his club?"

Before anyone could make sense of what we were seeing, the sound of car doors shutting out front got our attention. Hope surged in my chest that it might be Hollywood, so I started to walk toward the front of the house. Wheels grabbed my shoulder to stop me, hauling me back before taking the lead spot with Castor and Selene. All three of them had their weapons out, and Ru grabbed a pistol off the table, kneeling on the couch so she could peer out the window. I also grabbed a gun, just to be safe.

I'd never killed anyone before, but my brothers had taught me how to shoot when I was still in diapers. If this wasn't our family, I wouldn't go down without a fight.

"Shit," Castor said, turning back around to face us, his eyes wide with panic. "Hide, V. Hide. Go!"

It wasn't the SRMC, nor was it my mysterious stalker or the Kings of Carnage. When I looked out the window, six guys were getting out of a Range Rover in tactical gear, heading straight for my front door. Just as I backed away from the window, another SUV pulled up and I caught sight of men in black suits before Ru yanked me back toward the kitchen.

"Is that the Caputis?" Alba whispered.

"Go," Selene whispered, corralling the three of us toward the basement door. A loud boom preceded gunfire, but I couldn't stop. Wheels and Castor were still up there, and I left them because Selene, Ru, and Alba pushed me down the stairs. My legs shook and my knees threatened to give out on me; I kept going because I had to. Once there, Selene raced toward the back of the house where a set of cement stairs led to a slanted rusty metal storm door. Ru held her gun up as Selene forged ahead, unlocking the barrier before lifting it up an inch to peek out.

Hands trembling and heart racing, I reached into my pocket for my cell phone, managing to get a text out to the SRMC group chat that read "911! My house." Another set of gunshots rang out above us, and I clenched my eyes shut as memories from the night I'd been shot came rushing back to me. I couldn't breathe, I couldn't see straight, and suddenly, I wasn't in that basement with my sisters anymore. I was back in Saint's truck, staring up at Hollywood's lifeless face.

"No, no, no," I murmured, covering my ears as loud thumps hit the floor above us. My legs locked into place, my stomach churning as the pain surged through my chest again. Agony exploded in my body, and I couldn't move. I had to stay there. I had to get to my brother. I had to make sure Wheels had—

"V!" Alba shouted, grabbing my face so all I could see were her bright, sky-blue eyes. "You're okay. Just follow me. That's all you have to do."

I didn't want to walk. I didn't want to listen to her. I wanted to curl into a ball and pretend none of this was happening, but when she grabbed my hand and yanked me up those cement stairs, I found myself moving. When she raced across the backyard into the woods, hardly sparing a second glance for Castor and Wheels, I focused on my inhales and exhales, gripping the pistol tighter in one hand, her fingers in the other. Selene and Ru were a few paces ahead of us, disappearing into the tree line. Alba and I were almost there, and if I could just keep pace with her, we'd make it.

*Keep breathing. Inhale. Exhale. It's okay. I'm okay. I'm going to make it.*

Ten yards out from the woods, a burning hot stab hit me in the calf, and I dropped to my knees, wailing with the sting. Another bullet nearly got me in the shoulder, zinging past me and colliding with the tree immediately to my right. Bark exploded, hitting me in the face, and I blinked, hoping this was a dream, that I'd wake up in bed next to Hollywood.

*I'm okay. It's okay. Keep breathing. Inhale. Exhale.*

"Fuck!" I got back to my feet, limping to keep up with Alba and the others, but I couldn't take a step without the agony tormenting my leg and spine. I couldn't walk. I couldn't run. "Go! Go! Leave me."

"No fucking way," Alba said, coming back to wrap her arm under my shoulders, using her body weight to help me. But this would only slow them down, and judging by the shouts behind me, the Caputis were gaining on us.

"Granddaughter," called a female voice. "Stop running or I'll kill them."

Alba's steps faltered, and for a moment, I thought she wouldn't listen. I looked over my shoulder to see my brother and Wheels on their knees in front of the house, two guys standing behind them, pointing guns at their heads.

"Shit," Alba groaned, freezing just before we would have met up with Selene and Ru.

Selene kneeled on the ground behind a log, setting up her rifle on the fallen tree so she could peer down the scope.

"Get behind me," she hissed, trying to keep her voice low enough so the Caputis didn't hear.

"The MC will be here soon." Ru hunched down next to Selene, holding up her gun. "We just have to hold them off until then."

Alba and I stayed where we were, the sounds of Gabriella's footsteps growing closer as we turned around to face her.

"I'm not your granddaughter," Alba said, holding her chin up higher. "I'm a Rose, and I always will be."

Gabriella smirked, holding her fur coat tighter around her body as she sauntered closer, four men flanking her on either side.

"I promised you, Alba, one day you would know what a mother's grief could do." She put her hands in her coat pockets and stared at us with eyes so similar to the woman standing at my side. I could see the family resemblance, but where Alba's life had made her more radiant, Gabriella's had worn her down, turned her features drawn and ragged. "Today is that day."

"What do you want?" Alba said, taking a deep breath. My pulse thundered in my veins and my leg throbbed, warm, sticky blood coating the side of my calf and ankle. I clutched the pistol harder, waiting for the opportunity to raise it and blow this bitch's brains out.

"This is not about wanting anything," Gabriella said. "This is about blood."

"Haven't you spilled enough?" I hissed, sneering at the woman who had started this war. It was because of her Benito and the former SRMC president had gotten into a fatal dick-measuring contest. It was because of her Penny Wright ran away with Aris. Gabriella had started it all. "Haven't you taken enough from us?"

"Where is Leo?" she asked, ignoring me altogether. "If you tell me, I may let you go."

My stomach churned for Castor and Wheels, who still kneeled on the ground with their hands behind their heads.

"What makes you think we know?" Alba said. "We don't have access to the club's information."

"Hmm." Gabriella nodded and waved a hand over her shoulder, beckoning more henchmen our way. The guys standing behind Wheels and my brother hauled them upright and brought them toward one of the SUVs, but the queen bee didn't move. She just stared at us with hatred echoing out of her evil gaze.

"Not another step," came Selene's threat from behind us.

"If you don't come willingly, I'll kill both of them in front of you," Gabriella said, purposely ignoring Selene by putting one foot closer to us . . . then another . . . and another. I didn't know if she met Castor and Wheels or me and Alba, but either way, I heard Selene's frustrated groan before the sound of her dropping her gun to the ground.

With nowhere to run and no way out, I let go of my pistol and stared Gabriella down as her Caputi bastards lead us to their vehicles.

# HOLLYWOOD

If I thought dying was going to be easy, I had another fucking thing coming. They hauled me, KC, and Lore up, bound our hands and mouths, and forced us into the back of their SUV. I couldn't see Coins, but I heard his angry shouts as they did the same to him.

I was pretty sure my rib was broken and every breath racked my body with agony, but fuck it, ya know? I'd make it through this with a broken rib, and if I could do something to protect Lore and KC, I would or I'd go down trying.

Lore held his shoulder while it leaked down his arm and KC's leg had stopped oozing, but of the three of us, he looked like he was the closest to greeting Death. *Not today, motherfucker.* I just hoped if the bitch came for me, I was doing something that actually mattered. Trojan had gone out protecting Alba and Ru from these fuckers, and if I could do anything remotely similar, I'd make sure to hold out until I could.

I took a deep breath in through my nose, wincing when I struggled to inhale, and each bump in the road made my torso radiate with pain. I'd been shot three times, but none of those compared to this. On a scale of paper cut to "fuck-me-call-911," I hovered somewhere around "put-me-out-of-my-misery." Broken ribs were a son of a bitch.

A hard shove at my foot had me forcing my eyes open, meeting Lore's stern gaze from the other side of the SUV. He gestured to his boot, hitting me in the arm again before glaring down at the thing.

I couldn't remember if they checked us for weapons, but if they had, they'd done a piss-poor job. He had a knife sticking out of the top of the leather, right next to his sock. I tried to twist around so I could grab it with my hands behind my back, but I couldn't move in the right direction to get it.

*"Get your shit together, Matty,"* came a deep, familiar voice in the back of my head.

*"Trojan?"* I thought, grimacing as more torment sliced through my body.

*"No fucking shit,"* he said. *"Focus. Get KC's attention."*

I nudged my brother next to me, nodding toward Lore's boot and hoping he got the idea. KC's face had grown almost as pale as his shirt had once been before blood and dirt soiled it. When he understood, he twisted his body so he could grab it, but his fingers kept slipping off the handle, too coated with sweat and crimson.

When KC finally palmed the blade, he twisted it around in his grasp so he could saw through the plastic zip ties on his wrists. These stupid fuckers had put the three of us together and given no one to watch us, so once he got his hands free, he turned to me so he could get mine loose, too.

Once Lore was out, KC set his sights on the driver, who currently argued with the passenger in Italian, gesturing to the roads like they didn't know where they were or what they were doing. KC sat back in his original spot and held the knife like he was waiting for the right opportunity to use it. We turned into a driveway for a house I didn't recognize, and when the passenger turned around to face us for the first time in however long, he realized we were out of our bindings.

"Hey!" He unhooked his seat belt and murmured something to the driver, causing him to slam on the brakes. The three of us careened forward, KC's weight collapsing on top of mine, and I nearly screamed from how badly that fucking hurt.

But our cover had been blown, and KC hobbled forward, stabbing the knife into the driver's neck three times before the passenger pistol-whipped KC in the face so hard that he collapsed on top of me. The driver lost control of the SUV and it hurdled off the road, slamming into a tree.

That sent scalding torture through my chest so badly that I lost consciousness. Pain ripped down my spine and through the back of my legs before everything went dark. I hovered in that strange peacefulness for entirely too short of a time before I heard shouts, beckoning me back to consciousness. My brother's screams sounded from a distance, but they were too far away for me to make out. A hard smack to my cheek brought me back to reality, where two Caputi fucks dragged me out of the SUV and hauled me to my feet.

*God. Fucking. Damn. It!*

Everything throbbed and my head thundered so fucking bad I couldn't focus. And if I couldn't focus, I had no idea how we'd get out of this. They'd replaced the gag around my mouth so I couldn't communicate with my brothers. Instead, I tried to take in my surroundings while we walked.

A rickety run-down house stood up ahead, the rafters hanging off the shithole and the windows long since broken and decayed. Several Caputi pricks stood on the porch out front, most of them carrying assault rifles or loaded down with pistols. The three of us were vastly outnumbered, even if we weren't injured. Getting out of this was going to take a fucking act of God.

"That's it?" one of the Caputi guards said, walking closer as he eyed us up and down. "The boss isn't gonna be pleased about this."

"I told her they were carrying an arsenal with them," the fucker on my right said. "We lost five guys. We were lucky to bring in these four."

I glanced behind me and saw another two Caputis hauling Coins toward us.

"Where's the road captain?" another one said.

"Dead," came the response.

My heart sank at the thought of our lost brother, at his family and wife left behind.

*Fuck. We're so fucked.*

They pulled us up the wooden steps and across the porch, taking us inside the decrepit building. But my heart stopped when we got inside.

Kneeling on the floor were the girls . . . *our* girls. They'd been bound and gagged, and each had a Caputi standing behind them with a gun pointed at the back of their heads. Perpendicular to them, facing the front door, were four of my brothers—Skulls, Castor, Hollister, and Wheels. The first was supposed to be on guard duty at one of the storage locations where we'd planned to take our delivery from the cartel. I realized then that this had been a coordinated attack. We'd been outplayed.

Ru immediately met my gaze with an icy, pissed-off one of her own. Next to her, Selene silently seethed with her fury. I'd bet my left nut she was planning a massacre, even now. Alba saw KC and clenched her eyes shut, tears streaming over her cheeks as he struggled against the men holding him, screaming behind the gag, forgoing the fact he'd been shot in the leg in favor of trying to break free. But on the far end, staring up at me with those gorgeous violet eyes, sat *my* girl. My V. My Mistress.

I took a deep inhale and glanced back at KC, trying to tell him to calm down with my stare. If they were going to kill our girls, they would have already done it. More men walked in while our captors shoved the three of us to our knees, facing our MC princesses. They put Coins next to Skulls, right on the other side of V. He met my gaze with an angry one of his own, indicating he had plans of getting out of this as well.

My entire body shook with the effort to stay still, to not jump up and make a scene so the rest of them had a chance to get away. I'd have to find my opportunity and use it soon. Finally, the distinctive click-clack of high heels came down the hallway, and there she was.

*Gabriella Caputi.* In the flesh. She looked terrible, having aged at least fifteen years in a few months. She wore long dark red pants and a matching blazer, her thick diamond necklace matching her earrings and the gaudy paperweights around her fingers. Her dark hair had been pulled back into a chignon, and if it weren't for the desperate vileness in her eyes, I'd see the family resemblance to Alba. But where Alba was the very impersonation of her nickname Sunshine, Gabriella looked like a black hole, like she sucked all the joy out of every place she went.

"Now that I've got your attention," Gabriella said, sauntering into the middle of the abductee circle. "I'll ask again. Where is my nephew?"

I tried to grumble something around the gag, and the guy with the gun to my head yanked the wrappings down.

"What was that?" he sneered.

"Leo Caputi is dead." I winced at the stab in my rib, but now that the adrenaline was racing through my blood, the pain had started to subside.

Gabriella turned to me, narrowing her dead stare before coming to stand in front of me. "That is not true."

I forced a grin. "You stupid bitch."

The guy slammed his gun down on my face, and I whipped to the side, using KC's torso to right myself again despite the vicious twinge from the gash on my chest.

"I know that is a lie," Gabriella hissed, nodding to one of the guys in the corner. "Bring her in."

More rustling came from the hallway, followed by the familiar voice of Julia Caputi. Two Caputis carried her inside the room and threw her on the ground in front of us. She'd been beat up, her tear-streaked face more bruised than any of ours, and stripped down, her once beautiful dress now in tatters around her legs and shoulders.

*This fucking demon.*

I was going to enjoy watching her die—assuming, of course, I managed to get out of this situation alive.

"This one has been rallying support among *my* family to overthrow me." Gabriella spat on her niece like she was garbage. "After all I've done for her. After everything I've sacrificed. She betrays her own blood."

"Please," Julia whined, sounding broken and defeated. "Please, I didn't. I swear I didn't."

"Shut up." Gabriella nodded at one of her guards, who stepped forward and rammed his boot into Julia's gut. She cried out and curled in on herself, weeping from the abuse. I didn't know Julia very well, but she was an ally. According to Saint and Crow, she'd been helping us for years.

"Stop it!" I growled. "Leave her alone."

Gabriella returned her attention to me.

"Do you think your silly little motorcycle club is coming for you?" She tsked her teeth and shook her head. "I can assure you, they will be quite entertained for some time. My friends at the FBI are showing them what happens when you pretend at power."

*Fuck!*

We'd known Detective Jordan and her fucking pigs were hunting us down, but this had been an ambush for the ages. While the Caputis were rounding up our members on the run, the Feds had ransacked the clubhouse. How did we miss this?

She reached out to run the back of her knuckles up the side of my face and into my hair, clenching a fistful before yanking my head back. "Watch real power."

Gabriella nodded at the person standing in front of Coins, who leveled their gun at his head and pulled the trigger. I forced my eyelids to stay open while blood and brains scattered the wall behind him. KC screamed behind his gag as Coins's body fell lifeless to the ground.

*No!*

I'd known him since I was a teenager and watching him die while I'd been helpless to stop it sent blinding fury and panic through my veins.

"You see? *I* have the power here. *I* am the one you should fear." Gabriella let go of me and I slumped back on my feet, my heart aching for my fallen brother.

The Caputi bitch looked at KC, narrowing her gaze as she stuck her chin higher in the air.

"You're the one who killed my beloved Benito, aren't you?" She twisted her lips into a crooked grin as she pat his cheek. "Do you recognize this place?"

KC took a deep breath in through his nose, letting it out on a loud sigh, shooting daggers out of his eyes.

"This is where it happened." Gabriella pointed toward the front yard. "That is the spot where he died, where you bled him to death like a fucking monster." She made a sardonic laugh and shook her head. "I'm going to save you for last. I want you to watch me take the love of your life from you."

She went to Lore next, rubbing a finger over his eye patch. He seethed with hatred, staring up at her like he'd been planning her demise for months. "I must say, you look better this way. I think Leo did you a favor."

He pulled against his bindings like he was one second from getting free, but Gabriella only moved on, going to the man standing in front of Skulls.

"Do it," she said moments before he pulled the trigger, painting the wall with more Rose red.

I growled and yanked against my restraints, the sharp plastic digging into my skin at another brother's death. I didn't know him very well, but he'd sworn himself to the same MC as me. We were family by oath, if nothing else.

*I'll kill her for this. I will.*

The tape around my wrists gave, and I yanked farther, pleased when my own blood mixed with my sweaty hands and enabled me to slip my thumb through the opening. I minimized my movements, keeping my gaze on the man with a gun pointed between my eyebrows.

We were outnumbered at least three to one, but I'd faced worse odds and I'd bet these fuckers were underestimating our women. Selene had the best shot in this room and the worst bloodlust. She could get out of a pair of cuffs faster than anyone alive, and twenty bucks said she'd already thought through an escape plan. Ru and V had been shooting since we were kids, and all I'd have to do would be to cause a scene to get it started. KC had been training Alba since they got together, and I'd seen the piece she carried in her purse. She could handle herself much better now than the last time these Caputi fucks had come for her.

I eased my hand out of the bindings, forcing myself to take as deep a breath as I could before Gabriella went to Hollister, nearly a spitting image of his brother next to him. They had the same enchanting eyes, the same dark skin, the same genetic beauty they'd both inherited from their mother. I knew what it was to suffer through the loss of my only sibling, and I wanted to spare Wheels from that if I could.

*But how?*

I made eye contact with Selene, whose gaze darted between me and KC, attempting to get our attention.

*Are we doing this?* I tried to ask with my eyes.

She gave me one slight nod, as if to suggest she'd be ready if I started something.

Then, my attention went again to V, who gave me a red-rimmed stare with tears streaking down her cheeks.

*I'm sorry,* I tried to tell her. *I love you. I love you, and I'm sorry. Please forgive me.*

She shook her head, widening her eyes as if she could tell what I planned and didn't want me to hurt myself. But if it got her out of this, if she'd be safe, I'd do much worse.

"Hey!" I shouted, causing Gabriella to stop and turn to me. "You wanna know where Leo is?" I had to sit back on my heels to finish it, my lungs unable to inhale fully. "I'll tell you."

Seemingly intrigued, she came back to me, straightening her blazer with curiosity in her eyes. "Okay. Talk."

Julia widened her eyes, her poor broken body writhing on the floor as she looked at me, practically begging me to keep my damned mouth shut. But I'd seen enough. The time was now. If I didn't act, I was going to watch this cunt kill everyone I loved, and I had no desire to see that.

*You told me it wasn't my time, Trojan. I sure hope you're right.*

25

——————

# VERONA

y chest caved in on itself when Hollywood spoke up because I knew what he planned to do. I'd seen it in his eyes moments before he said anything, and I remembered what Selene had said about him. He believed himself to be dispensable, just a lowly MC grunt with no one in his corner.

That may have been true the first time he got shot for this club, but it wasn't anymore. I'd watched these heartless vultures steal two club members from me. I wasn't about to sit here while they killed the love of my life and the rest of my family.

"I took him to a safe house." Hollywood winced as he moved, and the blood pooling on his shirt had my heart in shambles. I couldn't tell how bad the injury was, and that made me even more anxious. Selene moved next to me, silently slipping out of her restraints. "I kept him there until his knee got infected."

"Infected?" Gabriella's shrill voice sent shivers down my spine. "What are you talking about? Where is he now?"

I bit harder into the gag around my mouth, trying to keep myself from crying out. My muscles trembled, adrenaline shooting through my veins, begging me to do something—*anything.*

"I told you." Hollywood twisted his features into a wicked smile. "He's dead. I killed him."

"Boss," said the man holding a gun in front of me, lowering the pistol. "Maybe he's right. We haven't seen any signs of Leo in months."

"No. He's lying. They're all lying." Gabriella growled and grabbed the gun out of his hands before walking over to Hollister, pointing it at his head, and pulling the trigger.

I sobbed as Wheels cried out, pulling against his bindings, trying to get up so he could take out his vengeance on this sadistic bitch. This wasn't an interrogation. This was a slaughter, and we were unlikely to make it out alive. Gabriella lowered the gun at Wheels next, his chin quivering as he held back his rage.

Julia's soft ridiculing laughter stopped Gabriella and sent a chill down my spine. She turned to her niece, who pushed herself up so she could stare down her aunt with the one eye that wasn't swollen shut.

"Look at you," Julia said, spitting blood at her aunt's expensive shoes. "Do you realize how weak you look? Chasing after my brother instead of ruling your kingdom?"

"I need him dead," Gabriella hissed, stalking back to the broken, bleeding woman on the floor. "I need to see it with my own eyes."

"You'll never defeat him." Julia shook her head with a broken smile. "You'll never defeat me."

Gabriella furrowed her brows, seemingly confused, before the roar of a truck came from outside. For a moment, my heart leaped and I thought we were saved. The sound of boots boomed up the porch and into the house, but I froze at the sight of two bikers from another club coming into the house. I recognized the one in the back as the guy from the Viper.

*Hoss.*

He made eye contact with me and grinned in a slimy, sadistic way, like he had big plans that didn't involve anything good.

"Ah," Gabriella said, turning to face them. "Just in time."

The tall gray-haired one at the front wore a Hell's Knights cut with the name tag, Crank.

"I'd never miss a pickup," Crank said, rubbing his hands together as he walked through the center of the room, gaze landing on me. "This her?"

"You wanted the president's daughter, right?" Gabriella pursed her lips and straightened, staring down her nose at the newcomers. "Verona Montgomery?"

"That's the one," Crank said, squatting down in front of me, bringing his decrepit-looking face toward mine. "Been watching you for a while, little girl. Ever since your daddy killed my brother."

I took a deep breath, trying to keep myself calm as Crank eyed me like a prized brood mare. This had to have been the guy that sent me those messages. *My stalker.* In the flesh. I shifted my attention to Castor, whose wide, panicked eyes confirmed he thought the same. The Hell's Knights had been following me and here was the proof.

"The information in exchange for the girl," Gabriella said. "Take her, and thank you for your business."

Crank chuckled to himself and stood, snapping at Hoss, who grabbed my biceps and yanked me to my feet. It took a moment for my brain to catch up, but as they hauled me toward the door, I realized I was being taken . . . that my family was about to die here and I'd been sold off to another club as repayment for whatever my father had done to this guy's brother.

I didn't know who that was. I didn't know what had happened to cause this. My world narrowed down to the race in my blood and the crazed look in Hollywood's eyes as I passed him. That set me off, making this real.

Screaming through the gag, I struggled against the two men, shaking my torso and kicking my legs out, but they easily overpowered me. Just when I'd been about to thrash harder, a sharp knock reverberated through the back of my head and the world went dark.

*No! Blink against the pain. Wake up.*

I forced my eyes open, trying to focus, and I caught a glimpse of the porch outside, the bright sunshine making my eyes water. Unconsciousness gripped me again as I clenched against the agony, but I swallowed it down, shaking my head to regain my focus.

*Wake up, V!*

Loud gunshots came from inside the shack as the Knights hauled me into the back of their truck, Crank sliding into the seat next to me before slamming the door shut. Hoss got into the driver's seat, cranking the engine to life, and my attention caught on a third person in the passenger seat before the world went momentarily dark again.

"You recognize my VP up there, don't ya?" Crank said, wrapping an arm around my shoulders, but I could barely understand what he was saying to me. More shouts and gunshots echoed through the midday air, eventually getting muffled by the truck's tires as we took off down the driveway.

"She's got a mean right hook," Hoss said with a laugh, looking at me in the rearview mirror. "Don't worry though. I'm gonna take that out on your ass later."

*Shit, shit, shit.*

My head ached from where they hit me and my heart pounded at the thought that Gabriella had just massacred my whole family. No one would come for me. No one would even know I was missing, not until the rest of the Roses figured out what was going on. If Gabriella was right, they had their hands full with the Feds.

I was on my own.

Tears blurred my vision and slid down my cheeks as I let myself sink into despair for a moment. *Only a moment,* I told myself. I'd survived a lot. Sure, this was pretty grim. I was outnumbered three to one by big, ugly men. But I was my father's daughter. I could get myself out of this . . . *right?*

"I bet you didn't even know we were there for you that night," Crank said, running a finger over my face to gather my tears. "At the Viper? We've been watching you for a while, *Mistress Mayhem.*"

I gulped, the bile rising in the back of my throat, resisting the terror in my chest and the remnants of the memory from that tiny apartment in Manhattan at the back of my mind. I could lose myself in it if I let it take over. My muscles trembled, and I gripped my hands together at the base of my spine, trying to figure out if I could get out of these plastic bindings. I could slip them down behind my legs to get my arms in front of my body, but these fuckers would notice if I did. I wouldn't be able to do it in time to grab a gun before they knocked me out again.

"Yep, that's right." Crank grabbed my chin and leaned forward, dragging his disgusting tongue over my cheek and up the side of my face, licking my tears away. I nearly threw up at the smell of his rancid breath, but the Knights in the front laughed, making me ache to kill them, too. "Your daddy owes me a life for the one he stole from me, and you're gonna pay up, little girl. We're gonna fuck you bloody, and then I'm gonna send your head to your daddy in jail. Do you think he'd like that?"

I shook harder at the mental image, now more determined than ever to get out of this.

*You have to fight. You have to fight as hard as you can.*

"Boss, we have a tail," said Hoss, glancing in the rearview.

"Are you sure?" Crank cursed and turned to look out the back window.

When I followed his gaze, I sobbed harder. One of the Caputi SUVs gained on us, and I honestly didn't know whether I wanted to stay in the car with these psychos or be taken by my family's sworn enemies. Both were a fate worse than death. If my family was gone, if Hollywood was dead, I'd rather follow them into the dark than survive whatever these sick fucks had in store for me.

But as the SUV got closer, I recognized my brother behind the wheel. And in the passenger seat sat Hollywood. I had only a moment to be thankful before another force slammed into the truck from the driver's side. I ducked down as we catapulted off the road, the crunching metal sound reverberating though my body. With my hands tied behind my back, I couldn't stop myself from careening into Crank, who shoved me back as soon as the chaos stopped.

He shoved the door open, jumping out onto the street with his guns out, the Knight in the passenger seat quick to do the same. Hoss slumped over the steering wheel, either knocked out or dead, but I didn't wait around to find out. Gunshots rang out into the air while I rolled onto my back so I could maneuver my arms down my legs and over my feet, screaming while I used my boot to snap the zip tie in half. My wrists protested and I burned the skin raw, but once I was free, I scrambled for the gun in Hoss's holster.

Once I had it, I jumped out of the truck, determined to help my family end this. Crank stood near the bed, aiming the barrel of his gun at Bear and Castor, who were hunched together near the SUV that had rammed into us. Hollywood had the other Knight in a chokehold near the hood while he elbowed my boyfriend in the face, trying to get him off.

I didn't even think. I raised the gun, aimed it at the back of Crank's head, and fired, blinking as his brains exploded down the obsidian fender and his body went limp. Then, I turned to Hollywood, stalking toward them like an assassin on a mission. I'd almost reached them when a hard grip circled around my throat, yanking me back against a tall, revolting body.

"You didn't think it would be that easy to get away, did you?" Hoss's voice whispered in my ear, the cool barrel of a pistol aimed at my temple. "Put the gun down, you little cunt."

I watched as Hollywood finally overwhelmed the third kidnapper, shoving him to the ground before rising to meet my gaze. He looked rough—bloody and bruised and barely alive on his feet. But he *was* still alive, staring at this new predicament with a hatred in his gaze I'd never seen before.

"No one move," Hoss said, tightening his arm around my throat, forcing me to straighten against him in order to breathe. "Drop your weapons, including you, little cunt. Go on. Drop them and I won't kill her."

Hollywood shifted his gaze between me and Hoss as my captor took a step back, angling his body so he could see Bear and Castor walking around the front of the truck, still aiming their guns at his head.

"Don't you see you're outnumbered?" I said. "Even if you kill me, they'll tear you to pieces."

"You think I'm afraid of that?" He laughed and shook his head. "I knew the risks when I decided to make a deal with the Caputi bitch."

Hollywood used his distraction to take a step toward me, but Hoss pointed the gun at him instead, firing two shots at the love of my life. The world went blank, a loud ringing in my ears making me incapable of understanding reality. Hollywood dropped like a stone, and terrorized screams tore out of my throat as I wrestled away from Hoss. Bear and Castor descended on him like wolves, filling his torso full of holes while I raced to Hollywood's side.

He'd been shot through the chest twice, his shirt drenched in his own blood. He met my stare with glazed-over eyes, pulling his lips into a shadow of a smile as he reached a hand toward my cheek.

"V," came Hollywood's shallow voice, the feel of his bloody fingers on my face making this real instead of the nightmare I wished it was. "V, it's okay. We're okay now."

"Shhh," I said, pressing my hands into his wound, trying to staunch the bleeding. But fuck, there was so much of it . . . too much of it. I blinked against memories of the last time Hollywood bled out in front of me, the horror of that night in Saint's truck so close to the surface now. "Don't move. It'll be ok-k-kay. You're okay."

"Is he alive?" Bear asked, coming to the other side of me so he could lean down and put his fingers on Hollywood's pulse.

"We n-n-need to get him to a h-h-hospital." I had to force the words through trembling lips. "Can you c-c-carry him?"

Castor grabbed Hollywood's arms and Bear got his legs, and together, they lifted him into the back of the SUV that hadn't rammed into the Knights' truck. I crawled in after Hollywood, lifting his head so it rested on my lap before putting my hands back on his wounds, pressing down so they'd stop bleeding. But they wouldn't stop. His blood just flowed and flowed, covering me and the back of the Range Rover.

We left the Hell's Knights fuckers where they were, and when Bear called Thor to let him know we were safe, he told the sergeant at arms we needed a cleanup crew.

"How's everyone at the cabin?" Bear asked. "Any casualties?"

*"Coins and Skulls,"* Thor said, sinking my heart into my gut. *"Hollister is still alive, but barely."*

"We'll see you at the hospital," Bear said before hanging up. But I couldn't focus on anything except the man slowly dying in my lap and the agonizing thought he might not live to see tomorrow. Suddenly, all those dreams about a future with him in it went out the window. Once again, Hollywood had sacrificed himself so I could live, and this time might actually be the last.

"You better not leave me, Hudson," I murmured, brushing the hair out of his eyes. "Stay with me. Please. I'm so sorry for everything I said. I'm so sorry. I love you. Please stay with me."

His eyes fluttered shut and he winced, but didn't regain consciousness. When we got to the hospital, Pollux's nurse took one look at us and let out a deep sigh. Hadn't we just picked up the survivor of our last run-in with the Caputis? Now, here we were again, and this time, we were just as fucked up and demoralized.

Julia, KC, and Hollister were already in the back when we walked in, but they took Hollywood immediately while the rest of us were put on the list and asked to sit in the waiting room. My leg burned, but now that I had a moment to get a good look at the wound, it wasn't much more than a deep scratch. I'd done worse to myself at the lowest points of my life, so I figured I'd get a few stitches and they would let me go.

Bear stood in a corner talking on his phone while the rest of my family tried to get their heads back in the game. We'd been hit really hard this time, much harder than ever before.

"How did this happen?" I asked. "How did we let this happen?"

"It was a coordinated attack," Thor answered from his spot where he had Selene's hand in a death grip. "They must have known the FBI would raid the clubhouse today. They knew our locations and our run routes."

"How?" Alba asked, running her hands under her glasses to wipe at her eyes. "Is there another spy?"

"It was the Hell's Knights MC," Castor said, running a hand over his dark curly hair. "They were spying on V and selling information to the Caputis."

"He said Dad killed his brother," I said. "Anyone know who his brother was?"

"A former SRMC brother," Bear said. "He betrayed the club to the Feds back in the '90s. Dad tore him to pieces."

"I'll have Switch check out your laptop to see if there's anything I missed," Castor added. "But we might want someone to reach out to whatever remains of the Hell's Knights to make sure no one else is after us."

Bear gave our brother a nod. "The prospects have cleaned up the mess from today," he said. "We'll regroup tomorrow to figure out next steps. Everyone get some rest. Try to heal."

*Heal.* When he put it like that, it sounded so easy. But nothing would ever scab over the events of today. I'd watched my family's sworn enemy take us out, one after the other, in the most callous way. I closed my eyes and I saw Hollywood's chest exploding, his limp body falling to the ground. My stomach churned with helplessness over the simple fact he'd needed me, and I couldn't do anything to stop it.

My body went numb, everything except for the scar in my chest, which burned hotter than it ever had before. I rubbed it, yanking my necklace out of my shirt so I could look at the bullet again, the one that Hollywood had taken for me so many months ago.

*You better survive this, Hudson,* I thought, knowing somehow he could hear me. Whatever connection had been formed between us that day had solidified in the months since. *I can't lose you. Please stay alive. Please.*

Hours later, after I'd been stitched up, I learned Hollywood had made it through surgery. Relief swelled inside me, but I couldn't fully relax until I saw him, until I could hold his hand in mine and kiss every inch of him again.

I pieced together the events after I'd been taken as everyone talked. I'd barely made it out the door before Selene, Hollywood, KC, and Lore jumped into action. Ru and Alba fought off their attackers while Selene and KC drilled bullets into whatever henchmen didn't run off. Gabriella, the slippery cockroach, still managed to get away.

It had been a coordinated attack between the Hell's Knights, the Caputis, and the FBI. While we were getting our asses handed to us by the mafia, the pigs were raiding the clubhouse.

"Detective Jordan finally had everything she needed," Bear said, his tone defeated and weathered. "She had a warrant for what had happened two years ago at the Holabird Docks. She said she had undeniable proof Crow and Aris were there, that they'd led the attack on the Caputis."

"Is she going after Gabriella?" Ru asked, her gaze emanating with the same rage brewing in all of our hearts. "Is she going after them, too?"

Bear shrugged. "I don't know."

"We've elected Bear as interim president," Saint explained. "KC as interim vice president, at least until the lawyers can get Crow and Aris out."

"Slip, Picasso, Skulls, and Coins"—Bear rubbed at his tired eyes—"they didn't make it. We'll talk about a new road captain and treasurer after we lick our wounds."

"You can't let this stand," I said, eyeing my brother with fury. "You need to find Gabriella and you need to kill her."

"It's not that simple," Bear said, glancing around to make sure we were out of earshot from any pigs that might be lingering around. "We had plans in motion, we had things brewing."

"Plans can change," Thor said. "We may need to move up your impending nuptials."

"Nuptials?" I narrowed my eyes at my brother. "What nuptials?"

Bear took a deep inhale and let it out on a sigh, shaking his head before running his hands back through his hair, tangling it up further. And that was how I found out my eldest brother was getting married to Julia Caputi in a desperate attempt to end this thing once and for all.

26

———

# HOLLYWOOD

"Look at your sorry ass," Trojan said, giving me one of his killer smiles. "Don't tell me you got shot again."

I laughed and nudged him with my shoulder. "Fourth time's a charm, or whatever they say."

My brother shook his head, his long chestnut hair glimmering in the dreamy sunlight. The sounds of bird, crickets, and cicadas sang from the trees on either side, accenting the calming rush of water over the rocks in the river in front of us. He held a fishing pole in one hand and a beer in the other, and all of it felt so damned familiar.

*We're in a memory.*

He'd taken me here during the weekends when things got tough, when it was just him and me trying to take on the world. I couldn't count the hours we'd spent in this exact spot.

"Is this real?" I asked. "You're dead, aren't you?"

Trojan shrugged and reeled in the line. "Who the fuck knows what's real anymore?"

"Am I dead?" A strange relief eased in my chest at the question, as if it might be okay with me if I was, as if being dead would ease the burden of being alive. At least I'd get to stay with my brother. At least we'd be together while we waited for our other family to join us.

"I don't think so," Trojan said. "I'm pretty sure you're dreaming."

"Oh." I took a sip of my dream-beer and grabbed my dream-fishing pole to check on my own dream-line.

"How ya doing, Matty?" Trojan reached across the bench to grab my shoulder, giving it a fraternal squeeze. "You taking care of everyone?"

"I'm trying," I said. "But it's fucking hard."

He barked out a laugh and nodded, resetting his line before casting it back out into the river. "No one ever said life was going to be easy."

"I've got a girl now," I told him, grinning as I thought of V and how much I cared for her. I could only pray she felt the same way for me, too—that when she thought of our love, she swelled with the same sort of heat and pride. I'd make things right as soon as I woke up. I had to. "It's Verona."

Trojan widened his smile, flashing the same dimples we'd both inherited from our mother. "I always knew there was something special between you two."

"She makes me happy," I told him. "Hey, if I'm here with you, where is everyone else?"

Again, Trojan shrugged. "Don't know. But it's peaceful here, isn't it?"

I nodded, letting my dream-self indulge in the symphony of that summer by the river.

"It's bad, isn't it?" I said, suddenly remembering the reason why I'd been knocked out so cold I was imagining the ghost of my dead brother. "Did we lose a lot of people?"

Trojan hummed to himself and nodded. "It's bad. But it'll get better."

I turned to face him, all the things I'd always wanted to tell him bubbling up in my chest. "I'm sorry this happened to you," I said, my eyes burning as I choked out a sob. "I'm sorry I wasn't there to save you. I'm sorry, I—I'm sorry I let Marissa run off. I haven't talked to her. She won't take my calls. I can try harder." The words were pouring from me faster than I could stop them. I had to get it all out, even if this was fake, even if this was in my head, I needed him to know. "I miss you so much, every day. I love you, brother, and I'm so sorry."

Trojan didn't say anything for a moment, just let me blubber the things I needed to get out. Once I caught my breath and wiped away the tears, Trojan bumped my shoulder with his again, drawing my attention back to his familiar friendly features, ones I'd been staring into ever since I was a baby.

"I know that," he said. "You don't need to say it. You don't need to carry it anymore."

"I feel it every day." I shook my head, taking another long sip of beer to clear the choking in my throat. "It should have been me. I should have died instead of you. They needed you more, the Roses need—"

"You shut the fuck up right now," he said. "If it shoulda been you, it woulda been you. But it wasn't. It was me, and you need to come to terms with that."

I winced like he'd slugged me in the gut. "What if I can't?"

Trojan made an amused sigh, shaking his head like he used to do when I'd fucked up at school over something stupid. "Still that same boneheaded idiot, aren't you?"

I narrowed my eyes, shocked he'd used whatever spiritual/memory/hallucination this was to insult me.

"You've got a good woman now, someone who loves you more than anything else in this world. Your job is protecting her, protecting the club. If you're so dispensable, she wouldn't have given you the time of day and you fucking know it." Trojan wrapped an arm around my shoulders and pulled me closer as I broke down from his words, the proverbial father figure consoling his son. Given the relationship Trojan and I had growing up, that wasn't too far from the truth. "And I better never hear you say you shoulda died again. I swear to God, Matty, I'll come back from the dead and kick your ass myself. Enough of this heroic martyr shit. You hear me? Enough now."

I nodded and sat upright, taking a deep breath to calm the sobs before I wiped my eyes. "Enough now."

"Hmm." He reeled his line in again before throwing it back out to the water. "It really is peaceful here, isn't it?"

"Yeah," I repeated. "Yeah, it is."

"Don't worry about Marissa," Trojan said. "I'm watching out for her. You worry about you and Verona. You worry about taking care of Mom. And when the time is right"—he set his stare on me again—"*really* right, I'll be here, waiting for you, little brother."

"You promise?" I didn't know why, but the thought of knowing Trojan still had my back, still loved me, still protected me, even if this was a hallucination, it made going back to the land of the living that much easier.

"I promise."

I sniffed and cleared my throat, drinking down the last of my beer in blissful silence. Something tugged at my line, just a small nibble at first but gradually becoming more feisty, and that too was from my memory.

"Oh shit," Trojan said, pushing to his feet so he could help me with the pole. "You got one."

"I got one!" I shouted, rising to reel it back in. "I got it! I got it!" The words were still on my lips when I opened my eyes to a dark, blurry room with loud beeps in the background and a warm body next to me. Everything hurt—my ribs, my head, my legs. I couldn't move, and when I tried, my companion stirred and sat upright.

"Hollywood?" came V's soft voice as she lifted her head from the pillow next to me, peering down at me with those big violet eyes.

"I got it, V," I told her, certain she would understand. "I got the fish."

"Let me get the doctors," she said, furrowing her brows.

"No." I tightened my fingers around her hand in mine, hoping to keep her close. "No, stay with me."

"Okay," she said, relaxing again. "How are you feeling?"

I winced and swallowed against a dry sandpaper throat. "Is there water?"

She reached for the cup on the table next to the bed and held a straw to my lips, letting me have barely a sip before she pulled it away again.

"I'm not sure if you're supposed to have any," she said, running her fingers over my face. "I love you, Hollywood. You scared the shit out of me."

"I love you," I tried to say. "I'm sorry."

"Me, too," she said. "About what I said before you left. I was scared. I *do* trust you. I do. And I want everyone to know you're mine. I want everyone to know how much we care about each other. I can't stand the thought of losing you. Ever."

I smiled, despite how drugged up I was and how hard my heart pounded. "Good."

"Don't almost die again," she said. "You hear me? You're not allowed to leave me. You and I are going to die at the same time, you understand? And not a fucking minute sooner."

"That's really fucking deep," I said, pleased as warmth spread through me that had nothing to do with the morphine drip. *That's my fucking girl.* Yeah, she was dark and gothy and would rather hiss at strangers than spark up a conversation, but I loved that about her. I loved everything about her, and I always fucking would. "I want you to be my old lady. Would you ride on the back of my bike?"

She leaned in to kiss me, delicately tracing her lips over my face before murmuring a quiet, "I'd ride with you anywhere, pretty boy."

It was with her affection and adoration warming my heart that I fell back asleep. I didn't dream of Trojan that time, and when I woke again, KC and Bear were on either side of my bed, talking over me like I wouldn't hear it. Bear stood, but KC had been relegated to a wheelchair.

"Berkshire says the charges are heavy. The judge is unlikely to set a bail," Bear said. "Dad's stuck there until we can figure out a way out of this."

"If there even is a way out," KC said, shaking his head. "I can't believe this is happening."

"What happened?" I groaned, blinking my eyes open.

"Hey, there he is," KC said, giving me a small grin. "You look like shit, but I'm glad you're talking."

"How do you feel?" Bear ran his hands back through his hair, but I noticed the dark, heavy bags under his eyes and the strain around his lips.

"You look like fresh, rotten hell," I said. "What's going on?"

"Don't worry about that right now," KC said, wheeling himself back as a team of doctors and nurses came in to check on my progress. They mumbled a bunch of medical shit I'd heard before. The bullets went clean through my chest and out the other side. I had a collapsed lung when they brought me in, not to mention the internal bleeding, but they managed to clear all that up. They wanted me out of bed and walking around to ensure I didn't get clots, but as long as things held steady, I could go home tomorrow.

The nurse promised to return with the walker to help me do a lap, but after they left, I returned my attention to my brothers.

"Where's V?" I asked. "Where's Crow?"

Bear sighed and shook his head. "The Feds raided the clubhouse. The place is a fucking clusterfuck. We lost a lot of people when the Caputis attacked us. Slip, Coins, Picasso, just to name a few."

"V's making funeral arrangements," KC added. "She'll be back as soon as she can."

"She hasn't left your side, brother," Bear said. "She really cares about you."

"I love her," I said. "I want to marry her."

"Goddamn, how long has this been going on?" KC's eyes darted from me to Bear and back again.

"Three weeks," I grumbled. "Since the auction." Fuck, that reminded me I hadn't even had the chance to take her on a proper date yet. Some boyfriend I was.

"Must be the pain meds talking." Bear snorted. "Let's talk marriage once you're sober, huh?"

I shook my head. Even though they'd been pumping the good stuff through my IV, I knew it in my bones. V was it for me, and no matter what they said, that would never change.

27

———————

**VERONA**

Over the next several weeks, we licked our wounds and cleaned up. They released Hollywood from the hospital and he moved in with me so I could take care of him while he healed. He'd been shot three times before, so he figured it was like riding a bike.

We buried our fallen Roses in the same cemetery where we'd buried Trojan and Alba's mother, Penny. I sat in the seat next to my brothers, rubbing the scar on my chest while Saint led us through a few prayers, reminding us those we lost would always be with us in spirit, if not in person. Rather than having separate funerals for each member, we did one memorial service for everyone we lost that day, preferring to rip the bandage off all at once so we could start to heal.

I looked down the row at Slip's old lady, Scribe, who sat stone-faced through the whole thing like she'd shut down her feelings when she heard the news and hadn't allowed herself to turn them back on yet. Next to her sat Shonda, Picasso's wife. Their daughter, Jinx, was only fourteen, and she hadn't stopped crying since the service started.

I remembered being younger than her when I sat in this very same cemetery to bury my mother. She'd died in the same car bombing that killed KC and Selene's parents, my aunt and uncle. Clenching my eyes shut, I tried to remember what my mother looked like or what her voice sounded like. When I couldn't, I wondered if the same thing would happen to Jinx. Would she wake up one day, unable to recall the sound of her father's voice or the way his eyes crinkled when he laughed? She was too young to go through something so horrific.

"Hollywood, you wanted to say a few words." Saint nodded to my boyfriend, who stood and walked up to the podium. He still struggled to take a deep breath when his emotions overwhelmed him, but compared to the dying man we'd taken into the hospital that day, he had almost made a complete recovery.

He glanced down at his index cards before looking back up at the gathered crowd. Everyone from the MC had made it in for the funeral, everyone who *could* anyway. What a fucking tragedy my father couldn't be here. What fucking monster would keep someone away from their family at a time like this? But the Feds hadn't authorized an excursion for him while he was still pending trial, and so he'd have to mourn his fallen blood brothers from the hellhole of a prison cell.

"There's a lot of people here." Hollywood forced a tight smile. "I hope I don't fuck this up." A few snickers came from the crowd, typical Hollywood making everyone smile before he started. Then, he cleared his throat and glanced down at his index cards. "I once knew a man who told me that family wasn't about the blood that ran through your veins. It wasn't about a name given to you, and it wasn't about the people on your birth certificate." Hollywood met my gaze when he said the next part. "It's about the people who love you when you don't love yourself."

Tears burned my eyes, dripping over my cheeks in thick drops I didn't bother trying to hide. A heavy weight swelled in my gut, permeating up to my lungs and making it hard to breathe.

"Scribe and Shonda, I never knew two greater men than Slip and Picasso. When I first met Slip, he taught me how to drive a manual transmission. He was the first person to teach me about engines and how to tear one apart. Picasso showed me how to appreciate art in life, how to find beauty in even the smallest of things. Coins treated everyone he met like his own child, like he was making up for the fact he didn't have any of his own by surrounding himself with adopted ones. It was a kindness so few people ever showed me."

He glanced at a few members in the back, clearing his throat before continuing. "I wasn't close with Skulls, but we were sworn to the same family, made the same oaths, protected the same people." Hollywood shook his head and brushed a finger under his eyes. "In many ways, they were more my family than my own parents ever were, and for that, I can never repay them for their sacrifice."

He paused to glance at Scribe, Shonda, and Jinx. "When I lost my brother a year ago, Slip told me the people we love, the people we call family, they're never really gone. Having almost died a few times myself, I can tell you with absolute certainty they are waiting for us on the other side of whatever this life is."

I tried to stop the stream of emotion pouring over my cheeks, but wiping the tears did nothing to stop it. I had to let it come, I had to let it be free.

"And one day," he went on, "when the time is right . . . *really* right . . . we'll see them again. Until then, I believe that our fallen brothers are looking out for us. Whatever this life brings, I know we can face it together, as a family, with our loved ones guiding us however they can."

He turned to the urns behind him, each carrying one of our deceased family with their names etched on the side. "Brothers, I salute you. Until we meet again, may you rest in peace and may your soul ride free."

"May your soul ride free," the rest of the crowd echoed.

Hollywood stepped down and everyone clapped while he took his spot behind me, reaching over the chair to grab my shoulder in solidarity. Saint brought the proceedings to a close before the cemetery attendants came to gather the urns and place them inside the headstones. The rest of the MC headed back to Bear's house for the wake, but I had another stop to make before I left.

Meandering through the cemetery, I walked along the path that led me to a spot I hadn't visited since I was a girl.

*Edith Scott Montgomery*

*Adored wife, loving mother, doting friend*

I bit back a sardonic snort at how her entire forty years of life had been boiled down to six words. She was so much more than that, so much more than I remembered. I kneeled so I could clear away the dead pine needles and mud gathering at the base of her grave marker.

"Hey, Mom," I said, choking down a sob as it threatened to barrel out of my mouth. "I'm sorry I haven't been to visit. I've been trying to take care of our boys the way I promised I would."

A chill blew around me, April's last fight against the impending spring, and I hugged my coat tighter against my body, praying for the strength to say what I needed to get out.

"I hope Hollywood is right. I hope you're waiting for us to greet you when the time is right. I hope you found our family and you're holding them close on the other side." I shook my head and dug my palms into my eyes as my heart shattered in my chest. My scar throbbed, aching painfully the more I berated myself for the horrible things that had happened to me, the horrible things I'd done to myself.

"She'd be proud of you, ya know," came a voice from behind me. I startled and turned to see Selene holding hands with Ru. They must have followed me here after things ended at the memorial. "And she wouldn't blame you for any of this."

"I could have done something," I said, pushing to my feet. "Instead, I just watched while she killed them."

Ru's features cracked, and she rushed forward to wrap her arms around me, pulling me into a tight hug while I sobbed.

"We were all there that day," Ru said, rubbing my back. "It's okay."

"We all could have done something," Selene said, shaking her head while she stared down at the headstone. "You know my parents are over there." She nodded to the right where another Montgomery headstone stood out against the gloomy winter morning. "I was the reason they were in Annapolis that day."

She'd told me that before, but I'd never believed Selene had been responsible for their deaths. It had been the Caputis that bombed the car containing our parents.

"I blamed myself for so long," Selene said, making me wince.

"Sel—" I started.

But Selene took a deep breath and straightened to look at me. "Horrible things happen, V, especially in this life we've chosen to live. We can't control those things, only how we react to them."

"You're too smart for your own good." I rubbed at my scar again, grimacing as the pain radiated down my stomach and up my neck.

"We share this burden with you," Selene added, grabbing my other hand. "When we get through it together, we'll share the victory with you, too."

Ever since I was a kid, I had cherished the friendship of these two women. I had run away after high school, hoping to escape this life, but now that I'd returned, I couldn't imagine it without them. We were the women of the Steel Roses, and we were indomitable. Our strength came from our empathy. We were the heartbeat of this family, and we fucking knew it.

Together, we would find Gabriella Caputi. We would dismantle her empire from the inside out, just like my father had wanted us to do, and we would make sure she suffered for what she'd taken from us. Until then, we would support each other and hold each other up.

That was what separated us from the Caputis. They relied on blood, on outdated ideas about what made a real family. But we were loyal to the ones who'd proved themselves, and as long as we still had that, we would make it through this hell together.

"The Hell's Knights won't stop coming for us," Dad said. "The motherfucker I killed was a snitch piece of shit, but he had three brothers I'm aware of. Crank won't be the last."

"My camming days are done." I winced as I said it, but it was true. Yeah, I was good at what I did and I made decent money, but in the days since I'd been sold to the Hell's Knights, only to be rescued by my lover and my brothers, the Beacon had reopened. I had my general manager spot back, not to mention the shows Hollywood and I could put on during the weekends. I figured going straight edge would make things a lot easier on me and my family, at least when it came to vetting the people in my life.

"Bear tells me you're seeing Hollywood," Dad said from behind the double-paned glass. He looked even worse than the last time I saw him. Big, dark bags hung under his eyes, more pronounced in the month he'd been behind bars, and he'd cut his hair short, damn near a buzz cut compared to the chest-length waves I'd grown used to. I'd tried to get here sooner than this, but the Feds wouldn't allow anyone except for his lawyer to visit.

"I am," I said, clearing my throat as I adjusted myself in the seat. "Is that a problem?"

Dad shook his head and sighed. "No, I guess I shoulda seen that coming."

"What?" I narrowed my eyes, scrunching my nose at his nonchalance. "Where's all that male bravado? No one touches my daughter!"

He smiled at my horrible impression of him. "I taught you better than that. If he made it past you and your brothers, I figure he's sticking around."

It had been almost twelve weeks since we'd started dating, and I didn't see any end in sight for this beautiful relationship that had sparked between us.

"I think I'm going to marry him one day," I said. "For real . . . not like whatever's going on with Bear and that Caputi bit—"

"Hey," Dad cut in. "Your brother's doing what he needs to do for the club."

My cheeks burned, but I gave him a firm nod.

"Besides, don't talk about any of that shit here," he said. "They're recording me. They're always recording me, waiting for me to screw up so they can use it against me."

I let out a sigh. "Detective Jordan's still up your ass, huh?"

Dad nodded and gave me a look that said I needed to keep my wits about me. "She's up yours, too. So watch out. She's relentless. If she wasn't trying to keep me in here for the rest of my life, I might admire the poisonous cunt."

"I tried to get Castor and Pollux to come with me," I said. "But they've been busy trying to find the bitch who killed our family."

"Listen to me, V," Dad said, leaning in closer and holding the telephone tighter to his head. "Things are about to get real sticky for Bear and the Roses. You need to be there for him, understand? You need to help him through this and make sure he keeps his head on straight. You know what I mean?"

After Dad and Aris had been taken into custody, the MC had elected Bear and KC to replace them. Hollywood had been named the new road captain, at least until Dad could get out to deal with this himself. But I knew my brother, and I knew what my dad meant by making sure he kept his head on straight.

While Bear had inherited the cool and collected side of our mother's personality, he had also inherited the Montgomery temper. It took a lot to get my brother pissed off, but once he hit that limit, he'd been known to go on a rampage that only KC, me, or my dad could calm. If he wasn't careful about this next move with Julia Caputi, the entire house of cards could come crumbling down around him.

"Yeah, I know what you mean." I held a hand up to the glass, blinking back tears when Dad did the same on the other side.

"I love you, kiddo," he said.

"Love you, too." I begrudgingly hung up the phone and left him there, praying he held out until the next time I could see him.

Hollywood was waiting for me out in the parking lot. It was a nice day, so we'd driven his bike up here, and now he leaned up against it while he smoked a cigarette, looking like some contemporary James Dean. Heat snaked into my lower gut, and I grinned as I leaned up to wrap my arms around his neck.

"How's Pops?" He stabbed the butt into the ashtray on top of a trash can and kissed me, pressing his forehead against mine.

"Pissed off and plotting." I hated seeing him in the pen, but until this shit with Detective Jordan got worked out, I didn't know how we'd get him out of it.

"So, the usual." Hollywood kissed me again before handing me my helmet so I could tug it over my head and climb on the back of his bike. He put the key in the ignition and kicked it to life, sitting back so I could circle my arms around him before taking off.

I'd grown up in an MC and all my brothers were bikers, so I'd been riding on the back of these monstrosities since I was a child. But nothing and no one made me feel as safe as I did when I was on the back of *his* bike, holding onto *him*.

If anyone had asked me a year ago whether I'd ever say that about Hollywood, of all people, I would have laughed in their face. Hollywood and I were seemingly opposites in just about every way. Where he had a smile for everyone and a joke poised on his tongue at any given moment, I'd much rather cut them down to size with the truth. I used to think it wasn't a good day unless I'd made someone cry. Now, I understood how we brought out the better side of each other. I made him give a shit about himself, and he reminded me that not all people were idiots, that being authentic didn't necessarily mean speaking my mind all the time.

He protected me, and in many ways, I protected him. I trusted him, and that was more than I could say about anyone else, save for my brothers. We needed each other more than either of us would admit.

I thought about Ru's question all those weeks ago.

*"Do you believe in soulmates?"*

At the time, I didn't know. I'd said yes because I *wanted* to believe. Now, I did. Perhaps it was a blood bond that brought me and him together, created when we were in high school and sealed when he'd risked his life for me. Perhaps it was our spirits that had recognized their twin in one another. Whatever it was, Hollywood was *it* for me. That was all I needed to know to finally be optimistic about my future here and my family's place in it.

28

---

# HOLLYWOOD

"Whew," Leo said, shaking his head as I came to visit him for the first time since everything went down. "I must tell you, my friend. I was happy to hear you'd made it out alive."

I snorted and shook my head. "Don't fuck with me. You'd be happy if she put a bullet in all our heads."

Leo shrugged and fiddled with a cuff link on his collared shirt. "Perhaps most of your brothers, but not you. You're one of the ones worth saving."

"Don't flatter me," I said, and he grinned in that friendly, charismatic way that made me want to forget the bad history between our families. The jury was still out on whether we could actually trust him.

In the days since Gabriella had attacked, Julia had been by to catch up with her brother and bring him some of his own amenities. Their interactions were still monitored by Bear just in case they decided to swing back to supporting their dear ole auntie. But I'd seen what Gabriella had done to Julia, what she had allowed to happen to her own niece. If I were Leo, I'd want Gabriella's head on a spike, so I was inclined to think he was on our side. Julia hadn't been back to her family's estate, but if our plan was going to work, she'd have to be even more clandestine than she was before. She couldn't stage a successful coup from the outside.

Clad in expensive trousers and designer shoes, Leo looked every bit the Caputi mobster he'd been raised to be. If I hadn't spent the better part of the last three months with him, I wouldn't believe he'd come around. But I'd seen him at his most vulnerable, and if there were one Caputi I could tolerate, it would be him.

"I never thanked you for this," Leo said, turning to face me while he shucked his jacket over his shoulders. "For helping me, for healing me."

"It wasn't like I had much of a choice." I crossed my arms, hiding a wince when my abused cock rubbed against my boxers. V had taken it out on me last night, making me come over and over again until I sobbed and begged for mercy. I could barely walk this morning.

"Doesn't matter why you did it." Leo let out a low, sardonic laugh and cupped my cheek, the cool metal of his rings brushing against my jawline. "You have me in your debt."

"Just don't fuck us over, okay?" I straightened and nodded toward the back door. "Bear is going to agree to marry Julia, and once we're family, that changes things, but . . ." I cleared my throat and shook my head. "Most of the MC is waiting for you to betray us."

Leo pursed his lips and narrowed his dark eyes. "Most of the support my sister has managed to secure has similar concerns about the Roses."

"Well, I guess we both need to be vulnerable and trust each other, don't we?" I held out my hand for him to shake, and he grinned before taking it in his own.

"My aunt has overstepped for the last time," Leo said. "I won't have her treat my sister like this any longer, and as you said, I am tired of this war. It was started by people who aren't even players on the chessboard any longer."

"The Roses feel the same way." I clapped him on the shoulder and brushed my hand over his Tom Ford, smoothing away a piece of lint. "Including Bear."

"Answer me this, Hollywood," Leo said, dropping his voice an octave lower. "Will he be good to my sister? Will he treat her with the respect she deserves?"

"Yes," I said immediately. I didn't even have to think about it. "He doesn't date very much, but when he does, he's serious . . . and he's serious about ending this war."

Leo nodded, seemingly appeased by this answer. "Well, then. I suppose we ought to get going."

A few brothers had come with me to escort Leo to church today, and if all went well, we'd arrange for a bigger meeting with the underbosses Julia had managed to sway to her side.

Of all the people in this mess with us, she walked the tightest rope. But Saint and Leo both assured us Julia had been playing this game for a long time. She'd be able to do it for a little while longer. Leo walked with a cane these days, but that added to his reformed mobster enigma.

I helped him into the back of the SUV before going around to the other side and hopping in so a prospect could drive us the few minutes to our clubhouse.

When I'd first gotten out of the hospital, the SRMC's home away from home had been wrecked by the Feds. We weren't morons, so we didn't keep anything valuable lying around there, but they had smashed everything to shit. Now all these weeks later, we'd set most of it right, but the place still didn't feel back to normal without all the brothers it had once housed.

Crow's and Aris's absence sat like a heavy weight on our chests, not to mention the people we'd buried only a few weeks ago. We'd lost five brothers in one day, and Hollister still had a shaved head, showing off the scar he would carry around for the rest of his life. He'd gotten lucky that Gabriella's hand had jerked from the recoil. Any lower, and he would have died, too.

We'd gathered for our first church since the change in leadership. And words could not describe the mix of excitement and pressure in my heart that this group of motley motherfuckers had elected me as their road captain. I'd never be able to replace Slip, but I was damn sure going to try. I sneaked Leo in through the back door, keeping him hidden in one of the back rooms until the time was right to bring him in.

Some of the Roses still had mixed feelings about the Caputi kingpin, so I didn't want him wandering around just in case anyone got a wild hair up their ass and decided to ruin this whole thing before it started.

"Is he secure?" Thor asked when I walked into the meeting room. As sarge, it was his duty to keep the Roses in line, and between the two of us, we needed to get Leo back to the safe house in one piece.

"He's secure, and he's ready," I said, walking to my spot at the SRMC table to the right of Bear. I nodded to KC across from me, who sat in the VP spot while Aris was in the pen, and looked at our enforcer, Doc, to my right, smoking a cigarette while he talked to Wheels, who had taken the treasurer position as Coins's replacement.

"Everything okay?" KC asked while the other brothers filled in around us.

"Peachy keen," I said with a smile, and once the rest of the MC had taken their place, our new veep stood to bang his rings on the table and bring church to order.

"Brothers," KC said, silencing the chatter around us. "We have a quick meeting today, so everyone shut the fuck up and listen in."

"Thank you, KC," Bear said, standing in the spot at the head of the table where his father had once led these meetings. "You know why we're here and what we have to do next. After what happened, we need to be more careful than ever. The pigs are breathing down our necks, just waiting for us to make our next move. The Hell's Knights have refused our offer of a truce. And there's a Caputi bitch that needs to be repaid for what she took from us."

Hollers of approval came from around us, and I caught bits of *"Kill that bitch,"* and *"Hang her head from the fucking rafters."*

"The last time we met, we talked about an alliance with Leo Caputi," Bear continued, and a hush fell over the group, the tension increasing with each passing second. "I agreed to marry Julia Caputi if it would bring an end to this blood feud."

"You don't have to do that," someone shouted.

"I agree," Doc said. "We should kill the entire family and be done with it."

"A war cannot be brought to peace with more blood," Bear said, glaring at Doc in a challenge for him to say more. "They own DC, and we'll never be able to take over the territory without their help."

Doc pursed his lips and inhaled deeper on his cigarette.

"So, I've invited our houseguest here so you can hear it from him," Bear said, giving the prospects at the back of the room a nod to bring Leo in. Leather rustled as the door opened to reveal the Caputi heir, looking every bit his namesake in his suit and diamond-encrusted jewelry. He leaned on his cane while he walked closer, but other than that one sign of weakness, he kept his head held high, exuding the confidence he'd need in order to stand tall in this room of killers who all wanted to bathe in his blood.

"Roses, this is Leo Caputi," Bear said, gesturing Leo to come stand next to him. "My future brother-in-law, our only hope to end this war."

My heart pounded, arguably the loudest sound in the room, when everyone went quiet and stared at him.

"Are you sure we can trust him?" another brother asked. "How do we know he won't kill us all the moment he gets a chance?"

"I could ask the same of you," Leo said. "Of everyone in your club, how many of you have killed my family?"

"No more than your family has killed ours," Doc sneered, returning his gaze to Bear. "C'mon, Prez. This is fucking batshit cr—"

Bear slammed his hands down on the wood, interrupting whatever Doc would have said after that, and leaned closer to the dissenting brother.

"Gabriella Caputi sold my sister to the Hell's Knights for information. She made our women watch while she shot our brothers in cold blood. Do you want your sister to share that same fate?" Bear raised his eyebrows, waiting for Doc to respond. When he didn't, the acting president straightened and glanced around to the rest of the room. "I have spent my entire life in this war. I've killed for it. I've bled for it.

I've lost family for it." He cleared his throat when he got choked up at the mention of his mother and our fallen brothers. "I'm tired."

"You've had time to speak your mind," Thor said, glancing around at our brothers. "This isn't a dictatorship, but it's also not a fucking democracy. This is what we're doing. If you can't live with it, see me about removing the patch from your cut."

At that, the tension in the club eased. They wouldn't risk being cast out over this, and even if they were wary, they trusted Bear's opinion. They trusted *my* opinion and Thor's.

"All right then," Bear said, turning to Leo.

"Thank you, Bear," Leo said, putting both hands on top of his cane as he rested it in front of him and looked out over the group of gathered bikers, his former enemies turned unwilling allies. "Gentlemen, let's get to work."

# EPILOGUE

VERONA

*Ten years later*

"**B**ut Daddy," came the soft voice from around the corner, "I'm scawed you won't come home."

"I'll always come home to you, bug," Hollywood cooed in the same soothing voice he used to calm me. "I love you to the moon and back."

"You pwomise?" Edie asked. At four years old, she still had trouble with her Rs.

I turned the corner and paused to take in the sight of my husband lying in the miniature bed with our daughter wrapped around him. Her bed of curly brown hair matched her father's, but she looked up at him with eyes a shade bluer than mine. Even still, with that adorable pout on her lips, there could be no denying she was his daughter through and through.

"I promise." He leaned down to kiss her forehead before glancing up to see me standing in the door. "Grandpa's here to watch you, but no ice cream before bed."

If there was one person our little Edie loved more than her father, it was mine. Hollywood long forgotten, she jumped out of bed and shouted a joyful "Yay!" as she ran past me to the living room.

Crow had come by to spend time with her so we could have a night to ourselves, something long forgotten in the early days of parenting.

"Well, I guess I'm chopped liver," Hollywood said, crossing his arms under his head on the tiny twin mattress.

"Welcome to the club." I smiled and walked to the space between his legs as he sat up to run his hands over the backs of my thighs, resting his forehead on my sternum, just under my scar. "I guess there's always next time."

"Next time?" He looked up at me, raising his eyebrows in quiet question. "You mean—"

I nodded and held up the sonogram showing our new little bean brewing in my uterus.

"Woooooo!" He let out a howl, causing two identical giggles to echo from down the hall, one much deeper than the other. "Fuck yeah. I knew I'd knocked you up again. It was only a matter of time."

I snorted and sighed, recalling the times we'd tried for a second and fallen short. "This one's further along. It's strong."

Hollywood bit his bottom lip and blinked against reddened eyes, clearing his throat as he glanced back up at me. "It's a boy."

"We don't know that," I said, cupping his jaw so I could tilt his face toward me and plant a soft kiss on his lips. "Right now, it's a fetus."

"If it's a boy, I want to name him after my brother."

"Hmm." I liked the sound of that. Trojan's real name had been Troy. "Troy Montgomery-Hudson."

"Trojan Montgomery-Hudson." He laughed, kissing the disgruntled scrunch off my nose before moving to my lips. "When do you want to tell everyone?"

"Let's wait until I'm showing." We'd made the mistake of telling people too soon before, and it had only ended in heartache.

"Deal." Hollywood pushed to his feet and wrapped an arm over my shoulder, leaning in close to me so he could whisper against my ear. "Are you ready for tonight?"

"Pfft. I was born ready." I glanced up at him, knowing he was responsible for the other end of this show. "Are *you* ready?"

"Fuck yeah." He bit my earlobe, sending a shiver down the right side of my body, but I caught sight of his chain underneath his shirt, telling me he'd been ready since he got up this morning.

We said goodbye to our daughter and my father, promising to return before sunrise, and headed out to Hollywood's bike. As I wrapped my arms around his waist, a warmth ran through my bloodstream at how *right* my life had turned out to be. Sure, it had taken a lot of blood and sweat to get here, but we *were* here. I had a family of my own, one I cherished and adored above everything else, and I had a man who loved me more than his own breath. In addition, he loved our children, and every day he reminded me of the same lesson he'd taught me all those years ago.

There were people in this life worth dying for, but more importantly, worth living for. And they make all the difference.

## HOLLYWOOD

"You look amazing," V said, rubbing her hands over my naked chest and stomach, reminding me she was my wife and she loved me despite what she was about to do to me in front of all these people.

I leaned down to kiss her, this beautiful woman who gave it to me like I wanted it, who had given so much purpose to my once pathetic existence.

"Baby, you look good enough to eat." I grinned at the blush on her cheeks, especially when she scoffed and rolled her eyes. But I took a moment to run my hands over her stomach, where new life had taken root, growing healthy, promising a future we'd both wanted for so long.

"Mistress Mayhem and her beautiful submissive, Mister Mischief," Ru announced to an explosive applause. In the years since the Beacon reopened, V and I had made a killing by letting people watch the things she liked to do to me. Since we had Edie, the only chance we got to play was when we were able to come here.

Honestly, my whole world these days revolved around our daughter, so there hadn't been much time for any of this. But I didn't begrudge that at all. Watching V bring Edie into the world had been the happiest day of my life. I had a family of my own, *finally,* and if anyone wanted to take it away, they'd have to go through me and my brothers to do it.

But those worries faded away as I watched the spotlights glint off my Mistress's leather bodysuit. Today was the tenth anniversary of the Beacon's grand reopening, so we'd decided to make a rare appearance.

I'd been wearing the cock cage all day, so when she led me to the St. Andrew's Cross, facing toward her, I leaned back against the cool leather and prepared for her to do her worst. We'd planned this entire scene down to the second, so nothing would be a surprise.

My stomach still twisted with butterflies as she cuffed my wrists and ankles into place. Trembles raced down my torso at the glint in her eye, the one that told me she couldn't wait to let her alter ego take over.

"Hey," I whispered as she stood to step away. She paused and glanced up at me, furrowing her brows as apprehension and confusion replaced the excitement in her gaze. "Do you still hate me?"

"Of course." She curled her lips into my favorite grin, the one that made her cheeks rosy and lit up those violet eyes. "Does it still turn you on?"

"More than anything."

"Good." She pushed up on her toes to kiss me one last time before grabbing the nipple clamps off the stool next to her. "Now hold still while I hate you as much as I can."

# WANNA JOIN THE ROSES?

Thank you for reading! If you enjoyed this book, please consider leaving a review. They help other readers find my work, and because of that, they enable me to keep writing.

**DELETED SCENE**
In the first manuscript, there were two chapters where Hollywood takes V for a date and they have wild edgy sex afterward. But it took place at the end and I was told it slowed down the pace. I agreed, but it was too cute and steamy not to share. If you want more Hollywood and V, go to the link below to get it for free.
https://books.jenadoyle.com/Hollywood

If you want more **STEEL ROSES** content, check out the prequel novella, **THEY CALLED HIM SAINT,** when you sign up for my newsletter.
https://jenadoyle.com/join/

(No spam, only smut. I promise.)

Keep reading for a sneak peek at **BEAR** and **JULIA'S** story,
**RUTHLESS REIGN.**

# RUTHLESS REIGN

JULIA

I stared at the paperwork on the table in front of me, the words blurring as I scrambled to catch up to what my lawyer, Angelo, said.

"If the marriage were to be dissolved, my client will walk with all of the assets she had coming into the arrangement." He scribbled something into the margins of the contract before glancing up at the other people across the room.

"That won't be necessary," my brother, Leo, said. He tapped his forefinger to his lips and looked at me before shifting his focus to my betrothed. "Caputis do not believe in divorce."

"Nevertheless," Angelo said. "This is to protect your investment... and Julia."

I squirmed as he added my name on at the last second, like I was an afterthought in this whole charade, like I didn't matter more than what my name would do for us in this situation.

Leo pursed his lips and nodded. Angelo went on, reading the rest of the legal jargon that would dictate the entirety of my life from here. My attention drifted to the heavily tattooed man next to the other lawyer.

Roman "Bear" Montgomery. My affianced.

Sure, at first glance, he was beautiful. He had dark curly hair, deep soulful brown eyes, and a jaw cut from marble. But I knew the truth. He was the acting president of the Steel Roses Motorcycle Club and my family's sworn enemy.

That was until my brother made an alliance with him two months ago. Leo had been captured by the bastards last year, and now that he'd sobered up and gotten to know them better, he thought he could end the bloodshed between our families with a blessed union.

Which was how we found ourselves in this drab conference room, decked out with lawyers, going through the technicalities of a relationship that had been forged from hatred and decades of shared animosity.

Roman caught me staring at him and I quickly averted my gaze, but not before I saw him purse his lips and narrow his eyes.

What did he see when he looked at me? Did he see only the Caputi princess? Or did he know how I seethed with my own vengeance? Did he know how badly I wanted to take down my aunt for what she'd done to me? That the only reason I'd agreed to this farce was because I hated her more than I could ever hate him and his family?

"Section four, subsection three, paragraph six," Angelo said. "Cohabitation."

I took a deep breath as I prepared myself for this battle. I knew that Roman and Leo both wanted me to reside in Madison County. They believed it was safer for me, especially after Aunt Gabriella found out that I'd been spying for the Roses and set her men to beating me. The bruises on my face had only just gone away. I didn't see how I could continue to be of any use from such a distance.

The information I'd given to the Roses had gotten them this far. How would they stage a coup without someone on the inside? Of course, how effective could I be now that my cover had been blown?

I still had family members that were against Gabriella. I had cousins and uncles that were willing to push her out in favor of Leo. But my brother had insisted that we would figure it out, and if I needed to contact them, I should do so with a burner phone from the comfort of Roses territory. It would be harder for her to get to me there.

"We will live at my house," Roman said. "In Madison."

Leo scoffed and picked at imaginary lint on his suit. "I've seen your house. How do you propose to make a Caputi princess happy in such a hovel?"

Roman shifted and set a penetrating gaze on my sibling. "As opposed to some drug den easily infiltrated by anyone with half a brain? Or perhaps you mean the Rose house currently given to you as charity?"

The Roses had snatched my brother out of his mansion on the Eastern Shore one night when he'd been having a drug party. He'd been so high, he didn't know what had happened to him until two weeks later when most of that nasty stuff was out of his system. Since then, he'd been living in one of the Rose's houses, running the family business from there in order to avoid our aunt. Eventually, he'd have to go home. He'd have to make an appearance on Caputi territory in order to show the bosses that he was a strong leader, that he could undermine Gabriella and steal back his throne.

"A house is a house, Leo," I said to him in Italian.

"Not for my only sister," he replied. "You deserve the best."

"If that was the case, you wouldn't be selling me off to this Godless mongrel."

"Hey, I believe in God," Roman cut in with perfect pronunciation in my native tongue.

"I've already agreed to go along with this." I scoffed and rolled my eyes, muttering obscenities to myself. "I'll live in whatever shack my new *husband* deems appropriate for his bride."

"My house is perfect for two people," he said. "It's on a mountain and it overlooks the city. You'll be safe there."

*Sure. Out of one monster's land, into another.*

"So we've agreed," said Roman's lawyer, Berkshire. "Ms. Caputi will reside at Mr. Montgomery's residence until further accommodations can be agreed upon."

Angelo checked that item off before flipping the page. "Section Five, Subsection Two, paragraph three - last name."

"Caputi," I said at the same time Leo and Roman said, "Montgomery."

Shocked but desperate to hide it, I looked at my brother with murder in my eyes.

"This is an alliance," Leo said. "You must play the part if anyone is going to believe it."

I took a deep breath to calm the rising tide of fury in my gut, knowing it would get me nowhere. My life had always been rooted in doing whatever the men around me deemed appropriate. My uncle, Benito, had been the Caputi Boss before he died, and my father, Benito's brother, had been his most trusted advisor. I'd had to act a certain way, dress a certain way, conduct myself a certain way in order to appease their conservative mentality. This would be no different.

"Perhaps you'd be open to a compromise?" Roman said, looking directly at me. "Caputi-Montgomery?"

*Ugh, what a mouthful.*

I already had four middle names, but perhaps this was Roman extending a tiny olive branch over the vast divide between us.

"Thank you," I said. "But Montgomery is fine."

Roman cleared his throat, shifted in his seat, and gave Berkshire a glance of approval.

"Okay," Angelo said. "That brings us to the next section. Procreation."

I sighed, knowing this was coming.

"What?" Roman said, leaning forward, blinking incredulously. "What about it?"

"You will produce a child within a year," Leo said, his tone calm and dignified despite how manipulative this whole thing was.

Roman laughed and shook his head. "You must be joking."

"I am not," Leo continued. "The only way this works is if Rose and Caputi blood are mixed. We need to be family. A child will go a long way to smooth over any . . . opposition . . . on both sides."

"There is already a child of both Caputi and Rose blood," Roman said. "And surprise, surprise, she doesn't want anything to do with you."

"Alba did not grow up in the Caputi family. Aside from a few individuals, no one else knows she exists." Leo raised an eyebrow. "Besides, everyone loves babies."

Roman blew out a breath and shook his head with a sarcastic laugh. "Fucking hell."

"Language," Leo said. "Especially in front of my sister."

"Your sister has said worse to me, personally." Roman looked at me with a sly smirk, and I bit back my own grin at the thought of the first time I'd ever met him. He'd been keeping Leo prisoner for months, and my brother looked like hell. I'd read Roman the riot act for not taking better care of him.

"Nevertheless," Leo said. "Show some respect."

"You're okay with this?" Roman asked, brown gaze trained on me. "Be honest. If you're not, we'll shut it down."

"Julia will do—" Leo started.

"I'm not talking to you," Roman said. "You're not the one I have to fuck, are you?"

I bit my lip as Leo adjusted his hips in his seat and let out a low growl of frustration.

None of this was how I'd ever imagined my life would go. Once upon a time, I'd been in love with with a beautiful boy from my high school. Hugo. From the moment I met him, I had stars in my eyes. I'd always thought we'd run away together and have six kids by the time I was thirty. Now, I stared down the barrel of my thirty-first birthday and Hugo was dead and I hadn't even been married. When Leo first proposed this asinine idea of wedding Roman Montgomery, he'd convinced me by suggesting that Gabriella would give me to an underboss's son, and if I'd been less conniving about maneuvering myself in other directions, it would have already happened.

After Alba's mother died / ran away, I became the eldest Caputi princess. A rare jewel. Worth more than a marriage of convenience to some underboss's dusty boy. So, I thought "Fine. Why not marry for an alliance? Why not end the bloodshed?" Never mind the fact that they'd killed my eldest brother, Julian. Never mind the fact that Roman's hands were so soaked in Caputi blood, it might as well be dripping from every venom laced move he made.

Could I push this aside for the sake of my family? Could I lay back and think of Italy anytime I had to couple with him?

To be fair, he wasn't the ugliest guy I'd ever slept with nor was he the most violent. I could imagine sex with him might even be enjoyable...if I got over the fact that he was a Rose and a Montgomery and my family's worst enemy.

"A child within a year," I said with a nod.

Roman made a low noise of disbelief and leaned back in his seat, running the length of me with an assessing gaze. "Is there nothing you won't do for your brother?"

"You have three siblings of your own, don't you?" I said. "Isn't that why you're sitting at this table?"

He considered for a moment before asking, "And if we can't produce a child? Lots of couples have problems with infertility."

"If that is the case," Leo said. "Julia has enough sense to seek out a doctor. There must be an effort made, you understand? There can be no pretending in this marriage. You must be committed to each other. There must be an alliance."

"Fine," I said, raising an eyebrow at Roman.

"Fine," he repeated.

"Wonderful," Angelo concluded, flipping the pages of our contract closed. "That settled, we have no further arguments."

"We are in agreement," Berkshire said before reaching to another stack of papers for the one on top. He handed it to Roman and pointed at a spot on the bottom. My betrothed picked up a pen, signed it, and pushed it across the table to me.

*The marriage certificate.*

We'd agreed to the contract, and now came the final step. After this, there was no going back. I picked up my pen and glanced at Roman one last time, steeling myself against the ever simmering rage in my belly for him and everything he stood for.

Then, for the very first time, a hint of kindness echoed out of his gaze, like he sympathized with me, like I could see deep down to his soul and it was good and sweet and generous. Perhaps this marriage wouldn't be as horrible as I feared. Perhaps there was a solid foundation to our relationship, however screwed up and ridiculous as it began.

I signed my life away right next to Roman's.

"By the power vested in me by the Commonwealth of Virginia," Angelo said, "I now pronounce you husband and wife. Congratulations."

# ACKNOWLEDGMENTS

Dear Reader,

Thank you for reading V and Hollywood's story. This book has meant so much to me while writing it, if only because I have also struggled with mental health and depression. A lot of V's backstory came from my own history with mental illness, and I feel like it's something that's commonly overlooked in fiction. By talking about it, we de-stigmatize it.

Depression lies. It's a monster lurking under your bed, waiting until you're most vulnerable to strike. I once saw a quote on Tumblr that said, "I don't make characters, I break myself into pieces and give the pieces names." I've never related to something more, especially with V.

If you're struggling, know that you are seen. You have worth. You belong on this earth. There are people out there who would do anything to keep you alive. Remember that when times get most dark.

Keep. Fucking. Fighting.

If you're in the States, you can always dial 988 for crisis support.

There are a few people I want to thank for this book. Firstly, my friends at the Tuesday night Shadow Work circle. Nae, Amethyst, Willow, Becca, and all the others — Thank you for being the light when times were most dark. I couldn't have crawled out of my filthy gutter without you. You kept me going if only by listening and commiserating. Together, we are stronger.

To my beta readers: Leslie Grace and Maggie Sims, thank you for all of your wisdom and advice. Thank you for letting me show you pictures of sexy men for the cover and helping me decide between a flogger and a paddle for the section breaks. I am truly blessed to have you in my writer's circle.

To Rebecca Hartwell, one of my beta readers for *Blood and Whiskey.* Your advice on that book helped shape this one. I owe you!

To my editors, Misha and Kimberly, you both are rock stars. When I emailed you in January and said I wanted to release six books this year, you both had my back 100%. You are such lovely people and I'm forever grateful to have you on my team.

To my ARC readers, thank you from the bottom of my heart. I can always count on you to catch that last minute typo that somehow gets through the ten times I read it and multiple rounds of edits. That's not your job, but I am thankful nonetheless.

To my wonderful partner, Adam. Sorry I killed Slip in this book. Thank you for loving me and supporting me while I hid away in my girl-cave, struggling to keep up with my deadlines. Even with Slip gone, there is a little piece of you in every book boyfriend I write.

To Rock Hudson, one of the world's first gay icons whose last name I took for Hollywood. You were beautiful beyond compare, and you deserved more from your legacy. I hold you in high esteem, and always will.

To the person who inspired Hollywood — I pray you never find out about this. But thank you for being a part of my story so that I could use some of your best parts (and some of your not so great parts) to create the lovable Matthew Hudson.

And finally, to you, Dear Reader. This is book four in the Steel Roses MC, so if you've hung in there with me this long, know that I appreciate you so very much. Every time someone reads one of my books, I am humbled by the fact that you are purposely taking in the words that tumbled out of my silly little imagination. You and I have shared this adventure together. I have reached across the void of time and space and given you a piece of myself. I hope it has been worth it. It has for me. Thank you.

Until next time.
Cheers!
-Jena

# ALSO BY JENA DOYLE

### MIDSUMMER

We Wild Things (Prequel Novella)

Midsummer

Samhain

Solstice

Beltane

### STEEL ROSES MC

They Called Him Saint (Prequel Novella)

Crimson Chaos

Savage Saint

Oleander Oaths

Mischief Mayhem

Ruthless Reign

### ROYAL BASTARDS MC: HELENA, MT

Blood and Whiskey

www.ingramcontent.com/pod-product-compliance
Lightning Source LLC
Chambersburg PA
CBHW022119310726
48972CB00007B/2102